THE GUARDIAN

THE GUARDIAN

A. HART

authorHOUSE®

AuthorHouse™
1663 Liberty Drive
Bloomington, IN 47403
www.authorhouse.com
Phone: 1-800-839-8640

Published by AuthorHouse   07/09/2012

ISBN: 978-1-4772-3313-9 (sc)
ISBN: 978-1-4772-3311-5 (hc)
ISBN: 978-1-4772-3309-2 (e)

Library of Congress Control Number: 2012911825

To My Sisters:

Proof that God loves us and doesn't want us to be

alone in the universe.

ACKNOWLEDGEMENTS

So I've finally stopped screwing with my book long enough to see it in to the publisher. I have always striven to be a person of my word and finally, here it is. To all of the doubting Thomas' along the way, neener neener.

Next, I suppose it's proper to move on to all of the little people that helped me along the way ... Okay, okay I'm kidding, just kidding, geez. But seriously, thank you to my mom for reading to me when I was little and for praising me when I finally learned how to read to her.

Thanks goes to my dad who, even when he didn't agree, always said, "Whatever makes you happy dear."

Thank you to Melissa at AuthorHouse for showing an outstanding amount of patience and fortitude. If you hadn't called that day I was trapped on the I-5 who knows where we would be.

Cheers to my horrible ex-job. You know who you are. Thank you for making my life so miserable that I had no choice but to put my head down and plow through this story. Without you it never would have gotten done.

Thank you to my sisters, who helped me grow more in life than they will ever know. I would not be the person I am today without you guys.

And last, but only because you have to save the best for last, here is to my good friend Will. Thank you for caring when no one else did. Thank you for showing up when no one else would. I value your friendship more than I could ever put into words. We are kindred, you and I. I was lucky to find you in this life time. Thank you for pushing me to expect more from myself and for never being afraid to tell me which parts of my story were complete crap. Here's to the next excruciating manuscripts, mid-afternoon cocktails, and late night neurotic texting. From the best fecking rent-a-cop you've ever known.

1

A sliver of milk white moon was suspended in the endless black of the night sky. It leered down at the earth and me in my frantic flight with all of the maddening, unflinching resolve of a Cheshire cat. I ran, all flailing limbs and pale skin, my hair streaming out behind me like a wild banner.

In the movies, the woman running from the monsters is always perfectly scantily clad. She is always expertly coifed, no matter how long she runs. No drop of sweat ever touches her perfectly smooth brow and there is always a perfect C-cup set jouncing purposefully with every step.

In real life, the monster catches you half way through changing into your pajamas. I knew that no starlet had ever been caught (dead or alive) in pink shorty-shorts with Carebears and sparkling hearts all over them; or a tie-dyed green shirt that had seen two days of hard wear. Pieces of my hair clung to my face, drenched in sweat. And my bosoms, well . . . Since the eighth grade I had been and always would be a B-nothing. Some would say that that is more than most; but standing in a high school locker room with giggling girls draped in all of Victoria's flashy secrets, a B-nothing is like a large, furry mole in the middle of your forehead.

Another thing they never tell you about in the movies is the agony of the barefoot run. Initially there is the pain of embarrassment. I'll be the first to say that I am not a graceful runner. I run heel-to-toe, full tilt, arms and legs flung out from my body. Think along the lines of a new born giraffe with a debilitating case of palsy. Yes, it's that bad.

Secondly, running *barefoot* made the experience vividly excruciating. Even running down a paved road as I was, I found every stone, every pebble, every sticker and foxtail. The stones dug into my heels, shooting pains up my legs and deep into my bones.

The pebbles and stickers got caught between my toes along with those sneaky stray foxtails.

It had been the strangest two weeks of my life, and if I hadn't known better, I would have thought the damn things were working with the enemy.

I ran knowing *they* were behind me somewhere. It was that prickling awareness that the hunted has in the eye of the hunter. I hurtled down the dark, paved, back road with my skin pin cushioned by the knowledge. And not another person in sight anywhere.

To my left there were tall California spruce trees bordering vast, empty fields. It was autumn and the earth had already been harvested and turned. The soil was left strangely alien and menacingly lumpy. In the distance, tiny porch lights twinkled, looking as far away from me as stars in the sky.

To my right, there was a high embankment with a set of railroad tracks on top. I had followed the road and the tracks, hoping that one way or another they would lead me to civilization and people.

Ahead, a bright orange light throbbed; a steady beacon cutting through the dark. The only sign of habitation I had received in this darkest of nights. I was intent on my breathing and following the light, when a particularly sharp stone jabbed into my heel. I stopped in the middle of the road, jumping up and down on one foot, cursing aloud. If the enemy came out of the dark right that second, I don't know what would have pissed me off more. That I would be munched because of a stupid stone, or that I would be eaten while being so badly attired.

I picked the rock out of my heel and gimping along, kept running. No monster grabbed me or leapt theatrically from the night, but I could feel it's ever growing presence building in the back of my brain. This alone made me ignore the pain in my heel and stretch my legs, sprinting towards the light.

As I neared, a small white shack came into view. My heart dropped into my stomach. No house, no people, just a shack.

A single door stared at me in mute horror; two, small, rectangular windows and a black mail slot making up the parts of its eternally shocked face. I knew that this moment would be frozen forever in my mind, of how the face on the door had been so fantastically mocking.

I slammed into it, all one-seventy-something of me, hands frantically turning the knob. With a squeal of surprise falling from my lips, it opened as smooth as silk, hurtling me down to the cold, dark floor.

Strange things grabbed at my shirt and slashed my bare arms as I went down. I scrambled to my feet gasping and squealing like a Sumo at an all-you-can-eat buffet. My noise was accompanied by the clanging and tinkling of metal on metal. I blinked rapidly, willing my eyes to adjust. My legs burned. My lungs ached. I had the terrible urge to cry.

I am not brave. I have never aspired to anything greater than making it out of bed at a reasonable hour of the morning and putting in an honest day's work. And I only go to the gym regularly enough to get passes for free hoagie Fridays at Pete's Diner.

As my retinas adjusted, I could see tall mesh squares hanging from the ceiling. They looked like the drying racks at a donut shop. I scanned the dark and found myself seemingly alone. I remembered the door was open at my back and spun around. A second from cardiac arrest, I quickly noted the door way was empty, slammed it closed and engage the little push lock. The effort was laughable against what was coming, but it made me feel the tiniest bit better.

The shack was small and a creeping sense of claustrophobia nibbled at the back of my brain. But I quickly reminded myself that it was either the cramped, dark space or back outside with the creepers.

Scanning the room I noted that the only windows were about four inches tall and two feet long, high up on the walls. The orange light streamed in through them and it was as if I'd been swallowed by a giant jack o' lantern. I knew I would never look at one of those smiling gourds the same way again.

I bumbled through the shack, looking for some sort of weapon. The air tasted stale and slightly acidic. Even in the chilled space, I was sweating. The trays clinked softly as I moved around them. There were large spoons and ladles the size of my head hanging from the ceiling. Vaguely, I could remember that there was a dairy nearby and that this might belong to them. A storage unit. Part of me was wishing a farmer would wake up somewhere and have the undeniable urge to make cheese.

3

The heavy crunch of feet outside stopped all thoughts of rescue. An icy shiver wiggled its way down my spine. I eased myself back into a far corner behind a tall rack and held my breath.

The footsteps drew closer, crunching up to the shack, not even bothering with concealment. The shadow of a head entered the two orange squares of light on the ground cast by the door windows. It stood there for a moment and I had the strangest impression it was going to knock first. I slowly let go of the breath I'd been holding, eyes locked on the shadow.

Before I could inhale again, two enormous hands crashed through either side of the door and ripped it completely out. Pieces of splintered wood flew in every direction. I had just enough time to grab one of the giant ladles before a tall, dark figure rushed into the room and barreled through the rows of drying sheets. The noise alone could have woken the dead and it was more than I needed to spur myself into action.

I swung at my attacker when it came near, snarling at me with two gapping, serrated mouths. The ladle connected a home run to its head and as it fell sideways into the drying racks, I swung again. Drying trays fell on top of it from all directions and the ladle smacked them with a resounding *clang*. There was so much noise, for a moment I forgot to be scared.

The beastie swam out of the pile, snapping its mouths full of shining teeth, rolling its eyes that seemed to glow with orange faerie light. I hit it with the ladle as hard as I could. I put in all the pent up emotion of the past two weeks and every day before when a plate full of pastries couldn't cure me. I hit it with the same force I put behind my sledge and into my ratchet. It fell back into the trays and I pummeled it mercilessly. I hit it until my arms ached and my hands went numb. Warm spray came across my face and thick, viscous fluid drenched my t-shirt. I hit it until it stopped moving. And then a few more for good measure. My arms were trembling at my sides when I realized there was something thick and gobby hanging from my hair.

I stood there with the ladle hanging loose in my hand. My heart had taken refuge inside my head, my ears pounding with the force of my blood. My would-be attacker lay very still on the ground. The thin strips of orange light showed his body, tall and very human looking. The dark suit was tweed. Such a shame.

Two weeks ago if you had told me I'd be killing someone in a dairy storage shed, I would have laughed. I would have laughed and called a doctor for you.

The glob in my hair fell to the floor with a sickening *splat*. My whole body was shaking and my face felt like it was on fire. Something thick and not so nice had pooled around my feet and in between my toes. And here I'd been worried about pebbles and foxtails.

Two weeks ago, if you had told me I could beat someone to death with a giant ladle, I would have given a very sincere chuckle.

A tall shadow filled the doorway and flashed glowing eyes at me. Two weeks ago seemed like an eternity away. And I couldn't even manage a smile.

2

Two Weeks Ago

I stood in front of the little Fiesta feeling a mixture of pity and consternation. Four days of work, a helping of elbow grease and a handful of brain cells out the window for nothing. Dark fluid leaked from the engine block in steady drops. There was a hair-line crack four fingers long down the side like a greasy, brown lightning bolt.

As cars go, it was an ugly little thing, but it had been faithful and steadfast to the last mile. It was the color of burnt oranges with puke green pinstripes down the side. Spots of rust decorated the hood and roof in large bloody snowflakes; badges of automobile honor. Maximus (call me Max), was not going to be pleased. Even though I could've found more useful things under a rock, Max loved his Fiesta.

It had been a hard couple of years for everyone; what with the final gasping crash of the Stock Market, the president having a stoke, and the brutal downfall of the U.N.

America had undergone a transformation it hadn't seen in nearly six generations. Big Brother had squared his heavy shoulders, closed his gates and turned his attention to the poor, the tired and the huddled masses within his own home. Technology quickly lost its chokehold. People returned to a simpler time, not unlike that of the first Depression, farming the land and eking out a meager life where they could. Most had lost their jobs and homes. But gravest of all, their lives. Our town survived by the sheer fact that it had been living humbly off of the fruits of the earth since it was founded and would probably continue to do so until the end of days.

For Max, the final crash had truly been the end of the world. A recovering addict, he had lost his home, his family and his job all in the span of two years.

Yet through storm and hail, Max had remained clean and continued going to the NA meetings once a week. He still volunteered at the soup kitchen, and was an all-around nice guy. In my heart I feared the death of his little car would be the grenade that killed the camel. Or something like that.

I rubbed the side of my face, trying to coerce my brain into formulating the answer. I had to tell Max his car was a goner, but the part of me that said, "Hey! You're a nice person. And nice people don't go around dropping bad news like mustard gas." made my brain cells burble around in my head like nitric acid.

I thought about simply ignoring it. Imagining it would just go away. But in a town with a population of a little over three thousand, hiding just wasn't an option.

I found myself looking down the driveway behind the Fiesta. Off to the right, my grandfather's fence sat pale and warped next to the work garage.

It wasn't *really* a fence as fences go; maybe someone would have called it a hitching post for horses. There were three posts sunk into the ground in a line, parallel with the road. Four rough beams connected the two outer posts to the center.

In my mind's eye, I could see him perched on it, a strange gangly bird. Forever in his faded grey coveralls. His sleeves rolled up and an unopened pack of cigarettes tucked into one. My grandfather hadn't smoked in years, but the pack had remained. "It keeps me honest." He would always say.

Stains of all sort dribbled over him in multicolored rain drops, from chest to ankles. Even the tops of his tan boots were speckled and stained. There was grease and spots of oil on his snowy white undershirt, sometimes flecks of paint and the occasional handprint. My grandmother would lovingly wash every shirt, stocking him up on fresh ones as you would stock an artist up on new canvas.

His thin face was always younger than his many years, with his fine white hair cut close to his head. His pale blue eyes danced, seeing things that I could never begin to imagine. He would press two fingers lightly to his bottom lip; an unconscious tick from smoking. Forty years after quitting, the tick remained.

For hours he would sit thusly, staring at this car or that truck. His mind on whatever thing he was fixing in the garage. Nearly everything he had his mind set on fixing could be fixed by long hours of fence sitting.

I could see him hop down with a satisfied grunt, smacking the legs of his coveralls like dusting a rug. Then he would amble back towards the garage.

My grandfather could fix anything; cars, boats, motorcycles, motorhomes, plumbing, appliances; scraped knees, hurt feelings and bad dreams. I sat on that fence for two days once, and didn't get anything but pneumonia.

Shuffling my foot through the dirt, I looked up the road towards the house. I avoided looking at the Fiesta, rubbing a hand over the back of my neck.

The driveway went right up to the front walk and twisted back on itself. In the open loop, my grandmother had planted three wicked looking rose bushes with gigantic red blooms. In the late spring and all through the autumn, you could smell roses all over the house and far down the road. The bush farthest from the house leaned a bit to the right with a long healed dent in its side; the result of an unfortunate driving lesson. I could still hear my grandmother shrieking at us. *Stop you heathens!* Her face hidden in a spray of dirt and gravel. The memory made me smile, but only the tiniest bit.

The afternoon sun glinted off the shining picture windows on the second floor. On the left was my room, and to the right, my grandmother's sitting room. A large awning stretched all the way across the face of the house like a tarry black mustache. There was a porch swing in front of the living room's wide window on the right and two carved wooden love seats on the opposite end in front of the dining room window. The little white house practically gleamed.

At deep and meaningful moments, I'm able to spout forth all sorts of snide comments and tom-foolery. I plan on renting a big brass band for my funeral and a red dress, should I ever dare to marry. But looking at this house I couldn't think of anything that wasn't poetic and unreasonably sappy. Even the sight of the box hedges in front of the porch, newly trimmed, thrummed across my heartstrings.

A gentle breeze licked over my face and the little chime hanging beside the front door tinkled magically. The damn thing often drove me nuts, but my grandmother had made it with her own two hands.

So it stayed. A bitter longing rattled in my bones. If they were here they'd know what to do.

I pulled my eyes away from the house and back to the dilemma with four tires sitting in front of me. I rubbed two fingers between my eye brows, feeling the deep frown line that creased there. A sickening feeling had crept into my brain. A thought, at last, had been born. And not one that I liked one bit at all.

My head turned towards the garage, rust red but sturdy, and to the tarp covered lump beside it. The thought was almost unthinkable. I shook my head hard enough that I should have been able to hear the leftovers of my brains rattling around.

Beneath the lovingly fitted, pale brown tarp sat The Beast. My pride and joy. My first born. The Mustang had five thousand miles on its "hypo" 289 engine. The body was from 65 but the rest was built twelve years ago. Two years before I was even able to get my license.

Every nut, every bolt, every swatch of leather seating had been installed with my own hands.

With my grandfather occasionally grunting over my shoulder and a manual balanced on the steering column, I had lovingly restored, polished and painted every inch. Chrome rims glinted in the sun, peeking saucily out from beneath the tarp. Just that glimpse sent a shiver down my spine and tingle in all the right places. I could truly say that everything from the dip stick to the bottom of the cylinder banks was mine. Mine, all mine.

It was often my secret passion to drive at breakneck speeds, cackling (yes, cackling) and yelling. That cold worm of a thought did the cha-cha through my cerebral cortex.

Counting The Beast, I had three vehicles. My grandfather's 1950 Dodge truck sat in the garage, next to 'Old Woody', my grandmother's wagon. I couldn't bring myself to sell either of them. My grandparents were gone, but I couldn't give away their things. This left only the things belonging to me.

My stomach turned over and twisted into little knots and then one big knot. I desperately needed a scone, a cookie, something with absolutely no dietary value.

I turned towards the house and then back again, as if my feet and brain couldn't think of the same thought at the same time. *Do it*, a little voice in my head whispered. I grimaced and turned back to the house. I wanted to search for another answer. But it seemed I already had one.

Four and a half hours later, I sat at my dining table in front of a large plate of scones. There were two small jars, one of strawberry preserves and the other of orange marmalade. Both poised at the edge of the plate, along with a bowl of good sweet cream. All sat untouched.

The sun was setting low on the other side of the house, so the dining room was bathed in cool bluish light. The hand carved oak dining table had its white lace cloth on and it felt as if I were sitting in a pale blue cloud.

Grease and a multitude of black marks covered most of my face and neck. There were black hand-prints on the chest of my once white under shirt. My coveralls had been rolled down and the sleeves tied together at the waist. There was a long, cold line of sweat down the back of my shirt. This was the result of too much thinking.

I had gone back to the garage to think. Working on Mrs. Flicheman's toaster had turned into working on everything in sight. In my own method of what my grandmother always called 'self-soothing', I consistently rubbed my face and neck in slow rhythmic motions. The chest scratching came from thinking too hard.

My grandmother once told me she could always tell when I was having one of my "off" days when I came home from school with paint or pen all over my face and hand prints on my shirt. A product gained, she said, from my grandfather's side.

There was a little gray mark on my left ear that would always be with me. Once, while thinking particularly hard I had reached up to rub my ear, forgetting that I held a freshly sharpened pencil. Years later, the tiny self-inflicted tattoo served as a reminder to be more attentive to my surroundings while cycling through my thought processes.

After ruminating for a good while in the garage, I had finally given up. With shaking hands, I had retrieved The Beast's key and removed the tarp one last time.

The high gloss paint exploded in the sun with agonizingly beautiful ruby flames. The chrome around the windows winked at me. My heart did a little *pitty-pat*. Sinking into the driver's seat, with the smell of good leather rising up around me, I started The Beast and pulled away into the road. The purr of the engine sank into my very bones, melted my marrow. Tears had burned my eyes, but I held them back. Don't be a wuss, I had scolded myself.

All the way to Max's house I chanted a resolute little mantra. Suck it up. Do the right thing. I repeated it over and over, but the feeling of dread and loss refused to abate.

Max was sitting on his porch when I pulled up. Like most of the poorer people, Max live on the edge of town. His house was as faded and crumple as a piece of paper left out in the elements. Paint peeled, wood warped. One of the front windows was missing a shudder. The adjoining garage leaned precariously to one side.

Desolate farm land crouched behind the rickety place, bits of wheat bravely sticking out of the churned ground. It should have seemed homey, maybe even rustic, but it made the scene worse. Everything seemed sad and worn and tired.

I'd taken one look at the garage, pulling up the drive and convulsed at the thought of my baby living there. Feet and heart feeling like chunks of concrete, I'd gotten out of the car, Max waving to me from his chair. He had smiled a gap-toothed smile and watched me walk all the way to him. We exchanged pleasantries and before I could stop myself, the moment came. Sharp as a gun shot in the woods.

It came out of my mouth in a flood. My eyes had burned, watching the smile die slowly on his face, one word at a time, until he was slumped in his chair, nearly curled up on himself.

Never in my life had I thought to see a look like that on a man's face. It was the look of a man who has a glimpsed the deepest regions of hell. His eyes were hollow, as if someone had ripped out the very soul of him. Ripped it out, stomped on it, peed on it, lit it on fire and tangoed all over the ashes. Yep, that was about the look he had.

I'd started to shake, but before my nerve broke, I shoved my car keys at him. I could remember how his eyes had widened. More words falling unchecked from my lips and how the sun had come up in those big brown eyes. I remembered telling him the pink slip was in the glove box and his face had changed colors. White to red to pink to white. Then he stuttered at me like a bi-plane losing fuel in flight. Then he had cried. No, make that sobbed, wept, wailed, slobbered all over me.

When he was done, there was a smug of grease on his forehead. But I don't think he noticed. You could have shot him and he wouldn't have noticed. That's how happy he had been. He had graciously offered me a ride home. I had firmly declined. The walk would do me good, I had told him. He had insisted, but so had I. I could have said the sky was green and he would have agreed with me. I had walked all the way home with his voice in my head, *god bless you, oh, god bless you.*

I stared at the plate of scones. Usually a heaping plate of scones (or anything horribly fattening) was just the thing to break my bad moods. Some had cranberries and raspberries and blueberries in them, one had little pieces of apple and chunks of walnut. Two were vanilla bean and fluffy as sugar coated clouds. I stared at the plate and didn't feel the urge to do much of anything. And the day was really bad when *I* couldn't eat anything.

My eyes started to burn and I reached for a scone. That's when the doorbell rang. Hand hovering over the plate, I contemplated not answering it. I didn't particularly want company at the moment. I was happy mopping all by myself. It rang again, and I got up and shuffled around the table anyways. Saved by the bell, I thought as my hand opened the front door.

On the little woven mat that read "Welcome", stood my bestest best friend in the whole world. And for those that have never had a *bestest* best friend, I say woe to thee.

Her eyes, like melted bits of dark chocolate, widened at my appearance. Her nearly black hair was pulled back into a sophisticated French twist with little tendrils teased down at her temples. In the sunlight her hair has silky auburn highlights. She was wearing a loose weave brown skirt suit with the long sleeves puffed at the shoulder and a cute frilled hemline. There were bits of yellow in the brown fabric and the cravat-looking blouse was some almost nonexistent shade of pastel yellow.

Leila, as always, looked like she just stepped out of a fashion magazine. Right down to her brown satin Manolo Blahniks. Even her skin was pure untouched creaminess.

We had been friends since before I could remember. And by 'before I could remember', I mean since I was ten. How it happened, I don't know. But when I was ten, an accident killed both of my parents. I couldn't remember anything before my tenth year. Not even the accident that had apparently destroyed our house.

I had known the basics, like being able to read and beginning mathematics. But of my family there was nothing. Not a birthday party, not a Christmas morning, nothing. The only thing I had from before was a shiny pink mark on my right wrist, shaped like a backwards seven.

At my parent's funeral, Leila had been there. She had held my hand and wiped my face. I remembered her sitting with me in the park near the church. She was a familiar face when nothing else seemed to be. Even my grandparents had taken a little getting used to. But not Leila.

I glanced down at her shoes a bit enviously and studied a split in my cuticle. Sixteen years later, the two of us were still as tight as burs on a sheep's butt. Yet no two people were less alike.

We were like the female version of Laurel and Hardy, except neither of us is fat and mostly we're only funny to each other. So maybe not Laurel and Hardy, but you get the idea.

I felt like I towered over her heel-enhanced five-eight with my lanky five-eleven frame. My hair tickled my face, having escaped from the long ponytail hanging half way down my back. It was the color of wet brick and rich mud. I knew without looking that it was probably sticking up in every direction. My skin is pale, but I'm covered in freckles. My grandmother once lovingly called them 'Angel Kisses'. In the mirror it looks like someone splattered brown ink on my face. The sneaky bastards even showed up on my chest and legs if I stayed out in the sun too long.

Leila often tells me my eyes are the prettiest shade of green. They're not green, I always tell her. They're bog-water gray-brown with little dark pieces of weed floating on top. Leila hates my analogies, especially the ones I make about myself. Standing next to her on my own porch I definitely felt like the country mouse.

I was so distracted by my inner musings, that it took me a minute to register there was a covered container in her hands. It was rectangular and the tangy scent of something ethnic floated up to my nostrils. My mouth instantly began watering. My eyes floated back to her face. There was concern in her eyes and empathy etched between her finely shaped brows.

"Oh Vivian, I came as soon as I could." she said as the smell of roasted tomatillos wafted towards me.

Did I mention Leila's a chef? Reason Number Eight Million of Why We're Friends.

She'd attended culinary school in New York right after high school. A whole year without her had been murder. Thankfully, she came back just as poised as she left and full of righteous indignation. "They wouldn't know a Torte from a Quiche if it hit them in the face." She had told me. Which, judging by the level of her animosity upon return, it probably had. Either way, I was glad she was back. And her list of delicious recipes had grown. Thankfully, my waistline remained nearly untouched.

"It was awful." I groaned, stepping away from the door. Leila came in and headed for the dining room. Her eyes lingered on the untouched plate of scones.

"God, did hell freeze over too?" she asked, setting her container on the table.

"It's a freakin' tomb in here!" She shouted, heading towards the kitchen door at the far end of the room. She flicked on a switch and soft gold light filled the dining room. I followed her meekly, my eyes locked on the container on the table. She pushed through the swinging door into the kitchen. I could hear her rummaging through drawers and cabinets. I licked my lips and reached for the cover. Leila came back with two plates and a pair of forks in one hand. Two bottles of wheat ale dangled from the other.

"Sit and help me serve. They're getting cold while you stand there eye-raping my Pampered Chef." She said shouldering me back to my seat in front of the scones. We both sat. Leila is never one to mince words, especially around food. I popped the top on her glass baking dish and nearly drooled on myself.

"Enchiladas? Lei you're a goddess!" I said taking one of the forks and diving into the cheesy goodness. Leila grunted at me and opened our beers. She set one in front of me. A whole, big, cheesy pan of enchiladas (with the green sauce) all to ourselves. I could have died and gone to heaven.

Leila's Hispanic food makes cats and dogs live together in harmony. There was gooey cheese everywhere by the time I served both of us.

"When Max showed up in town with The Beast, I nearly killed him. I thought he'd stolen the damn thing." She said taking her plate. I had my fork half way in my mouth and stopped. My face flushed and my eyes burned. Don't ruin the enchiladas, don't ruin the enchiladas, I thought fervently. A tear tried to sneak out of the corner of my eye, but I covered it up by taking a swig of my beer.

"What were you thinking? Why didn't you just give him the wagon?" she shouted around a mouthful of chicken and tortillas. She called it the wagon, refusing to call it Old Woody because, as she put it, it was sexist and vulgar. I hesitated to tell her she had cheese hanging from her chin.

"I couldn't give him *the wagon*; it's not mine to give." I said quietly, taking a big bite of food. They were superb, delicious, great sex and fireworks at the same time good. I made the appropriate sounds of appreciation. Leila eyed me over the neck of her bottle, one eye squinted. She could be a Vogue pirate, with or without the cheese on her face.

Of course we'd had similar conversations before. About the vehicles, about the house, about the prices I set for fixing things. I kept the old ways because I liked them; because it made me feel closer to my grandparents.

My grandparents never charged anyone anything they couldn't afford. My grandfather once accepted a clutch of pheasant for fixing a radiator. I had a set of hand-made ceramic bowls I'd gotten in exchange for new tires on Mr. Bell's Caddy.

Leila felt I could be living better if I were harder, more cut-throat. I knew she wanted the best for me, but I *liked* the way I lived and didn't want anymore.

I watched her across the table, spinning thoughts around in her head. I watched her choosing what to say next. The pain of my grandparents was still felt fresh in my mind even after so long. In the way of best friends, she was weighing her options, but I knew it wouldn't be the last time we talked about it. She swallowed a bit of food and took a sip of her beer.

"It was a nice thing for you to do." She said after a long pregnant silence. My eyebrows went up my forehead and tried to disappear into my hairline.

"Nice, but stupid." She grumbled, finally wiping the strings of cheese off her chin. I smiled and flicked a small piece of chicken at her. Leila stuffed her mouth full of enchilada, chewed a bit and made grotesque faces at me. I laughed, nearly choking on my own food.

As fierce as she might act, I know she only does it out of love. Because, just as she is my family, I was more than sure I was hers too.

In all of the years that I'd known her, I'd only seen her parents twice, and both times from a distance. Both were dark haired and cream-complexioned. Her mother studies antiquities and her father is an honored historian. The nanny, Mrs. Wain, had been Leila's resident guardian.

When we were children, she only saw her parents four times a year. We almost never talked about them. When we did, it was Fredrick and Melanie, never mom and dad.

When Leila turned eighteen, we took hatchets and hacksaws and baseball bats to every room of their very expensive ranch style home. It was the only time I'd ever seen her feel anything about them except cool indifference. I was still shocked they never had us arrested.

Leila has her own apartment above her own bakery now. She makes all the cookies for the church functions and cakes for nearly every festival. Mrs. Wain still does her laundry every Sunday. Life is hunky dory.

"So now what are you going to do? Drive the wagon around?" she asked, serving herself another helping of enchilada loveliness. I envied that she could eat forever and never gain a pound. Sheer force of will and hard labor kept me secure about my triple digits.

"Yea, it was a thought. Or maybe I could take up bike riding." I left it hanging there and took big bite of food. Leila stared at me in horror.

"What? What are you gonna do? Ride around with a scone tied to the end of a stick hanging from your back? And what if a bear gets you? Or a mountain lion?" she shouted, and then proceeded to stuff her face. Like me she eats on the cusp of intense emotions. I tried to look studiously concerned, creasing my brow and tightening my lips.

"A scone? Seriously Lei, there hasn't been a scone involved bear mauling in years. And I think mountain lions are strict protein dieters. I'd give them high cholesterol at the very least." I quipped.

We stared at each other across the table. I tried my damnedest to hold it in but a smile relentlessly pulled at the corner of my mouth until it was almost a twitch. I felt it involuntarily slide across my face. Leila sputtered and gave a loud burble of laughter. A chuckle spilled out of my mouth and erupted into a riot of giggles. We sat there laughing while the enchiladas got cold. Blasphemy.

3

Red Glen is situated in the northern hills of California. Some years before the gold rush, a small Irish man named Herne Boyd and his rotund, overbearing wife Meaghan migrated there and set up camp. While life in the wilderness can be harsh and unpredictable, the Boyd's had stuck it out, and were soon joined by other families seeking to make their way. Red Glen began life as Chastity Village (compliments of Mrs. Boyd) in 1854, with a population of one hundred and fourteen people, practically bustling. In 1862, under the illustrious leadership of Mayor Martin Blackhorn, the town was rechristened Red Glen. Much to the consternation of Mrs. Boyd, it has remained the same ever since.

Red Glen has a current fluctuating population of three thousand and twenty-two people. There are three dominant streets that form the hub of the town; all old, brick-sided buildings with their painted faces, white-washed decorative moldings and the occasional striped awning.

The main street (aptly named Main Street) has the pharmacy, the general store, the hardware store, the grocers, the movie theater, and Pete's diner on one side; the bookstore, the feed store, Leila's bakery, two ladies boutiques, and a plant nursery on the other. Stalwartly sticking with tradition, Red Glen still holds an annual promenade down Main Street sidewalks, with funnel cake and delicious homemade ice cream.

Hold Street bi-sects Main Street and connects it to Victoria Street. From an aerial view, Red Glen looks like a big H planted in the middle of nowhere.

Hold Street has the hospital, the police station, the fire station, the post office and boasts the town's only bank. There's a pretty manicured park next to the fire station and a flower shop next to the hospital. The bank is squeezed in next to the police station, safe and sound.

Victoria is mostly residential, with the High School and Elementary School on the north end. Smaller streets branch out from Victoria, cluttered with houses and gated duplexes. There were at least two churches and a small synagogue that I was aware of.

All around, the Sierra Mountains stand guard over our little valley. Ancient oaks, spruce and pine are the watchmen; tall sentinels on the hillsides. And not a damn Krispy Kreme for miles.

Like most of the older families, my grandparents built their house outside of town in a southern wooded area. The little white house was about five miles from town and more than a hundred yards from the nearest neighbor.

There were puffy white clouds dotting the sky as I headed into town. The air wafted in through my side window, bringing with it the taste of a faraway ocean and a touch of warm dark earth. I needed a coil from the hardware store and Leila had promised lunch at her place.

The old Dodge rumbled towards the west end of Main Street. The glossy green paint reflected bits of the blue sky and the white of the clouds. It was a nice day for a drive.

People waved to me as I passed the general store. Any second I expected Doris Day to jump out from behind a lamp post and burst into song. I pulled into a parking space in front of the hardware store, but nothing happened. Darn.

The Panner is a modest establishment with big, shiny, front windows and a glass front door with a big silver bell attached to it. The bell rings out every time the door opens. Stepping inside, one is greeted with the scent of new rubber, fresh cut wood and a faint metallic tang. To the left of the entrance, there sits long pine topped counter with scales and measuring lines and tools of the trade. Reed Paddington (like the bear) stood behind it, a pencil tucked behind his ear and a pair of small gold wire rim glasses perched on the end of his nose.

Reed is five-five, with a shock of white-blond hair cut short on the sides and back, but left long and untamed on top. He's perfectly tan from top to bottom, with a smile that belongs in a tooth paste commercial. His body is as stocky as a bulls and he also wears the title of 'best friend'.

Reed whipped off his glasses and threw down a hunk of greasy metal as I walked in. He was around the counter and making a b-line for me before I'd gone five feet. Without a word, he hugged me and lifted me clean off my feet. I managed to suppress a very girly squeal of protest.

"Ugh! Let go of me you lech! You're wrinkling my shirt!" I yelled, wiggling in his arms. Half a foot shorter and he could still man-handle me. It was down-right embarrassing.

He gave me another good squeeze, and set me on my feet. I ran a hand down the front of my white scoop neck shirt even though there weren't any wrinkles. I glared at him but he was staring at me with a strange doleful look in his eyes.

"You are a goddess among women." He said softly, taking a hold of my hand. I could only hope the horror I felt was expressly reflected on my face.

Reed had been allowed inside that very secret center of girlhood for the simple fact that neither Leila nor I had any designs on him. Nor he us. At the age of twelve, being very fickle, nearly all boys had been off limits. Until eighth grader Debby Jovinski locked one little white haired boy in his locker wearing a girl's dress. Having also been the object of Debby's deranged interests we instantly felt a kinship with the tow-headed boy from the coast.

No one was *supposed* to let him out of the locker and Reed had come out snorting mad, giving Debby a fat lip she'd never forget. And just to show her she couldn't best him, he'd worn that ugly purple dress all day. That's when we knew he was a keeper.

Standing in the quiet of his store, holding his hand, gave me an all new level of the creeps. It was like having intimate encounter with your brother. Yak. I tried to pull my fingers away but he grabbed hold with the other hand too.

"Max came into the general store the other day while I was on the way home." He said softly. Oh that. I had almost pushed it out of my mind. But no good deed goes unpunished.

"It's no biggy Reed. Like I told Leila, it was the right thing to do." I said. With a jerk of his pale brows, Reed threw my hand away from him.

"The right thing to do my shiny copper toned ass! What? Were you on drugs?" he shouted, his eyes flashed the bright blue of cornflowers. My mouth dropped open.

"Leila says you refused to hand over the wagon. The truck I can understand ... but The Beast? Seriously?" he threw up his hands and walked off, ranting through the store. I didn't catch nearly any of it I was so stunned. He came back with three packages in his hands. Looking thoroughly disgusted, he shoved them at me.

"I hope you know I'm very disappointed in you." He said reaching over to the counter and grabbing his glasses. He slipped them on his face and glared at me. I was half tempted to tell him he looked like an old woman.

"You sound like Ms. Crabtree." I managed instead, digging into the pocket of my jeans. It was his turn to look shocked. He did a bon-a-fide soap opera throwing off of his glasses and jerked his body to one side. He tried to give me what might have been his come hither face, over his shoulder.

"How do I look *now*." He said in a strange husky voice. It made me chuckle.

"You look constipated." I told him. Reed sniffed and pouted. I knew he was straight, but sometimes I wondered. Leila says he spends way too much time around us. I was beginning to think she has the right idea.

"Well if that's the way you're going to treat me when I paid for *all* of your things." He said, sauntering back behind the counter, absently running his hand over the polished surface. I stopped digging in my pocket and tried to process what he said.

"What do you mean you paid for everything? That's over a hundred bucks Reed, you can't do that." I said trying to wrench my hand free of my pocket. When I finally did, I only came up with a twenty dollar bill and cursed. I'd wanted to wear the jeans that made my butt look good. This then the price of vanity.

I stalked over to the counter and began setting the packages down.

"Oh no you don't." He said picking them up again and pushing them at me. We did a mad push and tug for the manila colored packages before I was forced to grab them to keep them from flying everywhere.

"You're not the only person around that can afford to be charitable Vivian Cross. And you better get that into your head right this second. If you even try to give me money I'll go to the bank and tell them you dropped it in the street and to deposit it for me." He said and I stopped struggling. He *would* do something like that. We glared at each other for a long minute. I blinked first and shoved the twenty back into my pocket. Reed grinned from ear to ear.

"Next time I decide to do something nice, I'm gonna do it anonymously." I grumbled turning for the door. Reed's syrupy voice chuckled loudly at my expense. My hand was on the door when he called to me.

"We're still on for Thursday right?" I gave him a small glance over my shoulder and shrugged.

"I don't know. We'll see how *charitable* I'm feeling." I snipped. I pushed through the door and was followed by the sound of laughter. I threw my packages into the cab of the truck and walked across the street. Again there were people waving; Mrs. Lawrence and Ms. Burke standing in front of a sparkling clothes window.

Sometimes I detest living in a small town. It's like Cheers but with more nosey old ladies and lots of rednecks. Having lived in the same town since birth, everyone knew my name. Everyone knew my family. They probably even knew when I lost my virginity. I walked past the bookstore with old mister Beaker perched behind his desk and hurried towards the bakery. I could feel the eyeballs of two old women boring into my back.

There were three small, pale yellow tables sitting in front of the bakery. Each had two gilded steel chairs. Once upon a time, the chairs had been beautiful hand woven wicker. But some of Leila's customers are a bit zealous in their loyalty of her pastries. The sheer magnitude had been too much for the little things. Now they were gold-painted steel that looked like wicker.

They sat under the frilled goldenrod hued awning; their spindly legs etched with shining flowers. Like many stores in town, Leila's has wide glass windows. Today I paused in front of them and stared. All around the border of the windows were flowers. But saying that they were flowers hardly did them justice. They were blooms bigger than my head, painted to look like bursts of filigree in shades of crimson and gold and orange and yellow. I looked closer and saw oak leaves and birch leaves, pine cones and acorns hidden amongst them. There were even thorny gold berry vines with bright fruit twisted in long tendrils.

I took my hand away from the door and took a couple steps back. The overall effect was stunning, as if the wooden window molding had come to life, Mother Nature deciding to retake the bakery. I could have stayed and looked at it all day. But my stomach rumbled.

Entering Leila's bakery is like stepping into a cube of buttery gold. The walls are yellow, with tan paisley designs. Glass lamps shaped like calla lilies hang inverted from the ceiling and spout from the walls in gold and pale amber. The brightly lit, gold edged glass viewing cases, stretch from the right of the door and curve to the left, forming a big L. A big L full of deliciousness.

Decadent tortes and cakes and tarts and Danishes beckon to customers like doxies in a tavern and the further down you go, the better it gets. A sugar-coated peepshow.

There were four different kinds of quiche, made fresh daily. Bright little marzipan and beautiful squares of baklava. On the savory side there were meat pies, smoked meats, and little, Italian, fried rice balls filled with ragú and cheese called arancini.

Off to the left there sat four more little yellow tables like the ones outside. At the end of the twenty-three foot case of heaven, was one table, close to the glass. There was a small yellow sign on it with the word *Reserved* in Leila's flawless cursive. In case it was lost in translation, Leila's favorite color is yellow.

I grinned and headed for the table, nostrils flaring to drag in every last yummy scent that wafted through the air. It was only then I noticed the absence behind the cases.

Two swinging doors led to the kitchen, each with a small circle of glass about half way to the top. Through them I could see three different heads bustling frantically back and forth. I could hear machines running and metal containers clanging together. Over everything, there was a sound like the angry buzzing of bees. It was soft yet constant. One bottle blond head came bouncing towards the door and a second later Keely, Leila's apprentice, burst through.

Keely is five-four and built like a china doll. All small bones and perfect peaches-and-cream skin; small cute nose and full red lips. Her hair is the color of harvest ready wheat, cut into a perfect bob.

She has big eyes, and I mean big. Big shiny anime eyes the blue of glacial ice. In her over-large apron, with flour smudged across her forehead she looked about twelve instead of twenty.

At first glance, I had been terribly jealous of the little creampuff. Any female in close proximity with Leila deserved great scrutiny. I mean she was *my* best friend wasn't she? The initiation of Keely's apprenticeship had made things awkward at best, and I had been pea-green with envy. This girl got to spend all day with *my* friend, while I could only look on over the counter. Leila never let anyone behind the counter, she said it was unsanitary. But Keely was allowed because she *belonged* there.

One long Sunday over tea I spilled my confessions of insecurity to Leila, who in turn laughed at me for the rest of the week. She dutifully informed me that Keely was her apprentice and could never come between us. Except for the fact that the girl could whip up a meringue with perfect peaks and was an absolute sauce wizard, Keely had the personality of a wet mop. Leila assured me that Keely would most likely never breech the circle of friendship. Not to mention she was nowhere near tall enough to replace me.

Fully appeased, I could now give Keely a genuine smile when I saw her. This got bigger when she handed me a plate.

"Leila says she'll be out in a bit to fill you in on all the *juicy* gossip." She told me with a small roll of her eyes. She watched me ogling the plate with a knowing smile.

"Who did the front windows?" I asked, balancing the plate on one hand. Keely waggled her eye brows at me.

"The Norki boy did it a couple days ago." She said, leaning into the case. My eyebrows went up.

"The punk kid with the rainbow colored porcupine on his head?!" I asked, completely disgusted. I have no semblance of interest or wanting to know what goes on in the mind of a teenager. I barely liked *being* a teenager when I was one.

"Yea, but its blue and black now. Very cohesive for his whole angsty painter vibe." She said with another roll of her eyes. I grunted and shook my head. That's just what the world needed, another angsty painter guy.

Keely shrugged her shoulders before turning and flouncing back into the kitchen. I turned back to my lunch.

On the plate sat an epic standard for sandwiches around the world. Between two golden slices of Leila's Garden Herb wheat bread, there was turkey and pastrami and roast beef. There were lovely slices of red tomato and purple onions complimenting delicate leaves of romaine and sumptuous slices of avocado. A thick slice of Swiss finished the masterpiece. I knew there was mayo on both slices of bread with just a dab of good home ground mustard. Kalamata olives decorated the top of two toothpicks holding the confection together. A large pickle spear and a small glass bowl of rice pudding completed the meal.

Although I felt like I had died and gone to heaven settling myself down at my table, a really awesome sandwich could mean only one thing . . . I would be eating my sandwich alone.

Only something truly disastrous could make Leila skip a lunch date, so I gratefully took a big bite of my sandwich. Flavor avalanched onto my tasted buds. I groaned in ecstasy and stuffed half an olive between my teeth.

I was half way through my sandwich when the kitchen doors burst open again.

"Ugh! I *hate* my life!" Leila shouted, sliding a tray full of goodies into a case shelf. She huffed and puffed over to me and I nearly choked on my food. There was flour all over her. In her hair, on her face, all down the front of her apron. Everywhere.

"This is the worst day *ever!*" she bawled leaning over the glass case near me.

A statuesque woman entered the bakery and raised her thin brows over Leila's exclamation.

"Don't tell me," the woman said raising one graceful hand, "the Baileys have finally produced enough children to take over Red Glen . . . and you have ten minutes to make to make soufflés for all of them . . . climbing uphill . . . and barefoot?"

Leila's and I stared at the woman, speechless, before exploding into laughter.

Michelina Dorset, councilwoman extraordinaire, smiled broadly at her own joke.

One of the town's most illustrious residents, Michelina comes from old money and always lets people know she knows it. She helps in the community and lobbies for budgets. She sits on the PTA, and rebuilt the entire school library. Her pale brown hair was streaked with gray, but instead of making her look older, she seemed fierce. She always reminded me of a hawk or some other bird of prey. Her wide hazel eyes saw everything, but her sharp featured face revealed nothing.

She continued to smile as she glided to the counter. Along with having a seat in the city council, Michelina has a fierce addiction to Leila's Very Berry tarts. Because surely everyone needs a good vice.

"Worse," Leila said, her laughter quickly petering out, "the Duncans are getting married."

Michelina and I threw confused glances at each other. Weren't weddings a happy thing, especially when a certain person happens to own the best bakery for miles?

"On the same day as the McLaughlins." Leila finished, her face screwed up into a deep pout. I gasped, clutching my chest. Michelina echoed me and assumed nearly the same posture. There was nothing I could do but stare in pity and horror.

Long ago, in the time of our great grandfather's grandfather, there were two families that got off the boat in the east, and decided to head for the west. But problems had begun between them before they ever reached the shore.

According to one version of the legend, a Duncan girl, trying to impress a McLaughlin boy, had caught a fish for them both to eat. Yet being a prideful sort, the McLaughlin threw the fish away and decided that *he* would catch them a better one. Insulted, the Duncan had returned to her family and told them what happened. The elder Duncan, being a prideful man himself, took up his fine fishing net and set out to catch *more* fish than any McLaughlin could. Seeing the elder Duncan with his net, an elder McLaughlin set out with a crew and a row boat to spear an even better fish to fund their journey to America.

And so simply it had begun, a lasting competition between the two families. Each insisted on being better, bigger, badder or stronger than the other. If a Duncan bought a house, a McLaughlin had to buy a better one. If a McLaughlin won a prize, a Duncan had to win a bigger one. No amount of reason could penetrate the feud. So all of Red Glen watched, and sometimes snickered at, the Duncans and the McLaughlins. It made for great gossip. Yet more than anything, I would have spared Leila this headache.

"Monday is supposed to be the big day. And I'm making *both* wedding cakes, two groom's cakes, and all of the deserts. I think I'm going to die." Leila groaned, pulling out three tarts from a shelf. I could only stare. There was nothing I could say to make this okay.

"I have to cancel Friday and Sunday Viv. I'll need to work up to the line to get it all done. I'm sorry." She said. She had robotically wrapped up the tarts in a little yellow and gold box and slid it across the case. Michelina picked up the box shaking her head.

"I can only extend my greatest sympathies and well wishes to you my dear." She said in her purring voice. Leila nodded, staring out into space, running a hand over her face and hair.

Michelina turned and pinned those sharp eyes on me. For a moment all the hairs on my arms stood at attention and I had trouble swallowing a piece of avocado.

"And you dear. How are things with you?" she asked.

My mouth dropped open, probably showing of bits of masticated food in my teeth. Me? She was talking to me?

I could only stare at her and struggle to close my mouth. Michelina Dorset had never so much as looked in my direction unless I was at a town meeting, or attending some function. I was an entity of purpose but of little notice.

She was watching me with those eyes. I saw her face soften a little as she waited for my reply. At nearly fifty, she didn't look a day over thirty. My mother would have been about her age, I thought.

I nearly dropped my sandwich the thought was so abrupt. The loss of my grandparents was a deep ache even though it had been almost nine years since my grandfather had gone and seven since my grandmother. I almost never thought of my parents. The fact that I had made me push *all* thoughts back and away.

I pasted a smiled on my face and took a big bite of my pickle. Juice ran down my chin and onto my arm. Michelina frowned.

"I'm great. Just peachy." I said, talking around my food. The sharpness was back in her face and she gave a little nod. Without another word, she turned away and headed to the door.

"Until next time." She called, and swung gracefully out.

I looked to Leila but she was still lost in some train of thought. I glanced back towards the door and my blood froze.

Outside in the beautiful, bright afternoon, my arch nemesis stalked. Even from where I sat, I could see him across the street walking at a steady clip. He entered the street and started to cross. His long muscular legs flexed beneath tailored black slacks. He was wearing a pale gray, long sleeved, button-up with a dark tie that may have been black or some shade of gray. There were lean muscles under the shirt but it too was made to fit his broad shoulders perfectly, seamlessly.

I had the hope he was going to walk past the bakery. But I hoped wrong.

"Two o' clock!" I hissed at Leila, instantly bringing her attention. Her dark chocolate eyes narrowed and her face cleared of emotion. She would be a stone in the face of the enemy.

Me, I tried to hide behind my sandwich. I put my eyes on my plate and diligently chewed.

Malcolm DeHaven entered the bakery in a breeze of chill autumn air. His waving black hair was slicked back from his face. Slate gray eyes scanned the room with their long, lacey lashes. His skin was tan and flawless. High cheek bones, straight sharp nose, perfect masculine jawline. His tie was dark gray with beautiful abstract designs only a single tone lighter. My gorge rose. I hated him intensely.

We had been fighting since we were children. Years of pulled hair, punched arms; hours in detention for destroying each other's property, slashing the tires of a bike. Even separating our classes hadn't slowed us down. Though neither of us seemed to know why, the animosity constantly floated in the air. It was like the scent of dog doo long after you wiped your shoe.

His eyes instantly flickered to me as he stepped in. He scowled, hands clenched at this side. He'd only been back since the beginning of last year. Four years of college had obviously helped him with his emotional control. But the enmity was still there, floating behind his stern gray eyes.

I watched him through my lashes. He took a deep breath and studiously chose to ignore me. Every line of his body was tight with discomfort as he walked to the case. He ordered two croissants and a danish. I was instantly bitter. Bet he doesn't have to worry about gaining a single ounce, I thought putting my sandwich down. I saw Leila place the items in a little yellow bag. He paid and quickly left.

"Sometimes I've thought about putting laxatives in his croissants." Leila said aloud. The comment surprised a laugh from me. Even on her worst of days, Leila's loyalty is at its best.

4

Late Friday morning found me alone in the back yard. The sun was shining in a cerulean blue sky. A gentle wind rustled the trees and sifted through my hair.

I'd showered and left it down. Now it drifted around my shoulders and face in a wild tangle. I didn't care. I pulled my cardinal red, knit sweater close around me and leaned back in my chair.

I sat at the antique, iron wrought table that had been my grandmother's favorite sitting spot. It was dark green with curling flowers down the legs and beneath the glass top. There were two matching chairs.

The forest was at my back, whispering its wind songs. To my right, in the same direction as the house was my rolling bed of Black-Eyed Susans. The flowers grew knee high nearly all year long and I would be sad when the frost came to take them. They nodded their sunny heads in the wind, dancing to the music.

It was hard to admit and even harder to say aloud, but the simple blossoms are my favorite. My grandmother planted them for me shortly after I arrived and every year they came back more than before. Now they stretched all the way up to the house and had begun making their way down the side towards the front. Except for keeping them out of my grandmother's flowers, they had been allowed to grow as they pleased.

To the right of the back steps sat my grandfather's vegetable garden. Looking across the table I winced at its state of disrepair. It was nearly time to tear everything out. The plants hung from stakes and cages in dilapidated brown skeletons. Even with my grandfather gone, I replanted it every year.

The rest of the yard had been my grandmother's domain. The scent of hyacinths drifted in the air. There were colchicum in giant beds and delphinium and crocus, and a kaleidoscope of flowers I couldn't name. There were boxes of herbs, chamomile and mint, thyme and chervil. There were great spikey artichokes and fragrant wild garlics with their little white flowers. Plants grew wherever my grandmother had touched.

Then there were her roses, giant prickly beds of roses surrounding a small brown gazebo about thirty feet out into the yard.

My grandfather built the gazebo with his own two hands. An anniversary present. English ivy grew up the support posts and covered the entire structure. In the summer it was a great place to sit in the shade with the scent of roses all around.

The sun was warm on the top of my head. I had come outside with nothing in mind. I had a refrigerator and an old vacuum in the garage waiting to be fixed. I had gone to the garage twice, but couldn't get in the mood for fixing anything. I couldn't even get up the urge to eat something. So I showered, dressed in cream colored corduroy gaucho pants with a red scoop-neck shirt and my favorite red sweater. On my feet I wore cream colored flats with little red bows on them. Leila would have been proud.

I'd gotten dressed and walked out into the back yard. I'd been sitting for nearly an hour. A sort of quiet melancholy had come over me. I tried to think of Leila and her dilemma, or of Reed and how great our movie night had been the day before. Yet the only thing I could think about was my grandparents.

In my mind's eye, I could see my grandmother sitting across the table, white hair piled on top of her head, the tiny blue flowers on her white long sleeved shirt. There was soft lace at the wrists and little mother-of-pearl buttons at the neck, which hung open so she could feel the breeze. She wore an ankle length jean skirt and white roman style sandals. There was a tiny chain with four little bells around one ankle. It jingled as she tapped her foot. I could see her sitting there, humming and sewing a tear in one of my shirts.

My grandfathers memory floated about like the man himself had always done. First he was sitting on the top step in front of the back door. He was tinkering with a clock radio, a screw driver clenched between his teeth. Then he was in his garden with a small rake, grunting to himself as he attacked weeds and parasites alike. He had his coveralls rolled down to his waist and a straw hat on his head. He'd looked like tanned leather by the end of every summer.

The memories of them followed me wherever I went. They were so thick sometimes I wanted to take a broom and go chasing them out like rabid dust bunnies.

Leila and I had often talked about it. She knew how I couldn't let go, how I couldn't get past their being gone. No matter how long it had been. The memories of their leaving were the worst. They were clear in my mind and sharp as knives in my heart.

My grandfather and I had been working on a dune buggy. Heads together, we'd spent the whole afternoon working out kinks in the suspension and turning it into a serviceable piece of machinery. It was spring. I was seventeen.

I remember turning a bolt near the front end while he was greasing a hinge, when suddenly he stood up. I thought maybe he was going to move to another area or let me finish while he put tools away in the garage. But he just stood there. He stood there so long and still it made me look up.

His blue eyes reflected the sunlight as they searched the line of trees. His nostrils flared and his face had this faraway look, as if he was listening to some distant, familiar music.

I remember standing and looking out into the forest. I remember squinting into the trees. I'd made my breath shallow and strained my ears to hear even the smallest noise. But there was nothing. Not even the wind was blowing. The day was mild and calm. After a long moment, I looked back to my grandfather. There was a tick in his cheek. The look in his eyes had gone hard. I'd never seen that look on his face before and I knew the memory would always be sharp in my mind.

"What's wrong pa-pa?" I whispered. Some part of me felt the need to whisper, as if someone might be listening. I remember how he blinked and looked at me. His eyes had softened and there was sadness there.

"Just an old man and his imagination." He had said, clapping a hand on my shoulder.

We had gone back to work. My mind had lingered on the moment but shortly after, my grandmother called us in for lunch and the thought was lost.

One late night, nearly a week later, I had gotten up to use the bathroom. I could hear my grandparents whispering together. I stood in the dark hallway with my back to the wall. I couldn't make out what they were saying, but after a long pause I could hear my grandmother crying softly. I had gone back to bed quickly, without ever going to the bathroom.

The next morning found my grandmother still in bed. My grandfather said she wasn't feeling well. After a quiet breakfast, I remember him walking out the front door and out into the lawn. He was wearing a thick, green plaid flannel shirt and sturdy jeans. He had on his work boots.

I followed him outside in my pale blue flannel pajamas. I hadn't worn any shoes and the grass was wet on my feet. We stood in the grass for a long time. Neither of us said anything. I remember *knowing* that that would be the last time I saw him.

He had turned to me, looking every minute of his seventy-five years. He lifted one large, callused hand and cupped my cheek. I had started to cry and held onto that hand with both of mine as if I could keep him there with me forever. There were no words.

When he took his hand away, I closed my eyes. I couldn't watch him go. I couldn't see which way he went because I would follow him and bring him back. I listened to his footsteps across the lawn and into the undergrowth of the forest.

I stood in the lawn for a long time. So long that my grandmother finally came and got me.

We sat at the dining room table staring out into nothing. The moment was so untouchable; the pain so real, so numbing. We just sat until the sun began to set.

I remember my grandmother making tea and taking us both into the living room. We ate scones and sipped tea. Outside, night birds sang their mournful songs.

"The wind called to him." She had murmured softly. I hadn't understood what she meant, but I had nodded. I remember looking at her and wondering if she too would suddenly disappear.

Sometime later, we put up a headstone in the family plot at the back of the property. It was nearly two hundred yards from the house and bristled with old stone markers. There was no fence to keep the wilderness out but it stayed well away. Only a large willow wept there, its long arms guarding the beds of our ancestors.

I remember standing near my grandfather's 'grave' with dry eyes. I looked at the other headstones and wondered how many of them also lay empty.

After that first night, we never spoke of it. There was a sadness that lingered in my grandmother that almost never lifted. She tried to hide it, but I could see. And I was full of questions for which no answers were forthcoming.

Not long and I was full of anger. I raged at the world, at my grandmother, at anyone I could. I set off into the woods with a vengeance. I swore I would find him and bring him back. I would shake the living daylights out of him and shout the sky down. All of those things I promised I'd do when I found him, but I never did.

I returned to my grandmother's house full of sadness and confusion. I was sick with a fever for two weeks.

An *emptiness* filled our lives. The place where my grandfather had stood was a gapping void, with only his memories scurrying about. I watched as the emptiness consumed my grandmother, like the ocean washing out a seashell. I had only been with them for seven years, but my grandmother had married my grandfather at sixteen. I missed him dreadfully, but I knew it was nothing compared to her loss.

Day after day, I expected her to simply float away. Everyone was careful around us. My teachers, the townsfolk. Even Leila walked on eggshells when she came to the house.

Sitting with her in her garden, I waited for the wind to pick my grandmother up and carry her away like some stray bit of flotsam.

Two years were all I had to wait. A month after my nineteenth birthday.

I had come home to a quiet house filled with cool autumn light. There was bird song drifting in from an open window in the kitchen. The house was still. Too still.

I remember running up the stairs and bursting into my grandmother's room. She was there, lying down on the bed. There was bright light streaming in the window that over looked the back yard. A breeze fluttered the long lace curtains. She was under the covers, with her hands neatly folded on her stomach. I remember how my breath caught painfully in my tight throat. Her eyes were closed. Her face was peaceful, with the tiniest bit of a smile on her lips. My eyes had traced every beautiful wrinkle in her face, the laugh lines around her mouth and the deep crow's feet at the corners of her eyes. My eyes had burned at the sight of her. All the love in my heart was burning in my throat and scalding down my cheeks. And then her eyes opened.

"Tears for me?" she had said in her beautiful sing-song voice, holding her hand out to me. I ran to her, falling to my knees beside her bed. I'd cried quietly and while she petted my hair.

"The time has come, my little love," she said, and there was so much tenderness in her voice.

"You grandfather is calling to me from the beyond. I know you'll be sad but you must know how much we both love you. You must always remember that we love you." She said. I remember nodding, unable to speak. Again, I was numb with agony. I knelt beside her bed until her hand fell away from my hair. I watched the last light of life ease from her body with the setting of the sun.

Leila helped me place the headstone. A good number of townspeople came for a service. I stayed by the cemetery for a long time, my love burning in my throat and my heart pouring from my eyes and falling to the ground.

Now at twenty-six, the pain was as real to me in the present as it had been in the past. I huddled in my sweater and debated going back into the house. Yet I knew the memories would follow me.

In a part of my mind I didn't often think about, sat the memory of my parents. Why I don't think about them is a mystery to me. I never had the urge to ask and my grandparents had never volunteered any information. If I thought about it hard enough, I realized that no one ever really talked about them.

I thought maybe it was out of politeness. Because lord knew that this was a town that knew how to mind its manners.

But it was as if they had been forgotten. Erased. Even Leila never asked about them and she bugged me about *everything*. I tried to think about when they died. I tried to remember the exact date. My right eye started twitching with the effort, and a deep ache started in the back of my skull.

I began rubbing the back of my head, when the kitchen phone rang. I was half tempted to let it ring, but anything had to be better than sitting in the back yard moping. I got up and walked to the house.

Trotting up the three stone steps, I swung open the door and stepped into the kitchen. The phone rang loudly. It was louder than most phones.

My grandmother had had a hearing problem (not that she would have admitted it), so my grandfather had installed a louder ringer while she was out one day. The first time it rang, I nearly jumped out of my skin.

"Told ya it was broken." my grandmother had said to my grandfather as we stood together around the island in the kitchen. My grandfather and I had shared a look behind her back as she answered the phone. Even after they were gone, I had never changed it. I picked up the handset and pressed it to my ear.

"Cross residence." I said.

"Uh, Missus Vivian? Is that you?" a female voice asked.

"Yes ma'am it is." I replied.

"This is Eleanor Bailey. Daniel Bailey's wife." She said. It made me smile. Ah, the infamous Baileys.

"What's up Mrs. B?" I asked, still smiling.

"Well the tele's on the fritz. And I was wonderin' if you could come take a look at it. I got a whole slew of laundry to do and the lil'uns are getting restless." She said in a rush.

"Sure I'll come over. Give me about ten minutes to get there 'kay?" I said, leaning against the wall.

"Sure, sure. We'll be waitin'." she said and hung up before I could say goodbye. I shook my head at the buzzing handset. A TV on the fritz. Anything was better than nothing.

5

Five pairs of identical brown eyes watched me from a faded green couch. I had tried to hide myself behind the hulking body of the television, but still they watched, and giggled, and occasionally picked a nose. Yes *a* nose, it didn't have to be their own.

The Bailey family is made up of Daniel Bailey, his wife Eleanor, and their eight children. They range from sixteen to sixteen months. All of them are made up of sable brown hair and pale brown eyes. The oldest, a son, was away at school. The eldest daughter worked at the grocery store part time. Another older son was out back in the yard helping to chop wood. Eleanor waddled into the room. Her belly was enormous and heavy with the ninth Bailey child.

I stood and walked around to the front of the television. It was a relic among TVs. Its big wooden body sat on the shaggy blue-green carpet nearly four feet long and two feet deep. It had the aluminum nobs that clicked when you turned the channel and a pull switch to turn it on and off. I grabbed the nob and a quick jolt raced up my arm.

"YEOW!" I shouted jerking my hand back. All the little clones laughed. Eleanor shook her head with its long glossy pelt of brown hair. Her pale face had dark circles around the eyes. Her thin mouth twisted to one side.

"Told ya it's buggered. The baby grabbed hold of it this morning and nearly screamed the house down." She said. I rubbed my hand and could taste metal in my mouth. I could only imagine how a baby would have felt. I quickly unplugged it and stood back.

"Well I'll take it home and see what I can do." I said.

The older son came in from cutting wood and between the two of us we managed to get the TV into the bed of the truck. All the little clones came outside to watch me leave and I left them with the promise that I would get their precious babysitter back to them as soon as possible.

Back at the garage, after a great battle getting it in there, I stood staring at the TV. My reflection was grotesque and bulging in its dark gray face. I had removed the backing on it and its guts lay on the long bench that stretched across one entire wall. I took up a voltmeter and began searching for the short circuit.

The little yellow box beeped and buzzed throughout the entire mass of television innards. The garage was quiet otherwise, save for the sounds of birds outside. Long beams of sun shone in, filled with happily dancing dust motes.

After a long while, I replaced two wires and started the process of putting everything back together. As a last thought, I found a spare bulb, and replaced it as well.

From where it perched on the shelf, the electronic monster seemed to glare at me. I made faces at my reflection and plugged it into a wall fixture next to the shelf. There was no fire, no smoke, and no sound. So far so good.

I reached for the switched and pulled it out. The hair-raising sound of electronic energy swam through the room. The screen filled with black and white snow. I nodded to myself, and reached for the channel nob.

It has been found that the average American wall socket puts out about one hundred and twenty volts, with anywhere between fifteen and twenty amps. The average older television set can produce more than twenty thousand volts. Studies have also shown that as little as thirty volts or sixty-five milliamps can cause death in a healthy human being.

That being said, touching the channel knob, I instantly knew what a Christmas tree must feel like. Every hair on my body stood on end. As if my eyeballs had become the television glass, black and white shapes exploded behind my eyelids. A metallic taste burst in my mouth, as if I'd been sucking on rusty pennies. My only thought was of Mrs. Bailey and all her little clones and how their babysitter was going to catch a sledge. And then darkness.

There were birds singing. The trees were rustling and groaning as they stretched their arms to the sky. Someone was playing a harp in the distance. It was like rain on window glass, the trickle of a mountain stream. Little creatures were burrowing deep in the earth, whispering secret things, laughing strange tittering laughs. Deep in the forest, someone murmured my name.

I opened my eyes to a bright band of light overhead. The little dust motes were still dancing, oblivious to my dilemma. I groaned and sat up. The wagon sat behind me, I had come less than an inch from braining myself on the rim of its tire.

I rubbed my head groaning. The taste of burnt pennies was sharp in my mouth. Little white squiggles danced inside my brain and I could see them floating in my eyes when I blinked. Everything in the garage had its own red and gold outline, like devious little halos.

I stood carefully, but fell back a step. I caught myself on the hood of the wagon and just stood there for a moment. My face flushed hot and cold. From its place of the shelf the TV watched me, its screen gone gray once more.

"Bastard." I whispered. My whole body was shaking. I managed to push away from the wagon even though my legs felt like jelly. I turned to my right and stumbled out the small door leading from the garage.

The daylight was about eighty million watts too bright. I tripped over my own feet and slammed into the door of the truck still sitting outside. I hung onto its handle while my vision cleared. The world was bright and painful. Again everything was bathed in strange red and gold halos and there seemed to be things moving around in the midday shadows. Strangely shaped humanoid things.

I had to get to town. Something was seriously wrong with me. Leila and Reed would help me. Those were my only coherent thoughts. Everything else bounced around in my head like manic, Techni-colored marbles.

I opened the door to the truck and slid into the seat. The world wavered for a second, but in the shade of the cab it seemed more solid. I sat there, staring at the keys already in the ignition. There was a breeze blowing through the forest. It sounded like laughter and voices and wild arcane music.

I quickly turned over the engine, shaking my head. I started towards the house slowly, making my way around the loop. In a long slow blink, I nearly collided with the rose bushes for the second time in my life. And then I said a little prayer when I managed to make it away without incident.

Driving down the long way to town, I was grateful that the roads were clear, because the trees made strange shadows across the road and the bands of sunlight mocked me, weaving like broken snakes. I focused on the yellow lines and the white reflectors, and prayed.

After what felt like an eternity, I reached town. People waved but I focused on the road, on parking the truck. I slammed on the brakes, bumping my forehead against the steering wheel. One of the front tires lurched up on the curb.

Sliding out of the cab, I staggered towards the sidewalk and people were watching me. I could *feel* them watching me like tiny drops of ice on my skin. Their images wavered like heat stroke visions. I ran for The Panner's front door.

The bell clanged loudly as I pushed through. The entire store wavered with the strange shadows and bright demonic halos. The front counter was empty.

I ran down the long isle towards the tall white door at the back, meandering about like a drunk. The dancing black letters on the frosted glass that read 'Manager' jumped out at me. Without knocking, I pushed it open. My breath seemed to be coming out of my chest in strangled gasps as if I'd run a great distance. I took one step past the threshold and froze.

The thing sitting at Reed's desk looked up. It had two spiraling ivory horns sprouting from either side of its forehead. A ridge of amber colored scales arched along is brows and faded up into its shock of white hair. Its eyes were white, with oblong pupils slit sideways like a goats. Its fiery skin shined like copper in the sunlight that streamed in through a window at its back. Its mouth was full of sharp pearly white teeth.

"Vivian? What's wrong?" it growled and stood up from the desk. It pushed the chair away and came around the desk towards me.

I am not ashamed to say that I screamed. Loud and hard and not much unlike a five year old girl. I screamed and backed away frantically. In my haste I tripped, falling out of the door.

The thing came for me, large hands reaching with their sharp ivory nails. I scrambled to my feet and started running. I crashed into a few displays along the way and pushed them behind me, hoping to slow its progress.

"Vivian!" it shouted and I could hear it running through the store after me.

My heart raced. I hit the front door full tilt. The little bell flew off and clobbered me on the top of my head as I went. I stumbled out into the sidewalk and strong arms grabbed me.

I turned gasping, ready to tell them about the monster in Reed's office, about the fact that it was coming to get me. Except the face I looked into was anything but human. It was *green* and covered in leaves and what might have been moss. Its eyes were dark as a forest pool in deep shadows. There were oak leaves around its eyes and dangling from its hair. It held me with long arms gnarled like branches, its skin lichen covered bark.

Again I screamed. I pushed away from the creature hard. So hard that it fell backwards on to the side walk, spilling the bag of groceries that had been dangling from its wrist. It looked up at me with wide, alien eyes, stunned. My feet carried me into the street just as the horned monster burst from the door of The Panner.

It jumped over the thing on the side walk and stood next to my truck staring at me. I turned and stopped walking, frozen in terror. Across the street stood two women with faces as pale as fish bellies. Blue scales shined around their necks and framed their faces like sapphires. There was a man with a mane like a lion and vines of red berries hanging from his clothes. There were others even stranger still and they were all watching me.

If I had been more coherent, I would have read the shock on their faces, the sorrow. I would have seen the very human clothes on their backs, the packages in their hands. But I was out of my mind with fear. And standing in the middle of the street.

The horned beastie shouted at me in some tongue that I couldn't understand, waving its hand at me. I spun around, hands raised to fend off some unknown attacker.

The thing about standing in the middle of the street is that eventually, some numbskull driver isn't going to be paying attention. Which is why man invented crosswalks and sidewalks and stop ways. In the hopes that some numbskull pedestrian wouldn't run out into the street unguarded. Apparently I had never met any of those ingenious folks with their high hopes and ideals, and apparently, neither had the man in the ruby red mustang.

6

My first thought was of revenge. I swore acidly to every god, every deity and every supreme being I could think of that I would haunt Maximus Lee for the rest of his days.

My second thought was that the afterlife smelled of lavender and honeysuckle, and of moist wooded places warmed by the summer sun.

I opened my eyes and blinked in the brightness of a summer day. I was standing in a great clump of bluebells and forget-me-nots. There was a long white stone path leading between meticulous beds of white flowers and pale herbs bordered by shining white granite. At the end of the path stood a white gazebo with honeysuckle climbing the support posts. My heart soared. Heaven was my grandmother's garden. Or so I thought.

Off to my left, sitting at a small, white, iron wrought table, there was a woman. She had long waving hair falling down her back. It was a thick luscious color like wet red brick covered in chocolate. Her skin was pale and delicate as fine porcelain. From what I could see, she was wearing a long flowing dress the pale green of Spanish moss with dark green flowers embroidered along the v-neckline. There was a soft smile on her full mouth and she watched me with eyes the color of fresh clover or the most expensive of emeralds. She watched me with my grandmother's eyes.

I could feel my breath trembling out of my mouth. My heart raced. How could I have ever forgotten that face? It was so beautiful to me, like Botticelli's Venus, the Sistine chapel, and the Mona Lisa all molded into one flesh. How could I have ever forgotten?

I stepped out of the flowers, and onto the pristine white path. My feet carried me to the second chair beside the table. I felt myself trembling all over. She was smiling up at me, her eyes sparkling.

"Hi mom." I said. My voice seemed to float out of me on a breeze. I gripped the back of the chair and slid into it across from her. Small white bits of tree dander floated all around. The entire scene was very dreamlike. She slid one slender hand across the table holding it open to me.

Without hesitation, I reached across and placed my own hand into hers. It was warm and smooth and very real. Mine was a rougher replica of it.

I knew there were many questions I should have been asking. Things I should have wanted to know or have clarified. But sitting in this heaven, I was content just to look at her, to fill my mind with love for her.

We sat that way for a long time, until she sighed and placed her other hand over the top of mine. Compassion filled her eyes. There was love there too, radiating out at me.

"You've grown into such a beautiful young woman." She said and tears welled up in her eyes, sparkling like diamonds in the sun. I took my free hand from my lap and latched onto our linked hands.

"It's alright mom. Don't cry. We're together now." I said, squeezing our hands together. Those diamond tears trembled on her lashes as she slowly shook her head.

"Not quite my love." She whispered. I felt my heart sink into the pit of my stomach. My face flushed hot. I tried to take my hands out of hers but she held on.

"What do you mean not quite?" I said, my voice rasping out of me. I watched her lovely brow furrow even as my own confusion built.

"Your time has yet to come. I am only a product of your mind. Your being here means that something significant has occurred. It means that something has happened to the spells placed upon you. This moment only betokens the beginning of your journey." She said in her velvet soft voice. My mind reeled.

"Journey? Spells? What are you . . . what are you talking about?" I stuttered. I tried a second time to pull my hands away and she let them go, but reluctantly. I rubbed the back of my neck and the top of my thigh at the same time.

"What was done was executed with only the best intentions. The memory of me was placed here so that the transition might be easier, should it ever come about. You must know that you were never meant to remember. It was decided that you would simply be a normal child, with a normal life. It was something we never would have been able to give you." She said. Both of her hands still lay on the table, palms up, beseeching me. I stopped rubbing myself, but gently began scratching the flat plain of my chest just above my breasts with one hand.

"Not meant to remember? Not remember you and dad? Not remember my whole stinking life? What the hell good is that?" I shouted pushing myself back from the table. I felt the legs of my chair scrape along the grass and stick. The heavenly summer day seemed to lose its peace as my anger arose. She sat there, her eyes now dry and watched me, irritatingly calm and compassionate.

"There are many that would have put you to death. It was the only thing that could be done to assure your life. All that was done was done out of love . . . for you." She said and the tears were back in her eyes. My heart melted in my chest and my hands fell motionless in my lap. All of my anger drifted away. False figure or not, this was my mother.

"Who? Where is . . . ?" I couldn't properly formulate the thoughts tumbling through my mind. I sat up in my chair and searched all around the garden. We were alone in the flowery haven. My mother shook her head slowly, her hands clenching.

"He could not be here to meet you. In the end he used up all of himself to save us. He could not be here, but know that he wanted to. Never was there so much love in him as when you were born. Child of his flesh. Proof of his love." She said. Two shining tears fell down her alabaster cheeks. My heart clenched and my throat burned. I reached across the table and took her hands in mine. We sat for another long moment and somewhere in the distance a thrush warbled.

"I fear this will be a hard thing for you. But your heart is strong and I believe you will prevail." She smiled at me and I couldn't help but smile back. I ached with love for her and for my father who had given his life.

"Did my grandparents know about this?" I asked finally forming an idea in my head. My mother's eyes sparkled.

"Your grandmother was the root of all power. Without her it never could have been done. She was a Guardian, as you would have been had things turn out differently. Your grandfather was a simple Tinker, a son of the forest. Where my mother led he followed. Please do not think ill of them." She said. Her eyes were full of bright happy things and a wide smile curved on her mouth. I shook my head. I could never be angry at my grandparents.

"What's a Guardian? Is that why I could see all of those things? What am I supposed to do?" I began rapidly. The figure of my mother opened her mouth to answer and in the same moment, a frigid breeze blew over us, tangling our hair. Her hands clamped down on mine painfully and her face crumpled.

"No, it's too soon." She whispered. She began shaking her head, holding on tightly to my hands. I tightened my own grip, holding onto her even as the sky began to darken.

"Mom? Mom what's happening?" I asked. She was still shaking her head. Her beautiful eyes glowed with green fire.

"I love you. Remember that we both loved you so much. Always follow your heart. Shelter the weak . . ." her voice reverberated all around me and the darkness gathered closer until the green of her eyes filled my vision.

"Mom! Don't go!" I screamed, desperately trying to hold onto her hands, frantically trying to gather her to me.

". . . Protect the good from evil . . ." her voice said. All around me were shadows and the sound of her voice.

". . . and always remember . . . remember . . ."

The darkness closed in until it swallowed even the green fire. Whispering bits of her voice floated around me. I lost the feel of her hands and lost the ability to breathe. The darkness had plunged itself into my chest. A lance of pain jolted through me like a thousand hot blades. I tried to scream but nothing came. I felt myself jerking like a landed fish and out in the black, a voice called my name.

"Hold her! Hold her down!" someone yelled. Many hands were holding onto my body and something hard was pressed against my lips.

"Drink Vivian! Drink!" a voice yelled at me. It was familiar yet I couldn't grasp the recognition, bathed in a haze of pain. I opened my mouth to tell them to let me go, only to receive a warm rush of bitter liquid down my throat. I choked and fought in earnest. I tried to yell an especially colorful expletive, but my throat felt raw and swollen, as if I had already screamed a good amount.

"Hold her!" the voice yelled. There were many hands but still I was able to struggle. I was full up to the top in pure agony, a pain so acute that it overwhelmed everything else. I couldn't breathe properly. My breath was spasms in my chest, hissing raggedly out of my throat. I could feel the bitter liquid burning in my nose. There were more voices and suddenly they seemed so far away.

My body betrayed me. One at a time, my limbs stopped obeying. I couldn't see through the darkness but I was warm and the hands slowly let go. I had the impression I was floating and then I floated away.

A heavy blanket of cashmere clouds was spread out over me. Sunlight warmed my face and made a red curtain of my eyelids. Lead weights had settled inside my skin, pinning me down. The smell of lavender filled my nose.

Immediately I tried to open my eyes. My lids fluttered. I caught a flash of images. Not the garden, a room. A yellow room. I tried again and every muscle in my body seemed to strain with the effort. I could hear myself groan and grunt. And then a shadow hovered over me, blocking the sun from my face.

"Vivian?" a voice said. I slowly reassembled the parts of my brain that were tossed around like pieces of scrambled egg. A hand touched my shoulder and the shadow moved.

"Vivian? Can you hear me? Open your eyes." The shadow said. I struggled with the weight of myself. I felt myself grimace. One at a time, I dragged my eyelids up. There was a shadow bending over me. Its head was bathed in an auburn halo. Wide, dark chocolate eyes studied me. The name to go with the face slowly bubbled to the surface of my cerebral cortex.

"Leila." I said. It came out of my mouth in a croak. She moved away, and I was once again flooded in sunlight. My eyes instinctively clamped shut. I could hear her moving around somewhere above my head and then she moved past me in the direction of my feet in a waft of fragrant air. There was a sharp snap of blinds and the room was bathed in shadow. I opened my eyes again and found her standing over me. She had a cup in her hand.

"Drink this." She ordered holding it out to me. Her voice was icicles in my ears. I slowly lifted one wobbly hand and struggled to sit up on what I recognized as Leila's living room couch. Though calling it a couch wasn't doing it justice.

Leila said it was a chaise lounge. It was a couch with only one arm that curved up higher on one end. It was Victorian and horribly expensive like all the furniture in her apartment.

I manage to scoot myself into a sitting position without passing out. The day was looking up. I slowly took the cup from her. I realized at the same time that she had made no move to help me. As soon as the cup was in my hand, she stood back, watching me. Her face was very serious and her eyes looked enormous. She looked for all the world like an owl in human form.

I took a long drink from the cup and almost spit it out. The liquid was bitter and smelled like old socks.

"No, you have to drink it. All of it." Leila said sharply. I sat there looking up at her with my cheeks bulging. What the hell crawled up her butt, I thought. I squinted at her and she frowned. I was half tempted to spit the noxious brew out on her very expensive, plush, cream colored carpet, but she looked like she might jump on me if I tried. So I swallowed and held the cup out to her.

"No, you have to drink all of it." Her voice was frigid and she was still frowning at me.

"The hell I am!" I shouted, trying to get off the couch. I slid my legs over the side but that's as far as I got. My head started spinning and snowflakes danced in my eyes. I sat there holding onto the side of the couch, willing my body to comply. When my vision cleared, I glared up at her. She was still standing there. She hadn't moved an inch.

"Some help you are." I said in a strangled half sob. My whole body was shaking. She was supposed to be comforting me. I was the one that got electrocuted *and* hit by a car. But she stood there with her big eyes and that weird bird look on her face.

"The drink will help you." She said. I wanted to tell her to go to hell but I felt that if I said anything, I'd cry. And I sure as hell wasn't gonna cry. I drank the horrible drink, making the appropriate grimaces and shudders of revulsion. When it was gone I held the cup out to her again.

"How do you feel?" she asked, not taking the cup. I felt stupid for sitting there with my hand held out to her. And I felt pissed off that she was making me feel stupid.

"Just F-ing peachy." I snarled, putting my hand down in my lap. Her eyes tightened just a bit around the edges.

"The more you cooperate, the easier this is going to be." She said. The icicles that had been in her voice found their way down my spine. I could only stare at her. Who was this person? The pod people had stolen my Leila.

"What do you remember?" she asked in a flat voice. I expected her to turn on a bright light over my head while she brandished a pair of pliers. Her eyes were cold slabs of obsidian.

"I was at my house fixing Mrs. B's TV and it electrocuted me. I drove to town to look for you and Reed. And . . . I saw . . ." I drifted off, staring avidly at her face. It was only then I realized she was glowing. It was as if there were lights under her pale skin. Her hair still had its own halo of light without the sun. My mouth went dry.

"What? What did you see?" she snapped, taking a step towards me. I flinched and pressed myself into the back of the couch.

"Nothing." I lied. The cup tumbled out of my hand and rolled across the floor unnoticed.

"I must have blacked out, I just remember getting to the Panner and that's it." I stuttered. The pod-person Leila wasn't fooled. I've never been a good liar. I suddenly felt that this had been the most horrible time to try.

Those owl eyes scowled at me. All the little hairs on my body stood on end. She leaned over me.

"What did you see?" She ground out biting off each word. Her voice had been glacial before, but now it was an inferno. I literally felt scalded. And absolutely unable to lie.

"I saw . . . a monster . . . in Reed's office." I said softly. My voice was high and breathy, "And then there were more out in the street, with scales and fur and there was a . . . a tree-man . . ."

The not-Leila straightened. The plains of her face shuddered and her shoulders drooped. For a second, I could see my Leila peek out from her eyes. The corners of her mouth started to fall but in an instant, the pod-person Leila was back. Her face was smooth as a piece of glass.

"So the time has come." She said in the flat voice. I started shaking my head.

"The time for what? Lei what the hell is going on?" I said and stood up from the couch. I felt myself wobble a bit, but was happy when I stayed vertical. Leila backed up until she hit the wall across the way. Her eyes were back to looking big and owly.

"Don't! Don't come any closer!" she said almost frantically. Her nostrils were flared and her fists were clenched. I looked hard at her. I couldn't believe what I was seeing. The air around her shimmered like heat waves radiating off hot asphalt.

I slowly side stepped. I was so out of here. The level of weirdness had reached maximum capacity. I watched her the whole way as I stepped toward the small hall to the left. It opened to a flight of stairs leading down. Leila watched me the whole time, turning as I moved. We were like strange silent dancers.

I reached the hall and held my breath. We stared at each other for a long moment. Who would make the first move? I cursed myself in my head, and made a dive for the hall. As soon as the stairs were in view off to the right, I leapt for them. And almost fell down them. I'm no ninja, but I made a fancy bit of a slide into a roll right down to the bottom.

Thankfully, the heavy oak door at the bottom was unlocked. It opened out into the sidewalk near the front of the bakery. I was half blinded by the sunlight, but was grateful to see my truck still parked across the street. Its one wheel was still on the curb.

I stepped off the sidewalk and stopped. I quickly looked both ways. No sense in getting clobbered twice.

After thoroughly checking for runaway Mustangs, I started off again. My eyes swept back and forth over the sidewalks and storefronts. Half way across the street, it hit me. Where the hell was everyone?

The street was completely deserted. And from the looks of it, the stores were too. Every door was closed, every window darkened. This alone urged me into a run. I reached the truck and still there was no one. I looked hard and found not even a quickly pulled shade.

I got in the truck and found the keys still in the ignition. One of the little graces of living in a small town.

I pulled away from the curb with a thump. My heart had taken up residence inside my head. Just get home, I thought. Once I got home everything would alright. Yea ... and pigs fly.

I drove down the deserted road and somehow, in my heart I knew. Nothing would ever be the same again.

7

Every surface in the kitchen gleamed in the afternoon light. I stood in front of the sink looking out the small square window with its view of the garden. My fifth cup of tea was clutched in my hands, hovering just below my mouth. The scent of jasmine tickled my nose.

The previous day had passed and the night with it. In a wave of paranoia, I had resolutely locked myself inside. No stroll to the garage. No long sit in the garden. Nothing.

I'd spent the night wrestling through panicked bursts of sleep. Every forest noise, every sigh of the wind, every creak of the old house had been a foreign entity creeping. As soon as the sun had come up, so had I. Some inner voice warned of danger. I'd gone to every door and every window and locked everything. Every light in the house had been turned on to chase the even the most minute shadow away.

The world was suddenly new and unknown. Creatures that lived in faerie tale and legend were now jaunting around in my home town. God only knew what could be lurking out there. My imagination was rampant.

I'd created a circuit of sorts for myself. I paced from kitchen to dining room, to living room, to pantry and back. I refused to go upstairs unless I needed to. I was afraid of being trapped. I had the first aid kit and a bag full of necessities sitting on the dining room table. Flashlights, batteries, freeze dried camping food, clean underwear. Yep, I definitely had the priorities in order.

Now, I'd been standing in the kitchen for nearly an hour, with three trips to the bathroom. (Way too much tea.)

I watched the light in the garden dance and twist. The red halos were gone, but the light still did strange things, moved in ways that simple streams of light never had. And there were noises.

There were things out in the garden. Lively little things that I could almost see out of the corner of my eye. Or if I pretended to look at them through my lashes they were shapes half imagined. Sometimes they were tiny people shaped things or four-legged animal things. And sometimes they were the size of large dogs but in no shape that any dog had ever been. They played in the garden, flitting and leaping and lumping about. I gawked at them in horrified fascination because in general, they seemed to be having a good time.

If I cocked my head to the side and let the sound of the forest blend in with the garden sounds, I could hear them. Singing, laughing, tittering, tinkling, barking, farting. Noises only imagined in dreams. And there was music. Music made from instruments no human hand had ever touched. Melodies that caressed the ear and quickened the heart.

I was rooted to the kitchen floor. Mesmerized. I stood there in my favorite jeans, my green tie-dyed shirt, my most comfortable pair of white sneakers, and a cable-knit, green housecoat that hit me mid-thigh. The coat gapped open, the waist tie dangling along the floor.

I turned away from the window to make another circuit. I had to convince myself the house was secure. And that's when I heard it.

Vivian. I slowly turned back to the window, half expecting some horrible thing to be standing there.

It's at this point in most movies where you'll find me screaming and throwing popcorn at the screen. The heroine turns to face the monster instead of *running the hell away* like a smarter person. Run away, I would yell, run away!

Vivian. My hand started shaking so badly I had to set my cup down on the island behind me.

Somewhere out in the sun-shiny day, a who-knows-what oogie-boogie called my name. Like most female movie archetypes, I threw caution to the wind, straightened my coat, tying it tightly at the waist and walked to the door.

My hand gripped the door knob, only slightly sweaty. Holding my breath, I quickly threw open the door and jumped (yes jumped) out onto the first step.

Nothing happened. Nothing grabbed me or sprang from the woods. None of the *things* in the garden became visible to point and laugh at me either. And for that I was very grateful.

I closed the door tightly behind me, and descended. My eyes darted around the garden and along the line of trees. Searching for anything. Anything *not right*. But in an area so pastoral, I found myself jumping at the sight of squirrels and a small scream escaped me when a tiny finch burst out of a flower bed. Walking down the path that bisected the garden, I almost sprinted back to the house when a stately looking quail ran out of the gazebo in my general direction. Okay so it was flying in the complete opposite direction. Damn quail. But that's how on edge I was.

I walked past the gazebo trying not to think about the things I had half seen dangling from it. The smell of roses was comforting and I felt a single iota better upon reaching the back half of the flower beds. There were more herbs towards the back, and the profusion of scents bombarded my nose. I walked past them, trailing my fingers through the plants I could easily reach. I plucked a piece of rosemary and sniffed it as I went.

When I stood on the edge of the last bed, with its plucky border of beach wood, I stopped and took a deep breath. There were large patches of wild garlic here and it was one of my favorite places. I stood there breathing in the familiar scent, feeling almost calm.

Vivian. The voice was a whisper in my ear yet distinct at the same time. My veneer of calm shattered. A shiver raced down my spine. The little piece of rosemary fell from my shaking fingers. The sound came from off to the right, drawing my eyes diagonally across the large field that separated the garden from the family cemetery. It was off into the trees on the other side. Inside my head I could almost feel it like the needle of a compass or Theseus' string through the labyrinth. I took a step and stopped.

What the hell was I doing? Tromping off into the woods after some crazy whispering voice? My kind of adventure is taking an extra piece of pie at the summer barbeque or driving a bit too fast across a deserted field. I think maybe there was a cow tipping incident Leila and I might have been involved in. Maybe.

Danger is not my middle name. Not even destined to be the middle name of my children's children.

I like fluffy slippers and baking terribly fattening things. I like reading a good book or pretending to be an expert in horticulture. I knit, for land-sakes. I don't gallivant after strange voices and story book things in the woods.

My feet were moving before I could convince them otherwise. I plunged my hands into the soft pockets of my coat and trudged across land. The grass was past my knees and the thought of snakes stopped me again. Scanning the ground, my eyes fell on a stout piece of branch sticking up from the grass. I cautiously picked it up to rustle the vegetation as I walked.

The sun was getting low in the sky by the time I reached the line of trees. I clutched the stick in my hand and swallowed hard. I was sweating under my house coat even though the air was autumn chill. The forest was a writhing tangle of shadows.

I almost lost my nerve. Whatever waited, was waiting in the shadows. The owner of the whispering voice *lived* in the shadows. *Bathed* in them. Wrapped around themselves like mating serpents entwining their flesh.

The thought made me pause. It was a thought that wasn't entirely my own. I have my moments of poetic justice, but this thought, this thought was something new. And yet it wasn't. It was a new thought half remembered.

Still poised at the edge of the trees, a flash of a memory hit me. Hit me like a ton of bricks.

A man was holding my hand. I knew the man, loved him. He was tall and dark haired. He smiled when he looked down at my small hand in his. He smiled at me with my eyes. We walked through the park. Other children played in the background. It was a beautiful day. There were birds singing and dogs barking happily.

He was talking to me. I remembered his mouth moving. I hadn't cared at the time what he was saying. He was talking to me and that was wonderful. I felt like a flower turning its face to the sun.

He was talking to me. He was telling me about the darkness. He was telling me about the shadows. *Never fear the shadows, fear will cripple you.* He had said.

Gasping breaths wheezed out of my chest. I found myself leaning against a tree, my stick still clutched in one hand. I think electrocuting myself felt better. I dug my fingers into the bark of the tree and forced myself to do breathing exercises. Beyond me, the dusky forest loomed. No fear, I thought, no fear.

The trees whispered and hissed as a breeze wound its self through them. My mind flashed on the things in my garden. If those things lived in a simple garden, what creatures would be lurking out in the forest?

"No fear. Ri-ight. No fear." I whispered taking a big step past the tree line. Every nerve ending in my body was on high alert, skin tingling, brain sparking.

I stood in the shadows until my eyes adjusted. There was sunlight flashing and speckling through the canopy but it was few and far between. I flared my nostrils and opened my mouth, trying to scent the air. And what exactly does a supernatural oogie-boogie smell like? I asked myself sarcastically, snapping my mouth closed.

I started off in the direction my inner compass still pointed to. Trudging along, I was immediately grateful that I had worn jeans. The undergrowth snagged on the fluffy fabric of my house coat and scraped over my legs. Above me and all around, the forest whispered.

I thought if I stopped suddenly and whirled around shouting 'BOO', I would see a multitude of figures racing through the brush. I did not stop. I kept walking, using my stick to part the foliage. I stepped on top of a fallen log and perched there. *Never step directly over a log,* my grandfather had said. I bent forward and used my stick to shuffle the leaves around. No sense in getting bitten before I ever reached the looming danger.

I snorted in ironic amusement and jumped to the other side of the log. No sense in being half-dead before the boogies can kill me, I thought. Now wouldn't that be a shame.

The forest seemed to go on forever. I was well and truly sweating from exertion. The sun had set even further, leaving me in sultry twilight. I missed seeing a particularly vicious root and almost fell. The bushes and trees snatched at my clothes like greedy hands. I gripped my coat and slashed at the branches with my trusty stick.

Before I realized it though, the trees opened up all around. I had stepped into a small clearing well ensconced by the reaching canopy of surrounding trees, yet it was still light enough that I could see.

I was gasping, leaning against a sturdy oak, trying to catch my breath and that was when I saw them.

If I hadn't been having one of the strangest moments of my entire life, I would have missed them. They didn't just blend with the shadows; they were *one* with the shadows. They were cloaked in them and formed of them in the same instance. I got the impression of man-shaped beings of varying heights. They stayed along the trees, churning in the growing evening gloom. There could have been twenty of them or a hundred. With the way they stirred and blended their bodies against the trees, I couldn't tell. They were nearly one flesh, until a single entity stepped away.

He was of average height. We were maybe thirty feet apart. He, definitely he, flicked a bit of something over his arm. After further examination, I realized he was wearing a cloak and had thrown the longer portion over his arm. One arm was tucked behind him in the small of his back in the way of a gentleman of olden times. Ever so slowly, I could pick out the features of his face. Broad cheekbones, wide square jaw, bulbous flaring nose. His twisted lips were pressed tightly together.

It was the sight of his eyes that instantly made me regret my adventurous decision. Glaring at me, they were the perfect shape of almonds, but no almond had ever looked like that. They were somewhere between yellow and white, the color of pus from a sore. There were flecks of green disease at their corners with enflamed veins streaking to the pupils. The edges of the lids looked chafed raw. I pushed away from my tree, clutching my stick feebly.

"Nice night for a stroll." I said, trying my best to put on a brave smile. No one laughed. The one in front continued to glare at me. The smile faded from my face.

"You have come to us as a lamb to the slaughter, half-breed. You are more inferior than we could have thought possible." He growled. The voice was deep and grave and full of dark, terrible things. It spilled out of fleshy misshapen lips. All my little hairs were standing up. Fear needled me. But a part of me was kind of pissed off. Half-breed? Inferior? What the hell?

"I am not inferior! Who the hell do you think you are? With your-your whispers and shadowy bodies. I have half a mind to-to . . ."

I trailed off. My half tried bravado failed. What was I going to do? Beat him with my stick?

The obviously-bad-guy had raised an ebony eyebrow high on his broad charcoal colored forehead. If I didn't know better I would have thought he looked very amused behind his gruesome mask of a face.

"You'll what, little human?" he asked in his growling voice. I could only stare at him. He had the posture of an iron rod. And beneath the blackness of his attire, I could make out a barrel of a chest and arms thick with muscle. Well I sure as heck wasn't going to arm wrestle him.

I licked my lips, and couldn't find anything to say. Those eyes took the wind out of me. They seemed to bore into my heart and spread their disease into the core of me. It was as if they could see and manifest the deepest darkest terror of my soul. I clutched my stick in both hands and just stood there. That made him smile.

It was a horrible smile. His mouth was full of sharp, shining teeth. They were egg-white, with black and red rot spreading out from the roots. I had seen similar teeth in pictures of meth addicts our school had provided during drug awareness month. In the photos, most of the addict's teeth were broken or missing. The shadow man smiled at me with a full set of gleaming chompers.

"Allow me to educate you on the severity of your predicament." He said, taking a step towards me. Night had almost completely fallen and the shadow men at his back followed like a gruesome writhing train.

I would have run then, but I couldn't bear the thought of turning my back on him.

"I am Duhán Agas, First son of the Svartálfar, minion of Ymir. I am the lord of darkness and soon to be ruler of this pitiful realm. I, little Halfling, am the face of your demise." He paced the clearing as he talked but stopped and turned towards me. He was grinning maniacally, his eyes wide and bright. Bright as a child's on Christmas day. The gravity of what he said slowly sunk in.

"Who's Ymir?" I asked sweetly, thinking to knock him off of his soap box. My second thought was, what the hell was I doing? This guy was seriously loco. My chief necessity was to get back to the house, not engage in wordplay. I had to get out of the freaking woods and far away from these crazed shadow men. The grin on the minion's face faltered and fell.

"Ignorant morsel! I shall enjoy picking my teeth with your bones!" he snarled, taking another step towards me. Run, my brain screamed, run! But my feet were glued to the spot. I lifted my little stick, facing him.

"I can't possibly imagine dental hygiene is very high on your list of things to do." I said, my voice shaking. Sure piss him off, I thought, that'll make him kill you less. He snarled again and leaned forward. His back curled itself into a mountainous hump, flesh bubbling under his clothes, until his grotesque head was settled below his massive shoulders. The cloak slid off of his arm, swirling behind him in a living black cloud. He held one large, gnarled hand out towards me. It had claws as long as kitchen knives and could have palmed my entire face easily. I swallowed hard, but something inside me refused to retreat. The vibrant yellow streak in my spine screamed bloody murder.

"I will enjoy this immensely Halfling. Arrogant to the end, just like your father." He said. The barb struck home. My chest tightened and suddenly I knew I was about to do something really, really stupid.

"Bring it on asshole!" I shouted. He snarled, spittle falling from his lips, and launched himself at me.

Standing at the apex of all stupid things that I have ever done in my life, I spurred myself into action, running *towards* the shadow man.

I was less than four feet away from him and raised my stick. The whole world slowed. I could see the gruesome gnarls of his skin, the blazing flash of red in his eyes, the impossibly wide angle his jaws had stretched to.

I was afraid somewhere in the back of my mind, but my anger had over-ridden it like the sun next to a candle. Only the winsome remnant of fear curled through me. Warm retribution flooded my veins, heated my arteries and coursed through my brain. I watched myself in a picture show of movements. I felt as if I were standing outside of my body. I was amazed at my own strength, the snarl that twisted my own face as I lifted my arms to strike.

The shadowy minions rose up behind their leader like a dark tidal wave. They were of a similar body, all gnarled features and twisted deformed bodies, endless rows of sharp, gnashing teeth.

With all the strength I could muster, I brought the stick down on the shadow-man. It slashed across his face with a satisfying *whack* and to my utter amazement he screamed, stumbling backwards. His minions faltered. I could see confusion in their terrible rolling eyes.

The shadow-man clutched his face. The breath that hissed out of him in agonizing gasps was loud in my ears. He turned back to me and slowly lowered his hands. From his left temple to the right side of his chin, there was a deep, angry weal, almost a gash. My mouth fell open. I looked from him to the stick in my hands and back again. Elation filled me. I could feel an insane smile filling my mouth. With a wordless yell, I attacked. I swung the stick as hard as I could, sweeping it back and forth. The shadows retreated and, shocking myself, I chased them.

The stick whipped through the air with a whistling hum, reminding me of a time when I'd caught an overly ambitious bumble bee in my bedroom.

I chased the shadow-men back across the clearing feeling like King Arthur with Excalibur. They were backed up to the line of trees less than ten feet away. I stood there, swinging my little stick, feeling invincible. But of course things always seem the best, before they get waaay worse.

I swung the stick in a particularly vicious stroke to the right and it snapped. The longer portion went end over end into the trees, leaving me with about four inches in my hand. I looked down at that little piece of stick and my heart sank.

"Well damn." I whispered, looking up into the shadows. The night had closed in around us. I could see the hundreds of burning points of their eyes, the gleam of their terrible teeth. Now my feet moved slowly backwards. More eyes appeared in the trees, more shining teeth. Out of the darkness there came a sound. Soft and hissing at first, but growing in volume like the roll of thunder. It took me a second to identify it. Then I realized, the shadow-man was laughing. Laughing at me and my little stick.

I back peddled, slowly. My mind sputtered and refused to compute. No stick, no daylight, no nothing. This time I was well and truly in the dog house. Well damn.

I felt more than saw them move, an errant current of air. Like a wet cloth had been placed over my mouth, I struggled to breath. The night stole the warmth from my skin, raising goose bumps over my flesh. And still that horrible laugh rose and fell through the darkness. I think I closed my eyes. Which at the time seemed like a good idea. I felt the shadows coming and I closed my eyes and that's when the world caught on fire.

I cringed, my eyes clamped shut. A scalding wash of fire rolled over me, around me, through me. My eyelids were illuminated by a flash of white light. I put my hands over my face, and tried not to scream. But at least I wouldn't have been the only one. All around me, there were high-pitched whining screams, as if someone was torturing a giant mosquito. And as fast as it appeared, the fire went out. I could feel a new sheen of sweat under my clothes. My entire body was shaking.

"Vivian!" a masculine voice shouted and a large hand grasped my upper arm, giving me a shake. I open my eyes and my mouth fell open for the umpteenth time in too few days. Malcolm DeHaven stood with my arm clamped in his hand.

He was dressed in black slacks and a short sleeved black dress shirt. There were bits of fire all around us in the clearing. I started sputtering.

"We must go from this place. The fire will only discourage them for a moment. Run ahead to the cemetery and I will follow you." He said. I stood there and gapped at him. The last thing in the wide world I had expected was for him to show up. You could have fed me a piece of moon-cheese and it would have been more believable. He shook me again, his fingers digging into the tender flesh of my arm.

"Ow! Jerk face! Let up on the arm will ya!" I said, pulling away from him. He was looking at me in a particularly disgusted manner, one side of his upper lip raised.

"Clean the sod out of your brain and move your hide woman! I won't be eaten because of your stupidity!" he snarled. I planted both hands on my hips with my mouth pulled into a tight line.

"I am not stupid you creep! And anyways who asked you for anything! I think I'd rather be eaten!" I yelled. It was his turn to stare at me with his mouth open. We glared at each other for a long minute before he shook his head, snapping his mouth closed.

"No good will come of this. If you value your own life you must go. Now." He said from between clenched teeth. I was half tempted to stand there for a good long time and let him stew. But all around the clearing, the little pools of fire had begun to extinguish themselves. I took my hands off my hips just as a long, eerie yowl echoed through the trees. Malcolm gave me another little push and it was all I needed.

I turned and ran off into the trees at a breakneck pace. I leapt over logs and crashed through the brush, heedless of whatever might be sleeping or creeping there. Because the real danger was yet to come, sliding through the night veiled forest.

Far behind me, a loud thud sounded and then a roaring wall of fire rose up above the canopy, throwing the foliage into high relief. The shifting darkness threw off my vision and I tripped, catching my foot on a bush I'd started to jump over. I hit the ground hard, leaves and sticks jabbing into my hands. There was dirt in my mouth that I frantically tried to spit out.

Struggling to my knees, I heard the snapping of branches behind me. All my little hairs stood on end. A little voice in my head told me it wasn't Malcolm. Refusing to look back, I scrambled to my feet and ran. I ducked and dodged, twisting my body through the trees in ways I knew I was going to feel later. Branches tore at my clothes and whipped my face, bringing tears to my eyes. Yards ahead, I could see the trees thinning out. My heart soared at the same time something snagged my right foot.

I went down in a sort of half cartwheel, a very feminine half scream squeezed from my lips. I crashed through the underbrush with leaves flying in all directions. Thankfully, all of my appendages made it clear of the trees. I landed on my back, half upside down, with my butt up against a thick trunk. I lay there blinking, relearning how to breathe.

A shadow-man separated itself from the trees as if it had always been there, one step behind. It lurched towards me, stretched thin and at odd angles like a spider with only four legs. I was half grateful to the night for shielding me from the sight of him, because the gruesome head twisted back and forth on a serpentine neck much too long and thin to be human. The other half of me cringed at the sight of its enormous round eyes glowing at me like two disease ridden spotlights. There were wicked looking talons on the ends of its twelve long, knobby fingers.

Slowly, as if assured its victory, it came. Spurred into action by fear, I struggled to right myself. Something hindered my movements, bringing on a wave of panic. At some point, my coat had come undone and now I was tangled in it. I fought with it, finding the sleeve caught on something that refused to let go. I beat at it, making pitiful, high pitched noises. Bastard fluffy house coat! I screamed in my head. And still the monster came, snapping twigs as it pushed it's strange body forward.

I stopped beating at my coat sleeve and looked up. It stood nearly nine feet above me, arms stretched back from its body, poised to strike. I knew I should have been terrified out of my mind, but sitting there in the dirt with death looming over me I was overcome with a dreadful exhaustion. And I desperately wished I had a scone to ease the passing.

Ironically, there are some things in life that the human mind refuses to compute. Staring up the long way into the darkness, waiting for the final blow, it didn't occur to me wonder why the canopy above our heads had started to move. My brain rationalized it as being the wind or that I was near a faint and the world was starting it's off kilter spin. But the little tiles inside me started to click together. I don't faint and the air was still as death.

If I had had any tea left inside me, I would have pissed myself. One large tree wrenched itself forward. Gnarled and tangled limbs crashed themselves around the shadow-man and jerked it into the air. The night reverberated with its high reedy screams as the abundant arms thrashed it mercilessly. Thick bits of liquid rained down on the undergrowth. Some splattered me but I was locked in a state of terror. I sat there, jaw clenched, eyes wide, my one arm still caught on a bush, unable to move. Abruptly, the screams stopped. The tree wove itself back and forth through the air, its movements growing slower and slower. Until I blinked and it was as still as it had started out. Still as death.

Digging my hands into the carpet of leaves and dirt, I contemplated my next move. I sure as hell didn't want to be crushed by a frickin' tree. But in the same token, if I stayed, the shadow-men would surely find me. I was so locked in thought; I didn't hear something crashing through the trees until it was too late. The large black thing was moving through the trees quickly. There would be no steady savoring pause for this shadow-man.

I screamed and threw up my hands just as it barreled through the foliage and nearly stepped on me.

"What the hell? What are you doing?" Malcolm's voice cut through the trees. I lowered my hands and gapped up at him.

"The-the tree. The tree." I stammered. My voice sounded too high and too frightened for my liking. I watched the shadow of Malcolm turn, shoulders hunched, face scanning the dark. After a moment, he cautiously stepped over to the offending tree. I lost sight of his shadow and my stomach lurched painfully.

"DeHaven?" I whispered. My ears strained for sound as my eyes searched the gloom. An eternity passed before the Malcolm shadow came creeping back.

"An oak. Our luck seems to be holding. Someone has invoked a spell of protection as well. The Dark Ones have fled, but god only knows for how long. We must leave this place." He said softly, holding a hand out to me. My mind was in chaos. Slowly, I slipped off the house coat and stood. My legs were shaking and there was something thick and not so nice in my hair. I did not take his hand and he let it fall to his side. Without looking to see if I would follow, he tromped past me. I looked up at the canopy one last time.

"I don't think we're in Kansas anymore." I whispered to myself and followed my nemesis in to the dark.

8

When I was twelve, my grandparents took me on a camping trip up north. There was a spacious port-o-potty ten yards from our tents, and a newly built fire pit that you could grill over.

We had sipped our orange soda and roasted our marshmallows and even made burgers for the local fish and game wardens. I'd been enchanted by the enormity of our adventure, puffed up with pride over my solitary tent, and zealously smug at my vast tree identifying skills. The Great Outdoors.

When you're young everything is enchanting and magical. I could still remember every story my grandparents told on that trip and every trip after. I could remember the feeling of independence when waking up in my tent, the sun rising over me. I remembered tromping through the woods fearlessly. I remembered the poison oak I'd somehow managed to rub all over myself. And not caring a bit. It had been a glorious adventure.

In the oh-so vivid present, a branch snaked out and tried to pluck out my eye. There were buzzing insects hovering around my head and ears that I frantically tried to bat away. There was dirt down the back of my pants and what I prayed was a leaf of some kind. Monster blood had dried across my forehead in grizzly patches. Only Rambo could have called this night some sort of glorious adventure.

Malcolm hadn't spoken to me since the killer oak tree. He'd only stopped long enough to pick up a tree branch and light the end on fire. No lighter, no accelerant, just poof, fire. I'd gapped at him, which now seemed to be the regular way of things, and he'd grunted. We'd been walking for nearly an hour. Strike that, he was walking; I was huffing and puffing behind him trying not to get my eye taken out by a tree.

Any attempts at conversation were met with cold glances over his shoulder and noncommittal grunts. I was about to tell him to screw off and take me home, when a flickering light off in the trees caught my eye. I stopped dead in my tracks. My ears felt like they would strain themselves right off the sides of my head. My eyes were open as wide as they could get. I wasn't hallucinating. Surely enough, out in the trees was a light. It was soft yellow and swayed gently in the air. A breeze ruffled my hair and cooled the sweat at my temples. I took a step in the direction of the light, and a second appeared a little above eye level. This one was also yellow, but danced like a flame.

"Hey, someone's out there." I whispered, taking another step. A familiar angry hand latched onto my upper arm and nearly yanked me off my feet. I turned on him, scowling. He was glaring down at me, his face cast in wiggling sideways shadows. The firelight was unkind. It made him seem just as sinister as the monsters we had left behind.

"Don't you know anything? I have no wish to go chasing you through the entire mountain range till the end of my days. Now follow me and keep quiet." He said, giving me a hard shake. He let go and took off through the trees again. I rubbed my arm slowly trailing after him. Who the hell asked him to be my keeper? I thought with a pout. To my horror, I could feel my eyes burning. My arm hurt where he had grabbed me, the same spot as before. I was going to have a bruise. Bastard.

I slowly caught up with him. He had stopped and was glaring at me.

"You know maybe I wouldn't be such a bother if someone would tell me what's going on." I said softly. He continued walking as I entered the torchlight.

"It isn't my place to educate you." He said, not looking at me. I was staring at his back again, but he had slowed so that I had a clear view of his left profile.

"Then who's is it? 'Cause I'm seriously getting tired of this whole magic and monsters thing we seem to be doing." I snapped. At this he snorted and I could see his upper lip curling.

"You're tired. That is quite amusing. My family has been Serving since before the first Guardian came to this land. Before gold drew the hearts of man here. Before the red man and the buffalo were taken away. Before the time of the Great Crossing. *You're* tired." He said snorting again. I could only frown at the back of his head.

None of what he said meant anything to me. It was all just a bunch of mundane mumbo-jumbo.

"If you hate it so much why don't you just quit." I asked, tucking my hands into the pockets of my jeans. Things were bad enough without my arch enemy seeing me lick my proverbial wounds. Again there was that contemptuous noise.

"There are some that have forgotten their duties. *We* swore an oath. And *we* do not take our oaths lightly. Till death, and beyond. That is the nature of our service, and our honor. *Some* have forgotten this." He ground out. Till death. It made me shiver. Still I couldn't let well enough alone and let out a small snort of my own.

"To bad *we* couldn't dislodge the stick from our asses." I mumbled.

The thing about mumbling is that you probably shouldn't be standing within a distance the person you're talking about can hear. Because then you really shouldn't mumble, it's rude.

Malcolm stopped and turned on me with his iciest glare yet. The white gold flames on the torch shrank and sputtered. The fight or flight reflex in me wanted to back away, but I held my ground. Magic or no magic, we'd done this dance since childhood, there would be no retreating.

We stood there for a long moment with the shadows dancing all around. He turned away first, his jaw tightly clenched. I softly cleared my throat and jammed my hands as deep into my pockets as they would go. I will not gloat, I will not gloat I told myself. Malcolm stomped off into the trees and I trailed behind him, watching as the torch flame grew higher and brighter.

After a few long minutes, I begrudgingly admitted to myself that I was the tiniest bit grateful for the light and for not being really dead. And that's when I began to feel like an ass. A heel of the first rate kind. I almost felt the need to apologize.

"I guess it would be a drag to have to do something you didn't want to for such a long time." I managed, earning myself a glance over the shoulder.

"Where are we going?" I asked. He stopped and pointed outward with the torch. My eyes followed the movement.

"There." He said. My eyes strained. All I could see was darkness and a little muddled blob of more darkness.

Malcolm pushed through a curtain of tangled of brush that wasn't quite there and like magic we were in a cave.

I blinked a few times to clear my vision. Bright torches flickered down a long corridor of stone. Each burned merrily, flames licking the still air. Malcolm extinguished his burning branch, threw it aside. The ground under our feet was smooth as if it had been packed and trod by a great many feet. I whirled around in amazement. The only thing behind us was a long stretch of torch lit corridor.

Malcolm walked brazenly on. I followed closed behind, eyes darting up into the gloom of the cave. There was darkness above that the torch light failed to penetrate. I took my hands out of my pockets and hugged myself. I had the sudden startling feeling that we had been separated somehow, that this cave was apart from the reality that I knew. I hugged myself and shivered.

We followed the path as it curved and wound into the earth. The walls closed in on us until finally I could see it's pitted, slopping ceiling. Looking up with something close to mild relief, I didn't see Malcolm stop. I slammed into the back of him, my face connecting with his hard shoulder. I bounced off him like a tennis ball thrown against a concrete wall. Steadying myself I grimaced at him. He hadn't even budged. Looking past him, my mouth dropped open.

There was a man standing in front of a heavy set of wooden doors. But he was unlike any man I had ever seen outside of a National Geographic. And even then there were few that could compare. He was nearly seven feet tall, with shoulders so wide he seem to fill the entire doorway. Every inch of him was padded with thick cords of deep bronze muscle and tattoos. But calling them tattoos was to liken a puddle to the ocean.

Swirling blue spread like clouds over the broad plains of his cheeks and down the severe length of his nose. They spilled in a tumbling waterfall down his bull neck and cascaded over the barrel of his chest. I was mesmerized by the tapering swirls that disappeared into a satiny brown breech cloth. The tree trunks of his legs were equally marked all the way down to his trim ankles and the tops of his bare feet. He was the cover for the summer edition of Barbarian Play Girl. I snapped my mouth shut and tried not to stare at his . . . axe.

Yes, his axe. The double edged blade gleamed wickedly in the torchlight. It was nearly three feet wide and five feet long. I couldn't have lifted it with all my strength and a hand winch. He balanced it on his right shoulder like a child's toy.

"Move aside Deluk, we're here for the Council." Malcolm said. The giant ignored him and stared at me with hard black eyes. They were bits of jet in the bright whites.

"The Halfling is not welcome here. Return and await Judgment." It was like hearing a mountain talk. Or maybe a Bull Mastiff. I couldn't seem to stop staring at him, but I frowned. A small crease appeared between his black brows. We stood there looking at each other. I waited for Malcolm to intervene with his brilliantly snide comments and biting attitude.

Another time, I would have laughed at the irony of the moment. How easy I could pick sides when I found myself against a common enemy.

But Malcolm just stood there, and Deluk continued to stare. I kept frowning. After a stretching, uncomfortable silence, I tried to look at Malcolm and found I couldn't. I couldn't look away from his endless pools of onyx.

Again, I had the strange feeling of being very far away from reality. My skin flushed hot and cold at the same time. All the little hairs on my body stood at attention. And then there was a light.

Imagine the white light you see when you hit your head or when your friend catches you off guard and brains you with her clarinet. That shining white star of a light you see in the back of your eyes. It was like that except it hung in my brain as if someone was rummaging around in my gray matter with a flashlight.

I shook my head without taking my eyes off of the axe welding giant. The light refused to go and steadily grew. It spread inside me until it filled my eyes with brightness. Until everything was wreathed in bright light and Deluk was the center of my world, framed in its radiance.

How foolish I was. How insignificant. I should bow before my master, I thought. Yes. I should bow and worship him in his greatness. His beauty. His strength. I should bend myself to him and perhaps he would allow me to bask in his awesomeness for all eternity. See, my master, see how I fall upon my knees for you. Your glory is the light of my salvation.

I paused, feeling the hard stones digging into my knees. Your glory is the light of my salvation? What the hell was that? I didn't talk like that. Why the hell was I on the ground? I blinked and scowled up at Deluk.

"You asshole." I said. He blinked and his eyes were brown. Plain, unremarkable brown. Surprise raced over his features but was quickly replaced by anger. I wasn't sure what just happened. But I knew it was all his fault.

"A big blue asshole!" I shouted, getting to my feet. Malcolm stood off to the left, facing us. He was looking very smug. I turned on him.

"And you're an asshole too! Some help you are. Let me get brain drained by some blue idiot!" I yelled. His demeanor faltered and he shrugged.

"It was a test. And it was one I knew you would pass. I knew there was no danger." His tone was arrogant and detached. The same voice I knew too well. The steam started to go out of me, but what he said sunk in.

"You knew? You *knew* he was gonna try and do something to me? And you didn't warn me? Some protector! You are an ass-hole!" I shouted. He gave me a dry look and one dark brow quirked ever so slightly.

"I think we have established that fact." He said. I opened my mouth to yell at him, and couldn't think of anything to say. Damn him! I couldn't let him have the last word. But I couldn't think of one damn thing to say. Damn! I turned back to the blue boy instead. Full of righteous fury.

"And you! Get the hell out of the way. We're here for business and it's none of your damn business!" I shouted, advancing on him. To my extreme pleasure he moved one hand to the great curved handle of one door. But he didn't look nearly as contrite as I would have liked.

"You have bested me *halfling*. But there are things beyond that even your darkest dreams could not imagine. I pray you have the chance to explore them well." He said and with a mocking bow, pulled open the door.

I tried to think up something snippy to say, but Malcolm touched my arm. I looked at him and he shook his head. Well double damn. I waited till we were through the door and Malcolm's back was turned before I gave Deluk the one fingered salute. He slammed the door in my face and I smiled. Ah, victory is sweet.

Such a victory, even one so deliciously savored, is often easily extinguished. There are certain things that can take the wind out of your sails. Things that feel like a punch in the guts right after you have a root canal. I turned away from the door and found myself looking at one of those things.

We had entered a wide circular cavern with great pale daggers of mineral hanging from ceiling to floor. They glowed with soft light, luminescent ghosts trapped in stone. Instead of torches, enormous braziers with taloned black feet sat along the walls at intervals. Across from the door parallel to the far wall, there was a large rectangular table made of rough white stone. There were four people sitting and one standing at the end farthest away from us.

Pale, androgynous figures drifted around the room. They wore delicate, gauzy garments that seemed to float around their lithe bodies in creamy clouds. Hovering at unobtrusive distances, they gave off the impression of servitude, eyes down cast, faces averted. There were shining goblets and gleaming gold plates set out on the table, but even from where I stood, I could see they were empty.

My eyes flickered over everyone at the archaic looking table, noting them briefly, before riveting on a figure crouched beside a wall far to the right. I don't know what made me look, or how I knew it was him. In a single instant though, I was sure.

He was curled into a ball, facing us with his head on his knees and his arms wrapped around his legs. There was a long, thick chain leading from a peg in the wall to a metal collar that covered his entire neck. Bloody wheals striped his darkly tanned torso and what parts of his legs I could see. He was trembling and gently rocking himself. I could see blood matting one whole side of his shocking white-blond hair.

All the air seemed to go out of my lungs. My tongue was dried up in my mouth. I was walking to him before I could stop myself. My sense of self-preservation brought me to an instant halt as a figure moved out of the corner of my eye. The man at the end of the table had slithered forward at the same time I had. I should have turned but I had eyes only for my friend and the bloody welts oozing down his beautiful skin.

"Reed. Reed are you okay?" I called, and my voice echoed. I mentally kicked myself. Of course he wasn't okay, he was hurt and chained to a frickin' wall! I felt my blood start to boil. Somebody was going to pay for this.

I turned towards the table and got my second bad surprise. There was a familiar face sitting at the far end. Her attire alone should have made me recognize her at first glance. She wore a high collared, sleeveless dress the color of strong coffee. Glittering beadwork cascaded down the bodice. The richness of the cloth made her creamy skin glow. Around her neck she wore a string of amber pieces the size of Ping-Pong balls. She watched me with large dark eyes and her dark hair, with its wealth of auburn highlights, was pulled up in a graceful French twist.

I blinked a few times to be sure I was really seeing her. She looked so calm. So collected. So *cold*. Part of me wasn't even sure it was her. Maybe she had a doppelgänger or something running loose. Stranger things had happened.

But the longer I looked at her the less I could deny that it *was* her. I opened my mouth to speak and the standing man was on the move again. Straight for me. I took a step back and gave him my undivided attention.

He could have been Leila's twin but he was my height. Slim but well formed under his tailored black suit. He had that fresh cream skin. High cheek bones, strong jaw, full lips. His hair was a nearly perfect black that shined with dark fire. His body moved like a well-oiled machine as he walked slowly towards me. His wide, dark eyes captured my every move.

"This is the part where you strut indignantly and tell us we're all going rue the day we met you. Which, in other circumstances would be quite valid. But you see dear child, this truth has already come to pass. Your birth has plagued every one of us, every day of your miserable life." He said in a cool refined voice. His voice was velvet in my ears. I watched him and some part of me knew to be afraid, as a bird knows to fear the asp. Those eyes watched me in a predatory way and my nerves screamed. The bells and whistles on my internal proximity alarm screeched in warning. Instead of running, I stood there like a deer in the headlights.

"What? Nothing? How disappointing. I have heard many things about your extensive eloquence. I pray you have not lost your tongue." He said from nearly five feet away. With a complete lack of regard for how it might look, I backed away from him. I wanted to be as far away from this guy as possible. The next state would still have been too close.

My eyes flickered over to the table. Leila sat unmoved, watching us. Hurt and confusion flooded through me. I could always remember turning to her in my times of need. Now she sat still as a stone, as indifferent as a porcelain doll.

Strangely, seeing her like that made me think of Malcolm. He, I thought, would protect me. Yet I was afraid to turn around to look for him, afraid to turn my back on this man.

"This is what we have been protecting. This is what we have been reducing ourselves for. This half breed child. Look well on the values that have brought us low." He said waving his hand at me. My breath caught in my throat, half anticipating a blow. Those full lips twitched in what might have been a smile. Almost absently, he turned back towards the table.

I felt a measure of relief that he wasn't watching me anymore. The pressure of his attentions had been lifted. But somehow I didn't think the night was over so quickly. My anxiety level started to spike when my gaze fell on gliding figures that had entered the room unseen. They were dressed in rich, embroidered fabrics and costumes that hadn't seen the outside of a renaissance fair in centuries. Their faces were beautiful and terrible at the same time. They had eyes like flashing gems, skin of every hue cast in a dewy haze. Others looked as if they had risen from the very earth itself, flowers sprouting from their hair, moss trickling down their arms, limbs carved of stone. They lingered at the far end of the cavern, their strange eyes avid on the speaking man.

Like a wraith, Malcolm drifted up next to me. He watched the dark haired man with burning intensity. And when I say burning, I mean I was surprised Mister Dark and Sinister didn't catch fire where he stood. I expected to see him stop, drop and roll at any minute.

"I say, that the end of an era is at hand." He said turning like an orator, hands raised. That really bad feeling I'd been getting increased tenfold and my hands started to sweat.

"No longer will we follow the edict of the fallen. No longer will we be reduce to crawling before the *unworthy*. No longer will we be forced to live in the shadow of a . . . human." He punctuated the end of each sentence with the shake of his fist and the way he said *human* made my brain go, 'Dum dum duuuuum.'

I had to use every ounce of will power not to turn and run for the door. A fine trembling had begun in my hands and arms. The feeling of needing to flee was intense. So intense, that I was backing away and a moment of time had dropped away in a blink. My feet had grown a mind of their own. What was I doing? I thought it, and stopped moving. Malcolm had turned and was watching me with his dark brows raised. Every eye in the room was pinned on me.

I was pretty confused about everything myself, so I resorted to age old tactics. I smiled and tried to look harmless. Malcolm was back to frowning at me. The dark haired man laughed.

The sound was a thousand sharp, little knives stampeding down my back. It was pain so acute little white stars burst in my eyes. The knives were flick-flicking around in my skull, rendering my brain to the consistency of tartar. Someone was screaming. High, piteous wails. And that someone was me.

I had another one of those coming back into my body moments that I was sooo fond of. I dropped back down into myself. I had both hands on the sides of my head and was in the process of trying to pull out my hair. My mouth was hanging open from a scream cut short. I slowly put my hands down, trembling. My head felt like a glass full of champagne, brain cells floating pell-mell to the top. I moved with caution, feeling like I might break. I looked around and saw that the room had been busy while I was having a psycho-panic attack.

Malcolm stood toe-to-toe with the Orator. The two men that had been sitting were now standing, one to the left and one to the right. Deluk of the Big Axe was standing behind Malcolm, axe-less. Many in the audience had spread out amongst the men and an alarming amount was on the wrong side. For the second time in the same night, we were outnumbered.

My gaze slid to Leila. She was still sitting, and if I didn't know any better, I would have said she looked bored, as if she had seen the show before. How often did she do this kind of thing? I asked myself. What else didn't I know about the woman I called friend.

The woman beside her was standing. Her face was strained and deathly pale. But everything about her was pale.

Her hair was a shining river of snow tumbling past her waist. It was only a shade darker than her nearly translucent skin. Even from where I stood, I could see a delicate pink flush under her cheeks and the tiny blue veins in her hands. She wore what could only be called a toga. It was white and pinned at the shoulder with a large sparkling stone set in silver. The stone was half the size of a tennis ball and blazed with bright fire. I would have bet my favorite body part it was some kind of diamond.

She turned that pale face on me, and her eyes were like flecks of glittering citrine. They were fierce, pleading bits of citrine. Apparently I was being expected to do something other than stand in the middle of the room like a freaked out piece of stalagmite. Damn.

I walked towards the men with trepidation. I wasn't sure exactly what I was going to do and I sure as hell didn't want to go through the whole vocal Cuisinart thing again. I stopped less than four feet away from Malcolm, directly across from Deluk. He sneered at me and flexed his muscles. I resisted the urge to show him my driving finger again and turned my attention to the two men standing nearly nose to nose.

"Two cannibals are eating a clown. One looks at the other and says, 'Does this taste funny to you?'" I said and everyone turned. Malcolm had a half disgusted, half incredulous look on his face. Everyone else displayed different levels of confusion. It gave me a feeling of pleased familiarity. Aside from day to day congeniality, this was the usual reaction I invoked from most people.

"Now that I have your undivided attention, I just hate to interrupt your 'play time', but maybe we could find a way to do this without throwing my brain in a blender or killing each other?" I gave them my best big beseeching doe eyes as I talked. I could finagle extra scones out of Leila during a Sunday rush hour with those eyes. There was a slow round of grunting and grumbling and everyone moved back. We stood in a big circle like gunners at the O-K Corral.

"Once again you are on the wrong side of the line, Malcolm." The Orator bit off. He had his arms folded in front of him, mouth twisted into an ugly sneer.

"At least I have chosen a side, Uncle." Malcolm ground out. I gave a few spastic blinks and tried not to self-destruct. If my brain hadn't just been scrambled a few seconds ago I would have totally cracked up. Uncle?

"We must agree to solidarity DeHaven. Our people are sparse in this country and dwindling in the homelands. We must stand together against the children of Man." Said one of the table guys. He stood to the left, close to Malcolm's Uncle. Lest there be any doubt what side he was on.

He was tall, almost as tall as Deluk. As thin as a rail. And did I mention green? His slick black hair was tinted green. His face was thin and sharp featured with skin the pale yellow-green of a frog's belly. I tried not to stare at him and skimmed my eyes to the man closest to me.

It took me a moment to realize he barely came up to my elbow because the first thing I noticed was his hair. The copper of new pennies it was cropped close to his head and fairly blazed in the firelight. His face was all high cheeks and wide blue eyes. The lower half of his face was covered with a thick, well-trimmed, red beard with shining pieces of gold wire twined in it. An intricate gold torque lay around his neck like twin snakes, deep sapphire stones blazing in their eyes. He wore what looked like a half-sleeved, cream colored shirt with a wide piece of plaid cloth over one shoulder. The plaid fell just above his knees in shades of green and cream and gold. He had one of those pouches hanging from his waist. Surprisingly, I knew that it was called a sporran. It was trimmed with soft brown fur and gold wire. Everything about him screamed 'leader'.

Those pale blue eyes flickered to me and he winked. His face was the epitome of stoicism and if I hadn't been looking straight at him, I would have thought I imagined it.

An invisible ice cube slid over my skin, raising a million goose bumps. I turned and found the Uncle of the Hour staring at me. My face flushed hotly, as if he had caught me doing something naughty. With an arrogance I didn't quite feel, I raised a brow at him.

"Yes?" I snapped trying my best to sound haughty and overbearing. I'm not very good at it, so I made a mental note to ask Malcolm for lessons if we ever got out of here.

"You have no idea what's going on, do you?" he snarked. His lips twitched again. I stared at him steadily. I could see which side of the family Malcolm got his charming personality from.

"Not a freakin' clue." I said, and surprise bloomed across his face. I don't think it was an emotion he was used to, it looked almost painful. His surprise was quickly replaced by a deep scowl.

"Then I shall endeavor to enlighten you." He said untucking his arms. He moved and the circle shifted. I stepped back. Not wanting to be in the line of fire. The uncle stopped still, hands clenched at his side and glared at me so hard I could feel the heat of it in my bones.

"I am Gannon DeHaven. I am a scion of the Tuatha dé Danann. Our family has served yours since the first Cross child was born. We, of royal blood, have served like dogs! And for what? Three millennia of nothing!" He shouted. I bit my lip to keep from blurting out anything inappropriate and abundantly smartass. And be assured there was an abundance. Chiefly, I wanted to tell him that none of those things meant anything to me. It just didn't seem like the best of times.

His dark eyes shifted like the ocean in a moonless night and those lush lips of his peeled back in a vicious snarl over bright white teeth.

"But tonight, we lords of the dreaming times will rule once more." He ground out. And then someone grabbed me from behind.

There was a startled 'hey' from Malcolm and everyone was moving. I struggled against the hands holding me and saw Malcolm lock arms with Deluk. Several of the surrounding people started to rush them.

The red haired, kilt-guy suddenly had a sword longer than I was tall. He charged at green man with a roar. The green man's face shifted like ripples on a pond. He expanded outward as if he were quickly being filled with air. His green tweed suit tore at the shoulders and to my surprise, spikey branches and thorny vines burst out. His entire head had grown to the size of a large watermelon and his skin had taken on the texture of seaweed

"You mustn't do this!" the pale lady shouted. It was a little late for that I thought, fighting in earnest against the hands holding me. I looked down and found dark hands in a vice-like grip on my shoulders. No matter how much I fought, they never budged.

I wasn't really worried, until I saw Gannon walking towards me. Terror raced up my spine. More than anything in the world, I didn't want him to touch me. I knew that it would be bad and there was no one to stop him. Malcolm was now wrestling around on the ground with Deluk, dirt kicking up in every direction. Red haired guy was chopping pieces off of green man and two pale men with enormous, yellow fish eyes. I looked at Leila. She was still sitting, statuesque in her chair. Our eyes locked as I fought to free myself.

"Help me!" I screamed. I don't think I could have felt any other emotion but fear at that moment. But Leila proved me wrong. A long slow blink of her lashes enraged me.

I felt betrayed. I felt angry. I fought those dark chocolate hands and was suddenly free. They snatched at me, but I turned with speed I knew I shouldn't have possessed.

The man behind me was wiry and nearly a foot taller. His skin was midnight in flesh with chocolate highlights. His eyes were chunks of onyx, completely devoid of white. He wore a little white breech cloth that was the twin of Deluk's. When he reached massive hands out to me, I hit him.

I need to be clear about the fact that I have never been a fighter. I've been a veritable pacifist since grade school. Any strength I've ever gained comes from turning wrenches and lifting the occasional car battery or engine block.

When my fist connected with the guy's chest, he hit the dirt as if I'd slugged him with a battering ram. I caught a glimpse under his loin cloth as he skidded across the dirt but was too pissed and surprised to be embarrassed. I turned, ready to take on the world. A red haze had leaked into my vision. I felt invincible. In some part of myself I knew that I should be wondering about this sudden super-human strength. But I figured, everyone else had super neat-o powers, why not me?

I was still turning when a hand connected with my forehead. The first thing I was sure of was that it wasn't my own hand. There was nothing I had forgotten nor had I been struck by an epiphany. The second was that I was in a whole world of trouble.

I couldn't move. Every muscle in my body had seized up painfully. Gannon stood with his hand cupping my entire forehead and a good portion of the top of my head. Where his eyes had merely shifted before, a storm raged in them now. I trembled, unable to help myself.

"They will call me a liberator. And you will be less than a foot note in the annals of history." He hissed at me. I only knew fear for a moment before I was consumed.

Pain surge through me. The storm had raced in a tidal wave of chained lighting down his arm and exploded in my brain. There was too much agony to even scream. I thought maybe I imagined it, but I was sure I felt my feet come up off the floor.

Along with the pain, I felt a bone deep remorse. I wasn't quite sure what it was, but he was taking *something* from me. He was stripping me of myself. My life force, my soul. The cracks that I had made in my past, he was methodically tearing open and shredding them to pieces. I could feel that. I could feel him taking everything away. The new powers and crazed memories, I didn't mind losing. I didn't even think about missing the many lonely years trapped in my grandparent's house.

But then he burrowed down deep into memories that were far more precious to me. Memories that had been locked tightly away. There was a flash. I saw Leila and I at four years old, hand in hand, both of us in frilly little dresses. I saw my mother braiding my hair beside a crackling fireplace. I saw my father pushing me high on a wooden swing in a stand of trees. I saw Reed smiling through tea time with a flowered hat on his head. I saw my grandparents, hand in hand on the front porch. The memories were so real, so full of love, I felt my eyes burn.

With a vicious twist I felt the power, the sinister worm that was Gannon DeHaven, wrap around them and squeeze.

It tore a gasp from my throat. I felt him trying to prize each memory from my mind, as you would peel away the layers of an onion. Except that that onion was my soul. Mine.

In panic, I plummeted down inside myself, searching for any flicker of hope and in the deepest part of myself there was a tiny sleeping piece of shadow. Under the film of pain I was surprised to find it. I recognized it as the same kind of shadow as Duhán. How it had gotten lodged way down deep in the center of my being, I didn't know. But I touched it, and it didn't hurt, if anything it felt warm and familiar. It seemed drowsy but I pushed it at the Gannon-worm and like a shark scenting blood, it sprang to life.

I was seeing it all without eyes. Inside my mind, I watched the shadow burst apart into many tendrils like the legs of an octopus. I saw it engulf the worm, latching on with all of its strength. I watched with satisfaction as the worm was now the one struggling, the one trying to flee. I felt Gannon trying to remove his hand from me. But our fates were sealed.

Deep down, I saw the shadow turning and twining. It had nearly covered the worm when a bright light struck.

There was that moment of 'uh oh' and my body was thrown. I could vaguely hear people fighting. I could hear the air crackling with power. But slowly, ever so slowly, I was falling. The shadow had fallen away screaming. I thought about it briefly, but was mesmerized by my own fall.

More surprising, I felt Malcolm reaching for me. I *felt* him struggling with Deluk. I felt his frustration, his sorrow. I started to reach for him, but the light came again. The light knocked me to the ground. It filled me up and pushed all of the air out of my lungs. It came in a never ending wave. And all at once, there was nothing.

9

So, I was on the ground. Again. I could taste dirt in my mouth and there was a spot on the back of my head that felt swollen. One of those greasy bastards had probably dragged me across the floor.

I had mixed feelings about laying there like a bump on a log. Part of me was trying to be really pissed off at Leila's betrayal, plotting my vengeance against her. And another part of me wanted to scream and cry and generally throw a big crazy tantrum. I opened my eyes and watched firelight dancing over the stone ceiling. My throat tightened and I could feel the tears gathering.

How could she? How could she let them take me? How could she let them hurt Reed? There hadn't been a single sign of remorse. No flicker of emotion. She'd sat there like some stupid lump. Stoically viewing everything that ratfink Gannon had said and done. Sixteen years of friendship down the drain in one brutal swipe.

I prayed the earth would open up and swallow me whole. But I couldn't be so lucky. A chain jingled off to my right. My whole body tensed and I closed my eyes tightly. It's nothing, I thought, it's nothing bad. But it can't possibly be anything good. Crap on a cracker. I balled my hands into fists and slowly sat up. Turning my head in the direction of the noise, I opened my eyes.

I almost laughed out loud. I put a hand over my mouth the urge was so severe. The scene wasn't at all funny. But relief flowed through me. Finally someone I could trust. Sort of. Reed sat in a far corner still balled up, with his arms around his legs. He looked exactly the same as he had in the cavern.

"Reed." I whispered, tucking my legs up. He didn't move. Only a tremble in his shoulders told me he was even breathing.

I took a moment to look around the large oval room. There was small round wooden door behind me and not much else. Except stone and more stone. Oh, and metal rings set into the walls where other chains could have been. I was grateful not have one of my own, but looking back, I saw that Reed still wore his.

"Reed. Reed we gotta get out of here." I whispered and began crawling towards him. I was less than three feet away when his head came up. It was a sharp motion that made me freeze in my tracks. One of Reed's eyes was white as snow, the pupil elongated like a goats. In his hairline, I could see two shining ivory points. I scooted back till I was almost back where I started.

"Don't-don't come any-closer." He gasped. A shudder ran through him and sweat beaded at his temples.

I shook my head, maybe in denial, I wasn't sure. A wave of fear was building inside my guts, threatening to suffocate me.

"You . . . you . . . go." He said. It was squeezed out from between sharp, clenched teeth. I watched in horror as a spot of white spilled into his beautiful blue eye and the pupil stretched like two cells straining to separate.

"What . . . what's happening? Reed?" I backed up as I spoke and watched as Reed began to grow. His shoulders stretched and he let grotesquely lengthened arms fall away from his legs. Both of his hands had long white talons growing from his fingertips.

I didn't realize I was still backing away until my back hit the rough wooden door. I wasn't sure if I was frightened or resigned. It was turning into one of the worst weeks of my life. Reed was staring at me like I'd turned into a big slab of prime rib. I ran my hand up the door but there was no handle. Somehow I wasn't surprised.

"Look, can't we talk about this? We can talk about this. Like two rational adults." I said. I tried looking around the room again without taking my eyes off of him. There was stone all around and nowhere to go. A noise rumbled out of Reed that was a sickening imitation of a rabid dog. He watched my every move with teeth bared.

"My, my, grandmother, what big teeth you have." I stammered. He didn't laugh. I started sweating. Okay, I thought, be calm. No sudden moves.

Reed lunged forward and I screamed. I immediately saw that the chain was long, long enough for him to reach me. I got up and ran.

Where do you run in a room that's approximately thirty feet in diameter? In a great, big, freaked out circle, that's where. Like a rat in a wheel. Only the wheel is on fire and there's a giant saber-toothed tiger chasing you.

With Reed close behind, I darted around the room like a manic jack rabbit. Twice I found myself running towards him instead of away. His chain snatched at my feet and once I nearly fell. Taking away another ounce of my dignity, I screamed, long and loud and unchecked. I stumbled against one wall and scraped my arm so that it stung as I ran. In my mind a little voice whispered. What are you doing? Why are you running? So you can be extra tired when you die?

I tripped over the chain a second time and went sprawling. I spun, expecting Reed to be bearing down on me. My chest burned and there was more dirt on my face and in my mouth. I crab walked backwards until I hit a wall. I could feel warm blood dripping down the arm I'd scraped. I was shaking all over. Reed was across the room, crouched and panting. He was still looking at me, and I could see beads of sweat dripping down from his hair. I felt a small surge of victory. At least I was giving him a run for his money.

"Reed, please don't. Please don't do this! It's Vivian. I'm your friend remember? Please don't do this." I gasped. I watched him turn on all fours, muscles bunching. There was nothing human in the way he looked at me. And there was no one home for me to talk to. I braced myself against the wall. I might go down, but I'd fight him every step of the way.

I've always hated the parts in movies where the scene slows down for dramatic effect. Yet in that moment, when the whole world seemed to apply the brakes, I was thoroughly mesmerized. I could see every detail of Reed's face; every bunch and flex of his body, the flickering patterns of torch light over his skin.

In my own body I became very aware of every breath that passed my lips, the very blood cells burbling through my veins, the cool stone under my hands.

I knew the exact moment when Reed took that final leap in my direction. I could see it in the droop of his head and the tension in his shoulders. In slow motion, I saw his entire body leave the ground. I saw sweat rain down from his skin, speckling the dirt. I felt myself react in the same instance, skin flushing, eyes dilating. I expected my heart to race, but it slowed to a deliberate, even thrum. The air grew tight all around me. I felt cold. Cold as ice. Cold as stone.

After everything that has happened in my life, and after all of the recent completely weird things that had occurred. I thought that I couldn't possibly be surprised about anything ever again. I was wrong.

Looking at Reed I had a string of thoughts. Stop. No. Don't. And that string of thoughts turned into a feeling. Not an emotion, but a *feeling*. I could *feel* the stone. I *was* the stone. All around, I became aware of its *essence*, the cool touch of solid earth. I had a moment to think, 'hey neat', before the stone moved. My mind zeroed in on Reed as if he were suddenly the center of the universe, the truth north of my compass. And I thought, Stop.

If I had expected him to merely stop, that would have been something to see. What happened instead was spectacular. The stone walls exploded all around. Like the grasping hands of a small child I felt the stone collide with Reed. As if I breathed inside of him, I felt his body slam into the ground. I fought as he fought. I raged as he raged. I shivered as his ivory claws tore at the stone. But with calm assurance, a detached sense of knowing, I *knew* that he would never break free. Unless I willed it.

And just like that it was over. I blinked and coughed and shook myself as if waking from a dream. The air was thick with dust and dirt, and I was gratefully alone once again inside my body. Sitting there, one shallow breath after another, I trembled like a leaf in a strong breeze.

As the dust settled I was left looking at a big mound of rock in the middle of the floor. It was oblong and suspiciously man-shaped. Getting to my feet, I walked tremulously over to it. At the end closest to me, there was a hole. A hole with teeth that gasped for air and growled. I stood over it and gave a great big sigh of relief.

There was a sudden scrabbling noise at the door and I turned just in time for it to swing open. I expected a lot of things. Monsters. Axe toting guards. Tree men with oak leaves in their beards. What I didn't expect, was Malcolm.

His hair was sticking up in all directions, so that I almost didn't recognize him. I'd never seen him anything short of suave and perfectly coifed. There was blood on his right cheek and his clothes were filthy. It looked like he'd been having about as much fun as me.

He looked from me to the growling mound on the floor and then back to me. His mouth hung partially open and he breathed as if he'd had himself a good long jog.

"You're-you're alright?" he said. I couldn't help but shrug.

"I was coming to rescue you." I joked, giving him what felt like a lop-sided smile. Not so surprisingly, Malcolm snorted. His eyes flickered to the thing on the floor once more and he shook his head.

"Come. We must be away before they rouse themselves." He said stepping back out of the doorway. I looked at the growling mound one last time. I wouldn't think about it. I wouldn't think about it, and it wouldn't hurt so bad. I turned before I could change my mind and fled.

Fleeing into the very core of the earth turned into less of a good idea by the minute. Again I was following Malcolm's broad shouldered back into the darkness with nothing but a single stolen torch to light the way. This time, the flame was low and blue-white, so that I could barely see a step in front of me. The better to hide our location he had said. And that had been the last of our conversation.

I stumbled over rock and stone, and trusted that he wasn't leading me astray. We had been walking for a long time. I played with the hem of my shirt, too tired to look around. My clothes were a mess. I thought about this absently until my face collided with the back of Malcolm's shirt. I stepped back and saw that a wide cavern gaped before us. The blue fire glittered on every surface, sparkled from every direction.

Somewhere close by, there was an unseen opening to the outside. I could smell cool, fresh air. Tiny winged creatures squeaked and fluttered over our heads. In my exhausted state, I thought of it all as a fairy land, a crystal dreamscape, some magical realm where no human hand had ever touched. Malcolm turned to me and there were dark circles under his eyes. He didn't look very magical.

"We will be safe resting here until we can go back to your house. It is still dark out. And I do not have the strength to protect us both." He said softly, looking about as tired as I felt. I could only nod and he led the way down a glittering slope. He walked us to a clear flat area further in. There were strange lumps just inside the clearing. Malcolm knelt next to one and I saw that they were two canvas ruck sacks. I wanted to ask him if he'd hidden here before, but I couldn't seem to work up the energy to even move my lips.

He pulled out four rolled up blankets, and handed two of them to me. I watched him as he stood and went to wedge the torch into a large cracked stone. He came back to me and I continued to watch lamely as he spread out one of his blankets on the ground.

"We are safe. Come, you must sleep." He said. I looked down at the blankets in my arms and couldn't move. I couldn't remember when I'd ever been so tired. Very gently, Malcolm took the blankets away from me and proceeded to spread them out on the ground next to his. If I had been in my right mind, I would have protested. Instead, I stumbled to my knees and squirmed like a broken worm to position myself between the blankets. Malcolm stared down at me for a long moment before shuffling to his own bed. He lay down next to me and the torch died.

"Thanks for rescuing me." I whispered. A soft grunt drifted to my ears. I heard him shift next to me. A balmy mantel of darkness was slipping over my consciousness. I heard him shift again somewhere in the distance of my brain.

"I'm sorry I hurt your arm." I thought I heard him say. I quickly tried to dismiss it. Surely it must have been a dream. But then I was asleep and the rest was forgotten.

10

In flashes of blue light and glittering stone, a figure watched us where we lay. Small, child-like and terribly waifish, he perched on a high boulder carved of alabaster flesh.

His two eyes were enormous. Limpid pools of black water reflecting eternity. They saw everything, watched every move, every breath, the flutter of a moth above our heads.

A rhythmic knocking filled the air, vibrating the stone all around. Knocking-knocking to the beat of our hearts. The throbbing pulse of the mother earth.

I lay dreamless, comforted, knowing we weren't alone in the darkness; knowing that we were safe as we slumbered.

There were birds singing. Their chorus echoed from every angle so that I opened my eyes expecting to be surrounded. I was warm in my cocoon of blankets. I watched the crystals covering the walls sparkle benignly. Somewhere far down the cavern, daylight was being reflected inward. There was enough light for me to see that Malcolm was no longer lying next to me.

I pushed myself up slowly from laying on my side. My whole body was stiff and sore. I wanted to call out for him, but who knew who else might be lurking. As far as I knew, Gannon and the others weren't restricted to night time frolicking. I knew for sure Leila wasn't and god only knew how far her betrayal went.

The sound of feet padding softly closer made me turn my head. Malcolm walked towards me. He was clean and his black hair was perfect once more. He wore black slacks and a black collarless dress shirt un-tucked. His quiet feet had on what I might have called moccasins. He was always so posh, my brain almost couldn't wrap around this dark bohemian side of his.

"I'm not particularly partial to Kool-Aid." I said when he came near, earning myself a deep scowl.

"Forgive me if I fail to chuckle." He said holding out a two plastic bags. There were moist towelettes in one, and what I suspected was jerky in the other. I snatched them up eagerly.

"I had the strangest dream." I said, pulling out one of the towelettes. Malcolm squatted nearby and watched me. His face was strangely open and serene. It made me nervous, so I busied myself cleaning my face and arms. Giving him a sideways glance, I quickly reached under my shirt and cleaned my arm pits.

"There were these little half naked people watching us while we were sleeping. I thought they were kids at first, but I don't know, I just knew they weren't. Pretty weird huh?" I asked, stuffing a piece of jerky in my mouth. It was sweet with a hint of rosemary.

"They are the Karzełek. This is their holy place." Malcolm said softly, and I nearly choked on my jerky. I could only look at him and try not to drool on myself. I should have known better. Nothing was as it seemed lately.

"What time is it?" I asked, stuffing the used towelettes back into the bag. There was still some jerky left but I handed both bags back to him. Malcolm took them and stood.

"A little after three." He said. I could only gap at him. Half the day was already gone. I scrambled up off of the ground flinging my blankets away.

"Well what are we waiting for? Let's get the hell out of here. Why did you let me sleep so long?" I hissed. My feet became tangled in a blanket and I almost fell. Malcolm's hand was instantly on my elbow.

"You needed to regain your strength. The games have only just begun." He said. We were very close together. He stood there looking very Zen. I had never seen this side of him. We were always busy being so angry. It struck me that I was actually beginning to trust him. Gasp! Maybe even like him. Double gasp!

"Yea well we don't know how long it'll take to get back to the house. I don't think I'd like to dance with those shadow guys again so soon." I said, gently extracting my elbow from his large hand.

"It is not far. And you'll be safe once you get back to your house." He turned away and went to tuck the baggies into a ruck sack. I followed his example and folded up the blankets. When everything was put safely away, we followed the light down the cavern.

"How do you know it'll be safe at the house? What if they get in, what do I do?" I asked. We walked through a narrow corridor of vibrant blue crystal and suddenly we were outside. It was like I blinked too long in the middle of my own demented picture show.

We were in the middle of the woods. Rich golden sunlight seemed to come from every direction. Leaves crunched and shifted under our feet. The scent of moist wet earth lingered all around. Those singing birds darted overhead.

I turned around in awe. There was no sign of the cave. No rocks, no stones, no mountains. Only trees as far as the eye can see. I turned back to Malcolm with my signature surprised, mouth hanging open face.

"You will not be able to find it alone. We have . . . ways . . ." he let it hang in the air and gave one of those irritating shrugs that told me absolutely nothing.

I nodded, unable to spring forth with a witty retort. I was mostly just happy to be out in the sun. Out in the daylight. All of the strange things of the world seemed far away. And that suited me just fine.

"I just want to go home." I said, still nodding. Yes, home sounded like a good idea.

I was standing at the bottom of my back steps just as the sun was sinking into its bed of trees. Sweat soaked the back of my filthy shirt. My once sparkling white sneakers were nearly black with mud and dirt and a little leaf was hanging onto my shoelace for dear life. Not far my ass.

Malcolm stood before me, and there was sweat at his temples. I wanted to say something snarky but I was barely able to catch my breath. Our trek had been long and fast-paced but thankfully uneventful.

"Stay in the house. I will return for you later. The Darklings cannot enter unless you let them in. Do not open the door. Do not leave the house for any reason." he said. I watched him run his hand through his hair, twice. It was a gesture he'd demonstrated repeatedly during the entire walk back. He'd look over at me for a long moment and then turn away, hand raking through his hair. Now, he caught me looking and put his hand down at his side.

"I won't leave unless you come. I promise . . . What about you? How are you going to get home?" this earned me a small smile.

"I will travel the usual way." He said, gesturing towards the trees. I shook my head at him. I had seen enough trees today to last me till the end of forever.

"Okay, but hurry. I don't wanna have all the fun to myself." I said. Malcolm snorted at me.

"Stay in the house." He said again and I nodded.

I slowly walked up the back steps and Malcolm stood on the edge of the garden until I had closed the door behind me with the lock engaged. I watched him wade through my Black-Eyed Susans and disappear into the trees. I instantly wanted to call him back. From the small kitchen window, I could see the night creeping over the land.

Every light in the house was still on. My electric bill was going to be hell this month.

My feet were heavy as they carried me up stairs. The upper floor was full of cool, undisturbed air. I shuffled towards my room, kicking off my shoes as I went. As I rounded the corner the light was bright from the open door of my room. I could see the butterflies on my wall paper and the fan with its big, spade-shaped, white blades slowly turning. I unbuttoned my pants and hobbled through the doorway with them around my ankles.

My queen sized bed was across from the door, still neatly made with its white down comforter and flowered blue throw. It looked so tempting. But a shower would come first. Yes, a shower sounded nice. I shrugged off my pants before I fell. My big white dresser sat off to the left under the big picture window overlooking the front yard. The world outside was cast in shadowy blue gloom. I ambled over to the dresser and quickly pulled out a pair of pajama shorts. I put them on so I wouldn't have to tromp around naked and threw my dirty underwear in the corner with a heartfelt promise to destroy them.

A deep sigh rattled through my chest. Fatigue had wedged itself deep in my bones. I closed my eyes, with my palms flat against the cool dresser top. The little bottles of perfume and other knick-knacks tinkled musically. A deep sense of calm flowed into my soul. Yet there's always calm before the storm.

I got that someone's-watching-you feeling. That hot-cold place in the middle of your back where their eyes are burrowing into you, the little hairs on the back of the neck standing at attention. I opened my eyes and looked out the window. There was a dark figure reflected in the glass standing behind me. Somehow I'd known. I'd known he'd be there. I'd noticed the open closet beside the door when I'd come in, with its deep shadows. Apparently, they didn't seem to mind electric lights.

Very slowly, I reached for the window lock and flipped it to the left. I tried to appear as nonchalant as possible. Slow and calm. The shadow remained unmoved. I could see that it was tall and broad and lumpy in a way that no normal human should be.

I slipped my fingers into the crack between the window and the ledge and took a long deep breath. It seemed like the whole world took a deep breath. And then I moved.

I threw the window up and launched myself over the dresser. Glass containers flew in all directions. I cursed out loud, unable to get up over the dresser in that first lurch. I had the front half of my body out the window, when the windowpane came down on my back, along with a cold pair of clawed hands.

I screamed. I couldn't help myself. It was like being grabbed by two giant ice cubes with talons. I felt them rip the back of my shirt like tissue paper. I screamed and kicked myself through the window jerking around frantically, doing my best impression of a landed carp.

The thing about jumping out a window, especially a second story window, is that the only way to go is down. Somehow I managed to wriggle free of those terrible hands. And then I was falling. Rolling through the air. I slammed into the roof of the porch awning, taking several tar flaps with me. I reached out to stop myself but it was too late. I was airborne again. It felt like I had a long time to wonder about the state of my predicament. My heart was a thundering in my skull. The air was chill as it raced past. I had plenty of time to think about these things before I crashed into the box hedges.

I lay in the bushes and blinked up at sapphire sky. I was relieved that I was still breathing, still in one piece. And horrified that I was still lying there. Get up! My brain screamed. I flailed around, beating at the bushes, leaves flying all over. I freed myself and rolled out onto the lawn. The grass was still warm and fragrant from the sun.

I scrambled to my feet and ran for the garage. The gravel tore at my feet in their socks and I nearly fell in my head long rush.

Plunging forward, I slid past the door grabbing for the handle. I jumped into the garage, and slammed the door shut, engaging the tiny slide bolt. Almost immediately, I slid through a puddle of something slick on the ground. It squeezed through my toes, soaking my socks.

I didn't waste any time worrying about the condition of my already dirty socks. I crashed through the dark garage and slid over the hood of the wagon. I got in and found myself keyless. I screamed my frustration and beat the steering wheel with my fists.

Of course there would be no keys. That seemed to be the way of my life lately. All I needed now was an elephant to fall out sky and crush me.

Not waiting for that rogue pachyderm, I quickly exited the wagon and ran over to the truck. I slid into the seat and took a moment to remove my slippery socks, only to find that the keys were gone from the ignition. I groaned. I vaguely remembered putting both sets beside my emergency bag in the dining room.

What now? I thought. My nearest neighbor was down past a long ten acres of trees. Malcolm was gone, and not likely to return any time soon. In short, I was up a certain creek without my paddle.

I got out of the truck and slowly walked back towards the door. I'd go back to the house. At least there I would have shelter, and possible weapons. I stood in front of the door and took a shuddering breath. Into that dark night I go, I thought.

I cracked the door and poked my head out. Nothing grabbed me, so I opened it a little wider. My eyes darted all around, to the tree line, down the road. I stepped out and strained my neck to see around the edge of the garage where The Beast had once sat. I stretched my ears, trying to hear every sound. Every whisper. A breeze tripped up my bare legs and made me pause. The open road was at my back. I felt it like a hand. I turned, my skin tingling with fear. It was empty. Wisps of mist trailed through the air like wayward souls. I turned back towards the house ready to run for those brightly lit windows. Towards my kitchen full of knives. I was ready to run and stopped dead.

A dark figure was standing before the front door. I'd almost missed it. It was bent at the waist and twisted off to the side. Its two arms were held out away from its body like a scarecrow hanging from a post. Its head was malformed and shaped like a strange potato. That head twisted around on an impossibly long, thin neck.

I thought about dodging around the side, going for the back of the house. But I remembered that it was locked. I was about to try for it anyways, when a second shadow walked around the right side of the house on all fours. It was man shaped, but raised its grotesque head to sniff the air like a beast to the scent of blood.

My breath caught in my throat. I wanted to scream, to cry, to rage at the unfairness of it all. *No one ever said life was fair,* I could hear my grandmother's voice say to me. I would have stomped my foot if I wasn't so scared.

Instead, I turned and ran. I ran down the dark and misty road, and out to my doom.

11

There was monster blood stuck between my toes. I couldn't stop myself from shivering. I clenched the giant ladle in my hand. If the end was near, I was gonna take a few pieces of them with me.

The figure in the doorway stepped into the room, tucking its hands into the pockets of a beautiful, black leather riding jacket. His perfectly formed face was frowning at me. But not too deeply.

"I thought I told you to stay in the house." Malcolm's velvety timbre floated through the air. I went almost weak with relief. I tried to laugh, but a sob escaped my lips. I dropped the ladle with a loud clang and eased my way around the dead guy on the ground. Malcolm silently took off his jacket and put it around my shoulders. He didn't even tease me about my shorts. Snide comments and cut tires on my bicycle I could handle. His kindness nearly undid me. We walked out of the shed and were instantly bathed in orange light.

Malcolm was wearing a black flannel shirt over a black turtleneck. His pants were black and jean. He wore a pair of rough looking black work boots. As monochromatic as ever. Still, it was another side of him I had never known existed.

"Black is not the new blue." I said, sniffling. The jacket was warm as I picked my way slowly over to the road.

"We can't all wear pink Carebears." He said, not looking at me. I stopped and stared at him.

"How did you find me?" He turned, hands in his pants pockets. His face was irritatingly blank.

"I placed precautionary measures around the house before I left. Just in case you decided to disobey me. It didn't take you long." He gave me a small smile and the quirk of his eye brow. It made my blood boil.

"I didn't let them in you jerk! They were already in the house to begin with!" I shouted, smacking him in the arm. He scowled.

"What do you mean they were *in* the house. That's impossible. Someone would have had to ..." His face fell and I watched a thought dance across his eyes.

"What? They would have had to what?" I pulled on his sleeve, willing his attention back to me.

"Someone on our side would have to let them in." he said softly, looking at me. My heart dropped down to my toes. No one had been in my house except ...

"Reed. He was the last person in the house. He let those things in my house." I felt like crying. My face burned. It was all too much. First Leila, and then Reed. I could handle him being all scary and trying to eat me. But so much betrayal was too much. Hot tears built in my eyes and spilled down my face.

"It could not be Reed. One, he would not betray the house of Cross. And two, he is simply not powerful enough to open the way to them. Please stop crying, you waste time on such things." He said gently, pulling out a kerchief from god knows where and handing it to me.

I wiped my face with it and then stuffed it in the pocket of his jacket.

"You're sure?" I asked and when he nodded, my heart lifted a few inches. Not far, but enough to keep me from shriveling up into a small soggy mess on the ground.

"Come, I have found us a place where we might be safe until a better plan can be amassed." I let him take me by the arm and together we walked down the road. I tried not to think about what I'd just left behind. Soon we would be safe. And that sounded real good to me.

More trees. We were slogging through the undergrowth. Thankfully, we had walked back to the house, lingering only long enough to procure a pair of jeans and shoes. There was no sign of the oogie-boogies. We left the lights on and plunged swiftly into the night drenched forest.

This time, I followed close behind Malcolm, occasionally bumping into or stepping on him in the process. He didn't mock me or make any off-color comments. He even let me keep his jacket, but he made me turn it around and wear it backwards. He didn't explain, and I for once really didn't want to argue.

95

There was no fire this time. That grinning moon managed to light the way perfectly. It was either that, or Malcolm could see in the dark. I was so stressed out by the smallest things at this point, I couldn't think about it. I needed an ally. A normal, no nonsense ally. And Malcolm was the closest I was going to get.

After nearly an hour of walking, the tiny yellow flames appeared once more in the distance. I grabbed ahold of Malcolm's arm and tried to rip it off.

"What are they? What are those things?" I hissed, stopping him. I watched him scan the trees and shake his head.

"They are follet. More commonly called will-o-the-wisps. They will not harm you so long as you don't go chasing off after them." He said continuing his steady pace through the trees. His surety of the situation made me feel less cowardly. If he said it was alright then by-gum, it was alright. I let go of his arm and followed, my eyes scanning the darkness in a never ending circuit.

"How much further?" I whispered. He glanced back at me with another shake of his head.

"Not much longer. We've had to travel the long way because of certain barriers I cannot cross. We are not, as they say, in Kansas anymore." He said and I was caught off guard. I couldn't wrap my brain around his comment. It was preposterous at best. Malcolm and Oz? Crazy. And to hell with Kansas. I wasn't even sure we were on planet Earth anymore.

I was about to ask him exactly what kind of barriers, when the barest of sounds from behind put me on the alert. A rustle of leaves. A shifting of the wind. A something.

Like all those big dummies in the movies, I stopped and turned around. All I could see were muddled black shapes backlit by a velvety sapphire sky.

"I heard a noise." I whispered. I turned back and Malcolm was gone. What the frickin' hell? I was alone in the dark. Again! This was becoming a trend I was quite un-fond of.

I wanted to call out, but my voice shrank in my throat. My tongue dried up in my skull. A piece of wood snapped loudly behind me. My body was instantly stiff and covered in goose bumps. I turned with B-movie perfection, eyes darting back and forth frantically.

Some yards away, a tree gently swayed in the still air. My heart jumped into my mouth. It's a just a tree. Trees are our friends, trees are our friends, I chanted in my head. The tree moved again and a large black lump detached itself from the gloom. Large black lumps in the dark are *not* our friends, my inner voice screamed.

The urge to urinate was strong as anything. The lump was well over ten feet tall. It moved steadily through the trees like a glacier drifting through the night. A hand gently squeezed my elbow and I almost screamed bloody murder. Another hand instantly clamped over my mouth and held on tight.

"No sudden moves. No loud noises. We are in grave danger." Malcolm's voice was barely a whisper, his breath warm against my ear. I nodded and his hand fell away.

"Back up slowly. When I give you the word, we're going to run. Run and whatever you do, don't stop." I could only nod. Icy terror filled me. The lump was moving faster than we were backing up. It was less than twenty feet away. Two red points of light glared out at us. I could make out an impossibly long snout and tusks longer than my arm. A noise straight from the bowels of hell trumpeted from that terrible mountain. It was the roar of an avalanche mixed with the screech of rubber on hot concrete. It reverberated through my entire body, turning my marrow to water. The foliage shook in its wake. Leaves blew in our direction, along with a hot, rancid wind of breath.

"Run!" Malcolm shouted in my ear. As if I'd even needed the urging. I turned and ran my ass off.

Somewhere in my mind, I thought, haven't we been here before? The cold, autumn air was whipping past. The branches of trees and undergrowth tore at our bodies. And behind, the monster was coming. It was like being chased by a train. I could hear it behind me tearing through the trees, roaring in its pursuit. My lungs burned and my legs ached. If I survived this ordeal, I was going to be a world class sprinter.

Malcolm ran ahead of me with long sure strides. I tried my best to mimic his body. Jump when he jumped, weave when he weaved. I was forced to bend my body in ways that I didn't know I could bend, just to keep up the grueling pace. And still the monster came.

I heard it roar and watched as Malcolm threw his body off to one side into the trees. I flung myself in the same direction, crashing through what felt like a wall of growth. In the same instance that my body hit the ground, the beast careened past. It was a dark blur melting into the night with its terrifying flash of red eyes.

"Get up, get up!" Malcolm shouted, yanking on my arm. He was already on his feet and pulling me with him. I floundered, wading through the bush I'd landed in. Then we were off again before I could even catch my breath.

We ran, and out in the forest I could hear the beast rage. I could hear trees falling and the ground shook under our feet. But most frightening of all, we were blind to it. We could have been running right towards it for all I knew, but I prayed Malcolm wouldn't lead us to our doom.

A sound like drum beats was coming towards us. I could feel it in the air. It quickened and grew in volume until it felt as if the drumming lived inside my head.

In a flash of vermillion and a rush of wind, an enormous figure burst through the screen of trees. It passed so close I could have reached out my hand and touched it. It was right on our heels. So close, I could smell its evil breath steaming around me.

Malcolm had released my arm and I was falling behind. I wasn't as fit as he was. The lactic acid was building up faster in my legs then I knew what to do with. He was six feet in front of me. I thought my heart was going to burst from my chest. Or that any moment I'd be gored by a giant tusk. I couldn't stop thinking about all of the horrible things that were going to happen if I fell or if I slowed down any more. Thinking about it though, made me pump my legs harder, willing my body to go further.

I watched Malcolm's shadow jump out into the darkness. It was a long jump and his legs stretched for distance. I counted the paces and as soon as I reached the point, I jumped. Some twenty feet across, I saw him crash into the brush, get up, and keep running. I was happy about this until I realized *I* wasn't going to be making it to the brush. In my mind's eye, I knew that I was going to come up short.

I braced myself for impact, arms stretched out in front of me, legs loose. I slammed into a bush on the outer edge of what appeared to be a ravine. My hands closed around whatever they could grab and held on tight. I slid downwards in a rain of dirt and leaves. Ironically, I ended up latched onto a bunch of roots, dangling into the ravine like bait. Behind me the beast snorted and roared and destroyed anything within reach. It couldn't reach me and gladness filled me. I might fall to my death on jagged rocks or timber, but at least some beasty wasn't going to eat me.

Dirt and debris rained down on me. I coughed and snorted and tried not to lose my grip.

"What are you doing!" Malcolm shouted down at me. He fell to his knees and grabbed my hands. I spit out a leaf and resisted the urge to pull him down with me.

"I'm knitting fecking a sweater! What the hell does it look like I'm doing!" I screamed. He hoisted me up like a sack of potatoes, depositing me neatly on my feet. Without even checking to see if I was in one piece, we were suddenly running again. We ran until the roaring of the beasty grew dim and finally faded away. There was a sharp pain in my ribs where something had jabbed me. My legs were growing stiff and moved like hardening glue. I dragged my feet and pulled on our linked hands.

"Malcolm! Malcolm, stop. I can't run anymore. I hurt. Please stop!" And like magic we stopped, toppling over onto the forest floor. Malcolm lay on his back gasping for breath. I reached under my shirt and found a small hole in the skin between two of my lower ribs. Warm liquid slowly trickled out with every gasping breath I took. It felt as if knives had been shoved into my thigh muscles. There were scratches on my face that stung. All in all, it felt good to be alive.

"I-turned around-and . . . you were-gone." He gasped. I watched him struggle to sit up, his arms braced behind him. His once neat hair was sticking up in all directions again. I would have said something, but I could only imagine what I looked like at this point. I didn't bother with sitting up. I lay on my back and dragged in the cool night air. My body had started sweating all over until my shirt was soaked and my jeans were damp. We stayed there for a long time, relearning how to breathe.

"I didn't expect him to be loose . . . I should have taken more precautions. You could have died." He said softly. I was still gazing up at the canopy, holding my hand tightly over the little hole in my side. It suddenly seemed like a bad time to tell him I was leaking like a sieve. So I pushed myself up and gave him a level stare.

"What do you mean you didn't expect him? What the hell was that thing?" I hissed softly, pulling the jacket around me and zipping it up as much as I could reach. Nothing hides blood like black.

"He is Oduon. He is a forest creature. His kind speaks and comprehends the human tongues. All human tongues. Yet unfortunately he also enjoys the consumption of human flesh. Thankfully he's not particularly intelligent. But he's usually kept away in his valley." Malcolm's voice was soft. I watched him feel around in the dark until he held up a large stick between us.

"Shield your eyes." He said and I quickly covered them. I heard him whisper something arcane and then there was a burst of light and heat. I uncovered my eyes to find myself bathed in golden warmth. Malcolm looked like he had war paint all over his face.

"You have a little something here." I said motioning to his chin. He wiped a hand over his face and grunted.

"I fell on my face." He said with a curl of his upper lip. It was a very unhappy face. A self-depreciating face.

"I ran a good length before I realized you weren't even there. I turned too quickly and fell over a root and slid through a great deal of mud . . . I shouldn't have allowed this to happen. It was a stupid mistake." I couldn't quite stand the self-loathing in his eyes. I balled up my fist and chucked him in the shoulder.

"Look, we're alive. Slightly worse for wear, yes, but nobody ever said adventure was clean. And Leila told me mud bathes are top of the line in Hollywood. Besides, if you keep tearing yourself down, what the hell does that leave me to do?" We stared at each other for a long moment. I watched him very seriously until a small smile was born under all that mud. He shook his head, valiantly trying to smother the moment of levity. He got to his feet and held a very dirty hand out to me.

"We must go. The night grows." He said his face carefully blank. I didn't really like the way he said that the night was 'growing' around us. I eased myself to my feet, being studiously careful to keep the pain off of my face. He was still holding his hand out to me so I took it. Chalk it up to a moment of weakness, but I kind of enjoyed it. Guided by the light of flame and the strength of our will to live, we headed into the trees once more.

12

Someone once wrote, '*All that we see or seem, is but a dream within a dream*'. I would probably look back on the length of my life and these words would still be buried within my soul. Yet I never really felt the depth of their meaning until this very moment, and I sincerely believed the author had to have had an experience similar to the one I was having.

We had entered a dream. At least that's what it felt like. The forest floor had given way to a tidy stone path. The stones were neatly edged in deep green moss and bordered by faintly luminescent wild flowers. Five yards down and we stepped into a wide clearing. Our entrance was heralded by two glass lamps on tall poles with cheerfully burning stubs of white candles. There was a little man sitting on one of the lamps. He was no bigger than my palm. His clothes were formed from bits of bark and there was a tiny gold hat on his head made from what looked like a rolled birch leaf. He watched us with dark beady eyes, his large bulbous nose twitching.

But that wasn't even the half of it. All around, tiny balls of light danced. Little black bats flitted over our heads, accompanied by tiny people shaped things with tiny bat wings. The air shimmered and sparkled. Little creatures I'd never even thought of outside of a story book ran, jumped, danced, cartwheel, or just sat and picked their strange noses. Some were smaller than a mouse, and some were tall as the trees; spindly as a spider or round as an apple. There were scales and fur and skin of all hues. My eyes were painfully wide trying to take in everything. And still there was more.

Down the path, its yard surrounded by a small white picket fence, there was a house. It was a house sprung up from the very earth. A single story mound, it boasted a sod roof with grass growing on it and more tiny glowing flowers. It had two square windows that glowed with merry light. Its spacious yard had overflowing beds of flowers and herbs. There was a pale statue of Artemis seated, alabaster hunting dogs sleeping at her feet and a little red sprite swung back and forth from the diadem on her forehead. There was an enormous bird bath parallel in the yard to it. Tiny blue-green mer-creatures played in it, while on lookers sat along the rim like some sort of pool party.

I was in awe. Every time I blinked, there was something new to see. The din of noise was shocking after such a long time in the quiet woods. There was tittering laughter, excited talking, and the occasional gentle bickering all in strange varied octaves.

A nervous giggle crept up my throat but I covered it with my hand. As if the slightest noise would send them into flight like leaves in the wind. I kept blinking, star struck in this unbelievable dream. Malcolm touched my arm and I looked at him. He had a strange look on his face. And then I realized he was smiling.

"The first time is always the worst for everyone." He said softly. It was my turn to snort at him.

"I feel like I've fallen down the rabbit hole." I whispered and he bobbed his head in agreement.

"I wake up every day thinking the same thing."

We walked carefully down the path. The little creatures running to and fro paid no mind to us. They were so immersed in their own world I thought perhaps we might be as imaginary to them as they had once been to me. A few looked up as we passed but they watched with calm eyes.

I was still busy blinking around. We were past the quaint little gate and up on the door step before I knew it. And then Malcolm was knocking.

My heart lurched when the door opened. Light came through in a wave, drenching us in warm, fragrant air. And there was a woman. My heart stopped.

Her long white hair streaked with gray was held back from her face by a long green ribbon. Sparkling green eyes regarded us. I wanted to cry. This *was* a dream. This was a terrible dream to have to wake up from. No wonder Malcolm was so damn cheerful. He was never so cheerful in real life.

She came out of the door way and took my hand in both of hers. They were warm and soft. The smell of beeswax wafted from her.

She was wearing a long sleeved brown shirt with bits of gold thread sewn through it and a long cream colored skirt. Brown suede loafers peeked out from the hem. I could have stood there holding her hand forever.

And then it hit me. I was so star-struck by our surroundings that it took me a long time to make my way back into clarity. The shock of it splashed over me like icy water. Her eyes were brown like sun touched earth and her long hair was completely silver. This was not my grandmother. I gently removed my hand from hers.

"Who are you?" It came out of my throat in a ragged whisper. She smiled that familiar smile.

"I am Gwyn of the Forest and *you* are Vivian Cross of Red Glen." She said. Her voice matched the rest of her, warm and supple. She turned that smile on Malcolm, snatching up his hand.

"And you dark boy, have been lax in the frequency of your visits. I have missed our games." She scolded. I was amazed as she drew him to her and pinched him affectionately on the cheek. My mind was further blown, when he actually blushed.

"I have been . . . busy, old mother." He mumbled softly. This made her laugh. Again my heart lurched. It was my grandmother's laugh. And yet, not. I couldn't seem to get past my confusion. I frowned at both of them.

"I'm dreaming. This is a dream." I said loudly before either of them could say anything else. Malcolm looked at me like I'd grown a second head. Gwyn only smiled.

"I can assure you child, this is no dream." She said. Only that and nothing more. So what? I was supposed to take her word? I reached over and pinched myself hard on the wrist. I looked hard at both of them. Nothing happened.

"Come inside. There is much to be told. And I've just pulled a batch of honey cakes out of the oven." She said. Malcolm motioned angrily to the doorway with a frown. Obviously I'd made some faux pas with him and our truce was over. Gwyn laughed and ushered us both through the door clucking like a mother hen.

The inside of her house was like standing inside a cocoon. It was warm and the air was thick with scents. They filled my nose and made me think of delicate spring and sun soaked summer. To the right there was a wide, arched hearth crackling away with a small antique sofa facing us and two plush chairs facing in with a low table in the center. Under foot, the floor was made up of dark wood covered by richly woven carpets. To the left there appeared to be a kitchen, with tall racks of herbs and spices lining the walls, copper and cast iron pots and pans hung from the ceiling. There was a large, white, cast iron wood stove, with a teapot steaming in one corner and a white china plate with small round biscuits in the other. Across from the stove under a pretty square window looking out into the yard, there was a small, two-seater pine breakfast table. It had a crystal vase on it filled with Black-eyed Susans. Directly across from the front door there was a dark archway leading off to other parts of the house.

I was as much intrigued as I was stunned by the appearance of this place. On every wall there was something to see. Pictures, figurines, bottles, vases. Chunks of stone and carvings of wood. Everything sparkled in rainbow hues or shined lustrously, beckoning to me in some strange, familiar way.

Gwyn had been busy in the kitchen while I'd been busy gawking. She handed Malcolm the plate of biscuits and beckoned to me with a tea set balanced on one hand. I followed them to the fire and plunked myself down on the sofa.

Malcolm set the plate down on the intricate wooden table and eased himself into one of the two chairs. Gwyn busied herself with pouring cups of tea for each of us. She plopped cubes of sugar and dollops of cream into them without asking. She was smiling to herself and bobbing her head in a way that made me think she was listening to music I couldn't hear. Again there was that feeling of familiarity.

"Oduon was loose in the forest this evening." Malcolm said nonchalantly. Gwyn glanced over at him, pausing in her ritual.

"I know. Someone has taken it upon themselves to release a great many of our more dangerous inhabitants out in the open. Be glad the pig-lord was all you ran into." She said, continuing with the tea.

I watched her hover over the table, gently stirring each cup with a delicate twitch of her wrinkled hand. I watched her eyes sparkle in the fire light as she handed Malcolm his cup. And then she turned to me with those gentle eyes and it hit me. I had my cup in my hand, when it hit me. I knew her, I *knew* this woman. We were still staring at each other as she sat in the empty chair. So I said it out loud.

"I know you. I don't know how I know you. But I do." I said. There was that smile and a nod.

"You do." She acknowledged aloud, taking her own cup from the table. She sipped it as I stared. I stared and frowned and I realized Malcolm was doing the same thing to me. I resisted the urge to stick my tongue out at him and took a biscuit from the table. It was soft and warm, which seemed to be the theme of this place. I took a big bite and honey filled my mouth. I was in ecstasy. It was quite possibly the best thing I had ever eaten. I chewed slowly, savoring it, when the memory came to me.

I sat ridged on the couch slopping my tea onto the leg of my pants. It was lightening running down my spine, snowflakes wizzing pell-mell through my brain. I crushed the little cake in my hand and was flung back with a gasp.

The walls melted into forest. I felt the wind whipping past my body, the moist earth under my bare feet. It was summer and I was happy. So very happy. Joyful almost. It surprised me that I had ever been so happy. So carefree.

The sun was warm on the top of my head. My hair waved behind me like a flag. I was so proud of my mane, so much like my mommy's. I was running, with no where or why, just running. This was my kingdom, my safe place. Nothing could harm me here. The trees watched over me, beloved sentinels. Nothing could hurt me, I thought. And then I fell.

I fell hard to the ground. The skin on my hands and legs were torn open. There was blood, a lot of blood. My arm was bleeding, pumping out my blood with every beat of my heart. I sobbed up into the trees. Help me, I thought, please help me.

I lay there a long time. With the sun shimmering overhead. The trees leaned their tops closer together to shade me. After an even longer time, I stopped crying. And she was there. With her funny shoes and long soft dresses.

I remember the way she knelt beside me and took me into her lap. I was so small then, I could tuck my legs up and fit like a roo in a pouch. She stroked my hair and held me close. I could hear her heart against my ear. It was like music, comforting music. She whispered something to me and like a flash, my pain was gone. I looked down at my arm and I was healed.

I hugged her and stood up on my own two feet. My knobby knees were unblemished. She handed me a honey caked wrapped in cheese cloth and patted me on the behind.

"Run along now my darling. Your mother will be waiting." She said. I nodded, turned, and ran away. I looked back once, and she was gone, like a mirage in the summer sun.

I was gasping for air. There was something sticky all over my hand and Malcolm was holding onto my shoulders, pressing me back into the couch.

"Well that was less pleasant than I expected it to be." Gwyn said wiping a cool cloth over my forehead. My whole body shook as if I were going into shock. Malcolm slowly let go of my shoulders, watching my face intently. Gwyn sat next to me on the couch, slowly leaning over to place the cloth on the table.

"You saved me." I croaked. She turned that lovely, aging face back to me and nodded.

"Who are you? What's happening to me?" I asked. I reached for the cloth and used it to wipe off my hand. Gwyn handed my cup of tea back to me. I looked down at it suspiciously.

"It's only tea child, it will help to calm you." I wanted to believe her. My mind was full of things I didn't know. I wanted answers, so I took the tea. Malcolm had resituated himself back in his chair. His rumpled hair and clothes made him look like a crow with ruffled feathers.

"To answer your questions, I must tell you two stories. Two stories so different and yet so intertwined that they would change the course of our world forever." She reached over and handed me another cake. I was sure when she said 'our world' that she wasn't just talking about the planet Earth. I nibbled my cake, watching her attentively.

"I suppose it begins as many stories have begun. A long, long time ago, when the scions of Olympus were new born, the Sovereign Arthur was but a twinkle in Fate's eye and the children of the Daoine Sidhe, ruled the land of Eire, a son of Man came to dwell in the mists.

He was called Cross and he was a shepherd. He lived alone on the shores of Eire with his flock and it was said he was the humblest of men. He had no things than what he had brought up from the earth himself. No food that he did not harvest with his own bare hands. It was said, that if ever an ambitious thought would have entered his mind, it would have struck him dead. He was a beloved of the Mother. This we know was truth.

Some two and twenty years had passed in the life of Cross when The Hunt came to his place. In those times, the sidhe preyed on one and all, even their own. Yet Cross was wise in the ways of the Underworld and in that time of danger, he took his flock into his hut and prepared to remain until the Huntsmen and their hounds had passed. All through the night, he sat with his clothes on backwards and a string of bells around his neck. These things, along with his crook of rowan, he used to keep the malicious wights at bay.

It was said that Cross dozed for a while and in a dream he heard a maid cry out for help. He was jolted awake by rolling thunder to find that it was no dream and that a maid somewhere cried out in the dark night.

With crook and flame in hand, Cross struck out into the enchanted, stormy night. Battered by wind and rain, it wasn't long before he came upon them in the woods, the Huntsmen and their diabolic feast. In their midst they held a maid captive and were set to consume her.

Cross had never before known a time of heroism. He had only the goodness in his heart lead him. Yet as a shepherd intent on the defense of his flock, Cross stepped boldly into the circle of their magic fires. He struck down the Huntsmen with his crook and chased them with his ringing iron bells.

These wights had never before been set upon by a son of Man, and they fled in terror. Cross took up the maid at once and they too fled, back to his hut. It was only there that Cross found himself trapped, trapped in a tangle as old as Eden.

The maid was the most beautiful he had ever seen and he was instantly in love. Some may argue that it is not such a lucky thing to love a daughter of the Faerie. Finola was the youngest daughter of the Queen of the White Ladies and she had been loved many times. She was wise in the ways of men, having lived ten score over the years of Cross' life. Still, she too was caught. Never had she been loved by one so pure and simple of heart.

Instead of returning to the forest as the sun rose, Finola remained with Cross. Their love was unspoken, chaste. By merely being together each prayed that the other would see it. They lived simply. Cross would tend his sheep, while Finola tended to his home. In the evening they would eat together and converse on the day. Always they slept separate, Finola in Cross' bed, and he out in the field with his sheep. They passed this way for nearly a fortnight before another storm came.

Cross and Finola were tending the lambs when it came. It was unlike anything either had ever experienced and they were afraid. Cross gathered his beloved and placed his body around hers. His sheep were scattered and all hope seemed lost. Cross looked at Finola to tell her, to tell of his love before they should die. Yet before he could utter a word, the storm ceased. They raised their heads, and all around were the sidhe of Eire. They were in all shapes and all creeds, and they were dressed for battle.

The King of the Tuatha dé Danann stepped forward, most tall and beautiful son of the Under Realm. In a voice that was all languages and none, he demanded that Cross return the daughter of his White Lady.

Cross, surprised, shook his head at the King and gave a bow. He meant no disrespect, he told him, but he was not keeping Finola, and she was free to leave at any time she wished.

The sidhe were disbelieving. Their brethren had told of the son of Man that had viciously attacked them in their revelry. The Huntsmen had told of the theft of their beloved sister and the wickedness of this shepherd.

So good and kind was Finola, so full of love was her heart that she was unafraid of her king and her people when she thought of protecting her beloved. She stepped out before them and shouted to them. The Huntsmen and his minions had misled them and Cross was in truth her rescuer. Finola told them the true story of her capture and near death.

The hill side was in an uproar. And once again the Huntsmen fled. Finola bowed at the feet of her mother and those of her king, and begged for the life of Cross. She told them what a good and kind soul he was, how steadfast and humble.

The queen of the White Ladies watched her daughter with shrewd eyes. She could see the difference in her child. She could see that Finola had given her heart to this son of Man.

After a brief counsel, the king invited Cross to come to the underworld, where he would live forever with them. To some this may have seemed like the opportunity of a lifetime. But the shepherd shook his head. His heart was heavy, for though he loved Finola, he had no wish to live forever. And also, there was his flock. He could not leave them behind.

The sidhe were shocked. Could a man be so selfless as to give up eternity? And try as they might, they could not sway him. Finola was heartbroken. No matter what, if she remained, Cross would grow old and die without her. She begged him to go and his heart too was broken, for he did not want to live without her.

It was the king, in the end, who found a remedy for them both. Seeing their love and their anguish was so great, he decided to let them stay. For Cross, he decreed that his line would forever hold a place of honor and power among the sidhe as a shepherd of their people, and Finola, he made mortal.

They were joined soon after and it is said that the celebration went on for days."

Gwyn took my hand in hers, and turned it palm up. She lifted the sleeve so that the mark on my wrist was visible.

"Since that union, every first born Cross child has been born with this mark on their body. Your grandmother, your mother, and now you. It is the Shepherd's Crook, and a sign of the kings promise." I could only look at her in awe. I put the honey cake in my mouth and took a big bite. It wasn't a scone, but it would do for the moment.

"So . . . what about you? You look like . . . I mean, I thought you were . . ." I couldn't get it out. I took another bite of my cake and licked the crumbs off of my fingers trying to ruminate. Her kind smile brightened.

"Only the first born bear the mark. But that doesn't mean the rest of us got left with nothing. Our family's power is legendary. It only seems so miniscule now that our line is dwindling." She said and a bit of the light died. I recognized the dull melancholy in her eyes because it was the same I saw gazing out at me in the bathroom mirror every morning. I took her hand and smiled.

"At least we have each other now, Aunt Gwyn." I said. She laughed and chucked me under my chin.

"That we do my child. That we do." She said and handed me another little cake. A half stifled yawn came from across the way and we both looked. Malcolm was looking at us with heavy lids. I was so excited about everything I had almost forgotten we'd been traveling all night.

"You look like road kill." I said sweetly to him. Those stormy eyes narrowed into slits.

"Obviously you haven't looked in a mirror of late." He growled. I would have snapped back with something else snide, but I remembered I was still wearing his coat.

"Now children, behave." Gwyn scolded, "Malcolm you may see yourself off to bed if our company is so lacking." He had the decency to look embarrassed. I was tickled pink. Ha! My auntie showed you! I thought and it was strange how right it felt to include her in the circle of my life.

"And you young lady, need not pick on your valiant guard. Me thinks you owe him much by now." She said turning those eyes on me. It was my turn to blush and I could see Malcolm gloating out of the corner of my eye.

"I think the two of you should get some rest. You've had a rough few days and you'll be perfectly safe here." She stood and let go of my hand.

"What about the other story?" I squawked, taking another bite of cake. She waggled her finger at me, motioning for Malcolm to get up and help her with the dishes.

"I'll tell you the other story later. Malcolm, you may sleep in your usual bed. And you my dear will sleep in the guest room." Gwyn said. I watched them clear away the mess with startling efficiency. Before I knew it, I had finished my cake and Gwyn was leading me through the archway opposite the door. It led to another small round chamber with five doors. Malcolm grunted at me and gave a small bow of his head to Gwyn before shuffling towards one on the far right. It closed before I could think of anything to say to him. It wasn't like he was very far away, yet somehow the room felt a little less acceptable without him in it. I quickly shook off the feeling and let Gwyn lead me across another richly woven carpet, to a door in the middle. She opened it and pulled me in.

It was a simple room, painted bright white with pale pink heirloom roses. The bed was a queen and covered with a white down comforter. There was a small white table with a white china basin on it. Across the way, under the room's only window, there was a comfortable looking plush chair in cream with more roses embroidered on it. Light struggled to peak in through the thick white curtains over the windows. I looked at the bed, and was instantly tired.

Gwyn sat me down on the edge of it and helped me get out of Malcolm's jacket. Her eyes lingered on the large dark spot on my shirt.

"You should have told him, he could have helped you." She said, helping me take off my shoes. My eyelids felt like ten pound weights, and I struggled to keep them open.

"I didn't want to worry him. He already stresses himself out enough for both of us." I said with a yawn. Gwyn turned back the covers and helped me slide under them. I sighed. The mattress was as soft as a cloud. She tucked me in and turned to go.

"Don't leave." I whispered, grasping at her hand. She turned back and sat on the edge, smiling down at me. It was familiar, as if we'd done it many times before.

"What is it my love?" her soft hand smoothed back my dirty hair from my face. I thought briefly about ruining her sheets, before letting my eyes flutter.

"I'm scared . . . I'm scared I'll wake up and you won't be here." I said. She chuckled softly.

"I promise I'll be here when you wake. Nothing could keep me from you now." She said her eyes fierce. My eyes closed and I thought I felt her kiss my forehead. And I wasn't even tired, I thought, and then I slept.

Two little pixies watched me from their perch on a crystal candle holder. I wouldn't have been upset except for the fact that I was naked. I was crammed into a small wooden tub, enjoying the most wonderful bath of my life. I couldn't straighten my legs or move around too much, but the water was hot and the soap smelled like roses and honeysuckle. And the company wasn't too bad either.

The pixies giggled and watched and brought me the occasional wash cloth. I couldn't understand what they were saying but they'd done pretty things to my clean hair, while helping Gwyn pile it on top of my head with a tortoise shell comb. They also had a tendency to drop little flowers on me and run away giggling. But anything was better than being dirty for two straight days.

Even better, when I woke up, my side had been completely healed. My side, my hands, my face, and anywhere else with hurts. I was good as new.

Gwyn came through the door with a pile of cloth in her arms. She wore a house dress cinched around the waist, with more flowers on it than should be allowed. They ranged in color from mauve to burgundy to pale baby pink. She dumped the pile on a nearby chair and came over to me with a towel.

We were in the first of the five rooms from the left. It was a small round room aptly designated as a wash room. There were other tubs leaned against the walls along with a variety of wash boards. The entire place smelled like clean linens, strong soap and beeswax. I sat in the middle of the stone floor in my tub.

"Alright missy. Jump out of there before you turn yourself into a prune." Gwyn said holding up the towel. I eyed the pixies before getting up as quickly as I could. Which wasn't very fast and I nearly fell out of the tub. Thankfully Gwyn came to the rescue and scooped the towel around me like a floundering infant. She wrapped it tight around me while eight or nine pixies went tittering around the room.

"Do they always watch people when they're bathing?" I grumbled from my towel cocoon. This made Gwyn laugh. She had such a nice clean laugh. It made my heart warm all the way down hearing it.

"They've been watching you since the day you were born child. There isn't much you have that they haven't seen." She chuckled. I looked up at the little creatures in surprise. Only three still danced above our heads, the rest had resettled around the room. My whole life? Were there such things as pixie stalkers? I hoped not.

I stepped out of the tub onto a length of rush mats. They were prickly under my feet. I dropped the towel around my shoulders and Gwyn went back to her pile of clothes.

"Why have they been watching?" I asked. Gwyn smiled at me and held up a piece of green cloth to my body.

"Because they were told to." She said. I had been getting a lot of those kinds of answers since waking up. She was open as a book one moment and enigmatic as a sphinx the next. She was as bad as Malcolm.

"I see, well I-what the heck is this?" I shouted at the green cloth she had handed me. She also handed me a pair of dark green silky shorts with bows on them. The long green cloth was a dress. I kept shaking my head until I thought it might come clean off.

"I am so not wearing this." I said trying to hand it back to her. She smiled and stepped away from my hand.

"You can't very well go running around naked can you?" She said. I snorted, waving the dress around.

"It not like anyone around here hasn't seen what I've got!" I snapped, throwing her own words back at her. She only smiled and pressed the dress into my hand.

"You always look so pretty in dresses." Her voice was a purr and I knew I'd lost the battle. Damn.

Gwyn turned her back as I dropped my towel and pulled the green fabric over my head. It was the color of pine needles or moss in the deep woods and it was soft as a clean baby's cheek. It had an empire waist, with a scoop neck, and small capped sleeves. The hem hit me just below the knee. All along the edge of the sleeves and hem someone had embroidered beautiful swirling flowers and vines with gold thread. I felt like a fairy tale reject.

My fairy godmother turned just as I finished putting on my under shorts. I expected her to exclaim something radiantly superficial and tell me how I should wear dresses more often. Leila always tried getting me into them. She was going to be jealous someone else beat her to it. What I didn't expect, was the near faint. Gwyn blinked at me in shock, face draining of blood until she was white as a sheet.

I watched, horrified as she sat down in the chair on top of the clothes with one hand over her mouth. I wanted to run to her, but I stood very still, doing my best deer in the headlights impression.

"Are-are you okay?" I asked. She had closed her eyes and was sitting there taking slow trembling breaths. All of the light had drained from her face. She opened hollow eyes to me and nodded unsteadily. See, this is why I don't wear dresses, I thought.

"I turned around and for a moment I thought your mother was standing there." I felt bad for her, but nothing could have made me happier, to know that I looked like her. I went to Gwyn and sat down on the floor beside her. I tried not to think of the rushes prickling my legs and butt.

"I think that's the best compliment I've ever gotten." I told her. That earned me a smile. She cupped my face in both of her hands and kissed my forehead. When she let me go, the light had come back a bit. I sat back and smiled at her. I would wear the silly dress if she wanted. And the stupid silky shorts. She took a deep breath, settling back in the chair.

"There are some things in this life that are beyond our control. Your mother was one of those things." Her smile was sad and I watched a tremor run through her chin.

"Even when she was born, she was completely without convention. Your grandmother was in labor for thirty-six hours because Junviere Cross would not be rushed. Truth be told, it was only through your grandmother's unwavering patience and tranquility that Junviere survived her first years. Your grandmother would tell me to bide and I would see, Junviere would be just fine.

But she wasn't. At least not for many years. She was as wild as the wind and as all-consuming as fire. Her teachers never knew what to do or say about her, only that she was a 'very spirited' child. Time passed and she transitioned from being a wild child to a rebellious teenager. Your grandparents could say red, and she would always say blue. Even if she knew they were right.

Only when your grandmother was teaching her the ways of the Guardian, was she able to sit quietly and listen. It was as if she was a plant and learning was the very fertilizer she needed to grow. Junviere would have been one of the most knowledgeable Guardians of all time. So thirsty was she for her heritage. But once she met your father, all was nearly cast to the wayside.

You must understand that there are many different kinds of other beings. They come from all walks of life and we take them all under our wing with kindness and understanding, and strength. It has always been our way to walk, ever since the beginning. And because there are many ways of being, with every ounce of good, there must be a bad.

Before the Tuatha dé Danann came to Eire, there were the spawn of Ymir. Dark hearted, shadow beings, the Svartálfar were born from Ymir's own rotting corpse. They spread their disease across the land with great relish. Incapable of love or kindness they are creatures of pure evil. They ruled for many hundreds of years, until the Tuatha dé Danann came and vanquished them. But not all were destroyed. A small band hid deep underground close to the heart of the mother, because even the mother dwells in part in shadow. There they were able gain enough strength to flee to the new world. It is not clear how they reached us here in our haven, but we were very aware of their presence when they arrived.

It is known of our people to be committed to one mate for the entirety of our adult lives. Some call it soul mates or true love. For Junviere and Caspian, it was as if the world had stopped and there was only the two of them left in it. But for Caspian to find any love in his heart for anyone, I think the world must have truly stopped. Because he loved your mother so much, it changed him in ways never thought possible. He was kind and thoughtful and dedicated. He did his best to push down his dark side so that he would be acceptable to your grandparents. He encouraged Junviere to continue her studies after a while, and helped her find a sense of calm in herself that none of us knew existed. And when you were born . . . well, never has a father so loved his child. It was as if Junviere were the sun and you the moon, lighting the way in his dark world.

But you can imagine that none of these goings-on sat well with the other Darklings. They confronted Caspian, and told him that he must kill his wife and child, and return to them. Their leader ordered him to help them take over all of Red Glen. Your father was unhearing. He was powerful in his own right, having gained the ability to walk in broad daylight, and he turned his back on them.

Yet the problem with turning your back on an enemy is that it gives them ample opportunity to stick a blade in it. I do not know how the Darklings were able to find the three of you. Your mother and grandmother, myself and a few loyal council members, created a web of protection around you so tight, we almost feared they might stunt your power all together. We were so careful and they found you anyways.

I felt your mother call to me in the dead of night. Her need was distinct and full of terror. I went as fast as I could. Yet by the time I arrived, your house was full of flames. Your father had stayed behind to draw them away from the two of you. He was still there, drained of life. Junviere had fled into the forest in hopes of safety. But they pursued. She hid you in the trees and led them away. I found them surrounding her motionless body not far from your grandparent's home. I fought them and nearly lost. It was your grandmother that rescued us both. She destroyed their leader, and drove them away. I have never seen such power as I did that night. But in the end, there was nothing she could do for Junviere.

We found you wandering through the trees like a spirit child. So star-struck were you that it wasn't hard for us to take the memories from you. There was no time to teach you all of the things that needed to be known. Your grandmother was too old to begin teaching again, and I knew none of the secrets of the Guardians. So in order to save what was left of your life, we made the ultimate decision. We had your memories sealed away and the ways of the Guardian went the way of legends."

Gwyn closed her eyes again. I could hardly move. My face was wet from tears that had run unchecked. My hands clenched each other in my lap so that my knuckles were deadly white. I had nothing to say, my mind was a tumult of emotions. Thoughts struck me in a whirlwind, a jumbled kaleidoscope of sensations.

They hadn't just died. They didn't leave me on purpose. They had loved me and had died protecting me. And those shadow men had murdered them. The same shadow men that were now chasing me, trying to murder me. I looked up and Gwyn was watching me. Her brown eyes seem to go on forever, filled with sadness.

"We did what we thought was best for you. We wanted you to be able to live a normal life aside from everything that had happened." She said gently touching my shoulder. I unclenched my hands from each other and roughly wiped my face. I slapped my cheeks. I wanted to wake up from this dream. I wanted to wake up.

I looked up and I was still sitting in a mound of a house surrounded by mythical creatures and being chased by some ancient, big bad guy.

"But it seems you cannot turn the hands of Fate from their course for too long. It will always find a way." She said softly. I frowned up at her. My destiny was my own. No one was going to tell me what was what. And no oogie-boogie was going to try and take my life without fight.

I got to my feet and brushed out the skirt of my dress vigorously. The pixies had ceased their flight and watched us from various places on the walls silently. One of the wash tubs had eyes and was watching us too.

"I'm not all that thrilled about what you guys did to me. But I love you. And I know in my heart that what you did, you did out of love." I said, and she nodded.

"But damnit, I make my own destiny! And I'm not gonna let these guys take me down without a fight!" I shouted, Gwyn smiled, and the whole room was suddenly in an uproar. The wash tub was dancing with a pair of long underwear. Pixies were zooming around our heads. There were little people in small pointed hats working themselves into a jig around our feet. And then someone pounded on them door.

"There are other dirty people in this house." Malcolm's voice sounded from the other side of the door. Gwyn stood and took my hands in hers.

"Well, if it's a fight you want, then it's a fight they'll get. And I'll be with you the whole way." She said, her eyes sparkling. She smiled and pulled me towards the door. A fight indeed.

13

Being full of piss and vinegar is great until the heat of the moment wears off. Hours had passed and still we didn't have a plan. Gwyn and I sat in the front yard watching the day tick away. Malcolm had disappeared into the forest and had been gone since the afternoon. I hadn't even known he was gone till I questioned Gwyn on his whereabouts. She'd kept me busy in the kitchen while he slipped out the back.

The culprit sat knitting in a chair beside her Artemis statue. If I had been in a different frame of mind, I would have felt very nostalgic. Instead, anxiety gnawed at me.

I sat on the grass across the path from her with my legs out in front of me and my arms braced behind. The bird bath burbled at my back. Gwyn would say nothing about Malcolm's leaving, and she dodged the subject every time I brought it up. He was *my* guard dog. It was my right to know where he was. If I didn't know better I would have said I missed him. Impossible.

I ran my eyes around the front yard for the millionth time and heaved a deep sigh. Most of the creepers had gone off to where ever mythical things go during the day. Only a few slunk or scurried around the borders of the clearing. And they didn't really want anything to do with me. Not that I could understand anything they said anyways. Only a tiny bogey, no taller than the length of my hand, with a grotesque face like a withered apple had found me unexplainably fascinating. He wore a little red and white mushroom cap for a hat and a tunic fashioned from ragged yellow leaves. He sat beside me, mimicking my pose in the grass.

The day was unseasonably warm. It was a sleepy kind of day with cicadas humming in the trees. A dragonfly hovered by my head and zipped off towards the trees. I started to close my eyes when a sapling at the tree line moved and there was a man.

I sat up straight, eyes wide, ears pricked. Gwyn stopped her knitting and looked in the same direction. She stood, a smile on her face. I scrambled to my feet, trying not to flash the whole world. Stupid dress. My eyes only left the tree line for a moment, but when I looked back, four more people stood there. Malcolm was one of them.

The lady in white was there, that impossibly white pelt of hair pulled back from her regal, porcelain face. Her long white robes looked like they were spun from pure sunlight. I realized the first man that had appeared, was the red head from the cave. He was in his cream tunic, with his plaid draped over one shoulder. There was a tall man next to him that I nearly mistook for a woman. His hair, which even from far away looked like molten gold, fell in shining waves to his waist. He wore a white dress shirt unbuttoned at the neck and pale tan trousers. There were beige Birkenstocks on his feet.

I suppose I chose to look at her last, because part of me couldn't yet bare the sight of her. Her luscious dark hair was piled up high on her head, with tiny wisps framing her painfully beautiful face. The sun danced in it with tongues of fire. She wore a yellow sun dress, with a lacy, white half-jacket over it. She had yellow flats on her feet, true to her ever fashionable nature.

I didn't know exactly how to react. The gears in my head were mashing together, trying to form an idea, but nothing surfaced. I was mad, and sad, and confused and betrayed. I now had memories that told me we had been friends forever. I was a loyal sort and even through my confusion, I was still mad because I still considered her my friend. Maybe if I cared less, it wouldn't hurt so bad.

I watched them step out of the trees and make their way to the front gate. My eyes followed them the whole way. I was ready for an ambush, another stab of betrayal. I don't know what I would do if Malcolm betrayed me too. I'd do my best to protect Gwyn. But what if she was with them too? That icy rush of fear raced down my spine. My eyes flickered over to her.

Everyone I knew seemed to be in the habit of turning me over to the bad guys lately. But the red head had fought for me in the cave, and I could still vividly recollect Malcolm's wrestling match with

Deluk. But what if it was just some ploy to crush me and deal the final blow?

Malcolm and his little parade had passed through the gate. They were headed towards us. I had one chance to make for the trees. *Someone on our side would have to let them in.* I heard Malcolm's voice whisper. My paranoia was spiking. I took a step back and something latched on to my bare leg.

I screamed. A short yip of a sound. Everyone stopped dead in their tracks. The tension was almost palatable. I looked down to find my little bogey attached to me, arms and legs wrapped around my ankle. He wove his lumpy little head back and forth, humming a soft nonsense song. Laughter bubbled up inside my chest, and spilled out of my mouth. It grew until I was giggling uncontrollably.

When I was able to gain control of myself, I shook off the bogey and looked up at the waiting group, wiping tears out of the corner of my eyes. Everyone was looking at me with different levels of confusion. Malcolm had his ever familiar frown plastered on his face.

"So much for a quick get-away." I said, stifling another round of giggles. No one laughed. Tough crowd. Gwyn had turned towards me, her pleasant face neutral.

"There is no need to flee from anyone here. These are our allies." She said, making me stare hard at her.

"If I'm not mistaken, *certain* people here didn't even move a muscle to help keep Lord Doofus from scrambling my brain." I snapped. I turned my head back, pinning Leila with angry eyes. Her pale face was frustratingly indifferent and she shrugged at me. She F-ing shrugged.

"Gannon is more powerful than I. It would be like a sparrow baiting an eagle." She said. Her speech was structured and carefully enunciated. She didn't even sound like the Leila I knew.

"How long have you been lying to me?" I asked. I felt tears sting my eyes and wanted to kick myself for it. I wanted to be strong in the face of her indifference, righteous against her treachery. Mostly, I just wanted to curl up with a warm blueberry scone and cry. Again, there was that graceful lift of her shoulders.

"I was ordered to keep the truth from you after your identity was taken. I did as my duty required." She said in that cool voice of hers. I felt my lips curling.

"And after I found you were devoid of your full powers upon waking, what sense would there be in preserving you?" she said, landing another painful blow.

"So, what? You pretended to be my friend all these years? After all we've been through? Even with your parents? My grandparents?" I said nearly shouting it and taking a step towards her. No one else made a sound and they didn't stop me from getting closer. I watched a spark fly behind Leila's eyes, a reaction at last. But it was quickly shuttered away.

"You weren't really my friend after the geas was laid upon you. I was ordered to remain close to you. To watch you in case you showed any signs of recovering. I would be the liaison between you and the rest of the supernatural world. Anyone that came to Red Glen seeking protection, I was to send them to the Council. The people you know as my parents are servants of my House. The house in Grandé belongs to Gannon. As for your grandparents . . ." she paused, pursing her lips. I waited patiently, steeling away my own emotions, every word she had said was a knife twisting in my guts.

"It was necessary for me to pay my respects to them. Your grandfather was a forest child. The finest of any I have had the privilege to meet. And your grandmother was a *true* Guardian. She deserved my respect and my loyalty." She said finally. The way she made a point of saying my grandmother deserved her respect, made it very clear that *I* did not. She had acted under obligation, not out of love or concern for me. It was a hard blow to my heart. I clenched my lips together to keep them from trembling.

"And Reed?" I asked softly when I was sure I could keep my voice normal. Her eyes were very steady on my face.

"A pet. Nothing more." It was almost more than I could handle. I nodded, trying to digest everything. I wasn't sure which I liked less, not knowing the past, or the realization that the grand majority of my life was one big lie.

"So what now? Are you guys gonna drag me off to Gannon and let him puree my brain? I suppose it might be more pleasant than whatever the shadow guys have planned for me." I said, letting my eyes drift over everyone else. Or this, I thought. I felt a great well of self-pity opening up inside me, but I swallowed the lump in my throat and steadied myself for the next batch of shitty news.

"The Lord DeHaven has acted against our wishes. The Council has always been a kind of democratic union standing behind the overall authority of the Guardians. But now that there is no one strong enough to oppose him, he wishes to place himself upon the throne." said the lady in white. Her voice was like a night wind through a stand of reeds. It was distinctly a very non-human sounding voice. Different, but not unpleasant. Those pale yellow eyes of hers were intent on me.

"What about you guys? You're obviously united, why can you take him?" I asked. Someone cleared their throat. It was the guy with the long gold hair. His eyes were the yellow of dandelions. I blinked, thinking I imagined it but they remained unchanged.

"I do not mean to interrupt this sharing of information which is obviously important to you Guardian. But I suggest we retire to a place of more security, even here, Lord Gannon has ears." He said. He had a nice normal, masculine voice. There was a round of agreement from everyone. I could only shrug. What choice did I have?

We all trooped after Gwyn to the back of her house where her enormous herb garden sat. It was a great profusion of various plants. To me there was no apparent pattern, but several small dirt paths ran through the entire place like slices in a pie. We took one that ran diagonally through the plants to a circle of softball sized, shiny, black stones. The circle was less than three feet in diameter. All seven of us crammed ourselves between the stones.

"You have *got* to be kidding." I said, grabbing onto an arm to keep from falling on my ass. The red-haired man held his face back from my chest, grinning.

"Begging your most gracious pardon." He said, but he didn't look the least bit sorry.

"You may want to close your eyes." Malcolm said over Goldilocks' shoulder. I didn't ask any questions, I just squeezed my eyes shut. My guard dog says run, I run. Guard dog says close my eyes, I closed my damn eyes.

I heard someone mumble something and then there was a *gong* in the back of my skull. At least that's what it felt like. Someone had struck an electrified gong and the sound waves were skittering through my brain. My feet felt like they'd lost their purchase on the ground, so I flailed, grabbing for anything close by. My left hand still had ahold of an arm, the other grabbed a big wad of something that felt like the fur of a baby bunny. Someone yelped in my ear.

"We have arrived, you may let go now." I heard the white-haired woman say. I opened my eyes and saw that I had a death grip on her arm. I quickly let go, stumbling on an apology. I looked at my right hand and it was wrapped in thick gold hair. Its owner's head was bent at a painful angle. I quickly released him, gently smoothing down the gnarls that had risen as a result.

"I'm so sorry. I'm really sorry." I stammered. He smiled, and took my hands away from his head.

"There is no need for such apology Guardian. I assure you, I have suffered much worse at the hands of a lady." He said, and laid a gentle kiss on the back of my hand. I would have gushed in my embarrassment, but then I caught sight of where we were.

We were inside of a gigantic dome woven from lush green foliage. Somewhere beyond, intense light boldly tried to filter in until it was as if we were standing inside an enormous sparkling emerald. Strings of morning glories line the walls. They were lit from the inside by warm shimmering light like some expensive Tiffany fixture. Other flowers I couldn't name glowed there too, all bright jewel tones. There were eleven white stone chairs in the middle of the room in a circle. Everyone else had gone to a chair and sat. Goldilocks let go of my hand and strolled over to one. Malcolm was looking at me, his eyes dark and squinty.

I ignored him and walked over to the circle. I was about to ask where I should sit, but one chair, larger than the others, had my name on it. Not my whole name, but the word CROSS was carved across the top of the tall back in intricate letters. I felt a little bashful, but I walked over to the chair, and sat down. Gwyn was on my left and Malcolm was two seats to my right. The chair on my immediate right was empty.

"Your mother would have sat there when the time came for you to succeed her. And your grandmother would have been here in my place." Gwyn said softly. I touched my hand to the empty chair and felt my throat grow tight. She should have been here. I shook myself and raised my eyes to the circle.

"Well, we're here, let's get crackin' on that plan." I said, and Red Beard coughed into his hand. It looked like he was trying to hide a chuckle.

"If it would be acceptable Guardian, perhaps we should begin with introductions." said Goldilocks. I smiled because I sure couldn't go around calling people by the nicknames I made up in my head.

"I am Kamac Vahail, ninth son of my House, and your loyal servant." He said, giving me a cheeky smile. He was on the opposite side of the circle, with an empty seat between him and Red Beard who sat to his right. Red Beard was on Gwyn's left with another empty seat between them. He inclined his head to me.

"I am Olione Alberichson. Servant of his most grand eminence Alberich. Born unto the children of metal and fire. Our forges nestled in the belly of the great Mother, we have pledge ourselves since the liberation of our people by Brand Cross, the seventh Guardian of your house." He said, and I returned his slight nod. I turned to the lady sitting on Kamac's left. She gave me a small smile and a tilt of her fair head.

"I am Lady Oulhwihn Vahail, First daughter of the House of the White Ladies, scion of the First Lady Mor Gwynn." She said in her airy voice. I nodded and rolled their names over in my head. They were familiar and not. The sense of knowing and not *knowing* was frustrating. I let out a small sigh and gazed about the circle.

"Okay, so we need a plan. Let's plan." I said, because it seemed like they were all waiting for me.

"As the lady Oulwihn has stated, Gannon has become a bit of a load stone around our necks. With him in our way, we were unable to sense the returned presence of the Darklings until it was too late." Olione said, gold twine glinted in his beard as he talked. Malcolm was nodding in agreement.

"My uncle cares for no one more than himself. Even should he gain the seat of power, it would be hard to believe that he would lift a finger to protect anyone outside of his own retinue. And as much as we shudder to think on it, the Svartálfar are our kin. Gannon will give them far more consideration than any human or halfling." Malcolm said, and everyone in the circle nodded. Except me.

"Well that sucks. So what do we do about him? Wait around for him to take over and go all mad monarch on everyone?" I said. Oulwihn gently shook her head.

"Lord Gannon cannot take the power from you." She said. I frowned at her, remembering all too well the little scene in the cave. Malcolm must have read the thought on my face because he pointed at me.

"He can do many things to you. He can strip you of your mind, crush your life force, even make you beg him to kill you, but he cannot take the power from you without your permission. You must offer it to him of your own free will. It is one of the rules of our kind." He said. This made me start. *Our kind*? I had never thought of Malcolm as anything other than human, even when he was doing crazy magic tricks and ushering us through alternate dimensions. I looked at him long and hard. He still looked like the same Malcolm. I drew my eyes away from his face and felt my brow wrinkling.

"Well is there some way we could trick him? Or maybe get him away long enough to deal with the shadow guys?" I asked. This time it was Gwyn who raised her wrinkled hand for my attention.

"We have already tried many things. We have been struggling to deal with him for quite some time now. Even when he isn't in the immediate vicinity, his fingers are always in everyone else's pies. Take Ergot for example; the water lord serves Gannon in many facets. He orders his wights to spy for Gannon or to carry out his bidding. And though many do not wish it, they are not strong enough to gainsay him. And there are people like your young friend Reed. He is one of a kind in this place and has no overlord to speak for him, so he has fallen prey to Gannon without choice or argument." She said. The thought of Reed made my blood run cold.

"So what you're telling me is that because I don't have the juice to protect everyone, things are going to hell?" I ground out, lacing my fingers together in my lap. Gwyn shook her head.

"It's not that you don't have the 'juice' my dear, it's that we did such a good job binding you up, we don't have the proverbial scissors to cut you free. We simply don't have the power to free you. Which is no fault of your own." She said, holding her hands out palms up. It was my turn to shake my head.

"First things first, we have to rescue Reed. No matter what happens, I want him safe." I said. I knocked my fist on the arm of my chair for emphasis. Kamac was shaking that gold head of his at me.

"We have already tried to free the young man, Guardian. But he was no longer a guest in Lord DeHaven's dungeons when we went to liberate him." He said.

"We believe he was freed by an outside source and has gone into hiding. The lad has many friends he does not speak of." Olione continued. I rubbed my hand up my cheek an across my forehead. My head was so full of things and ideas. All I wanted was to go back to my normal life. Or did I? I now had a family and memories and crazy stories I could tell to my grandkids . . . If I lived that long.

"Okay, so we need to cut Gannon's strings. With him out of the way, we'll be able to focus on the Salter-shadow what's-its. Hopefully Reed will be safe wherever he is. What I need to know is what I'm supposed to do and what rules do I have to work around? And who is this Ergot character?" I asked, still rubbing my forehead.

"Since you are of little use to us in terms of power, it would perhaps be best if you just stayed out of the way." Leila finally said in her smooth, cultured voice. The sound of it made me clench my teeth.

"I do not agree with the way Gannon has gone about things, but I believe in what he has said about the separation of humans and supernatural beings. No good has ever come from the twining of our lives to each other." She said. Each word was a blow to my spirit. Why was she even here? I thought, not even bothering to look at her where she sat on Malcolm's right. There was a muffled thump and I looked up to see Malcolm with his fist grinding into the arm of his chair. His eyes were locked with Leila's, trying to stare her down. I barely dared to breathe, their skin seemed lit from the inside, and Leila's eyes glittered like two dark gemstones in her face.

"An oath was made! Through kith and kin it has been followed, and honored. You disgrace yourself and our line with your actions." Malcolm growled at her, they were inches from each other's faces. Leila's lips curled back over her teeth. I looked around, but no one had moved a muscle to stop them. No one even looked worried. I turned back in time to see Leila slap a hand to her own chest.

"I? I have disgraced us? I have done everything asked of me! And for what? Nothing! Everything I had was taken and I was left to baby sit this-this . . . thrall!" she shouted, pointing at me. I would have thrown in a retort, but I felt Gwyn place a restraining hand on my arm.

"I have done everything I was asked! And you speak of disgrace? What about you? It's a wonder you even bother with our House anymore! The only thing you care about is-"

"SILENCE!" Malcolm roared. He was on his feet, towering over her and I hadn't even seen him move. I jumped at the suddenness of it. Olione was behind him with a restraining hand on his shoulder. It was like I had missed an entire frame of the scene.

"Easy son." Olione said softly. Malcolm was breathing hard and Leila was cowering back against her chair. The glow was gone from her face. There was real fear in her eyes. I couldn't see Malcolm's face, but half of me was glad. Olione was whispering something to him, and his broad shouldered back slowly relaxed.

"You will not speak of things which you do not understand." Malcolm said softly to Leila. I watched her nod, never taking her eyes off his face. He allowed Olione to guide him back to his chair. The small red haired man sauntered back to his seat, giving me a reassuring wink as he went. Talk about your family drama, I thought. Leila was smoothing her dress down and trying to make herself sit up straighter. I could see a fine tremor in her hands.

"As I was saying, without the benefit of your full powers, you would only be a target. In the interests of everyone, I believe that the Guardian should be placed in a safe house until we are able to contain the situation." She said, her eyes cast down to the ground. Gwyn's hand left my arm.

"You make a valid point Lady Orr. But there is nothing wrong in having another body on our side of the line, be it human or otherwise." Olione said. There was another round of nodding heads that included Leila. I was very aware of the empty chairs in the circle. I nibbled my lip in deep thought, rubbing the knuckle of my right index finger between my eyebrows.

"What many do not realize about our kind is that we are still tightly linked to the Old Ways." Oulwihn cut in softly.

"We cannot take that which you do not give. We can dissemble or twist the way of words, but we cannot lie outright. Even the strongest of us may be brought low by a rod of Ash or Rowan or any weapon formed of cold iron. Turning the clothes backwards on your body keeps the lesser sprites from leading you astray and a good whistling tune will chase away the smaller bogeys of the night. In the face of danger, show no fear. But perhaps the greatest word of wisdom I can give is that our kind cannot break our word once it is given. No matter what." She said. I put my hands in my lap and gave her my full attention.

"What about the Huntsmen? Gwyn said they lied to the king and everyone about taking Finola." I said. Oulwihn gave me a gentle smile and shook her head.

"They did not lie. Cross did indeed attack them and he took Finola away. It is all in the context upon which the subject is lain." She said. Exasperated, I decided to move on.

"What about this Ergot character?" I asked. I didn't really want to hear anymore today, but it didn't feel like we were much further than when we had started out. A little wiser, but no further.

"He is lord of the waters in Red Glen. His family has been with us a long time and he was once a trusted ally. Gannon though has managed to bend his ear. He was the great green toad you met in the cave." Olione growled, wiping his hands as if brushing something away.

"He is as slippery as the water he dwells in and clings to Gannon's backside like a leech." He said. A flicker of an idea was forming in my head.

"If we were able to get Ergot alone, is there any way you guys could take him?" I asked, searching the faces around me.

"We have thought of this, but at the slightest hint of danger, he goes to ground. There are many places he can hide. Anywhere from a puddle in the street, to a lake three states away." Leila said. I rubbed my forehead hard with the palm of my hand.

"Well do we have any water people on our side? Preferably female. He does like girls, doesn't he?" I asked. Gwyn was nodding at me, her brown eyes all squinting.

"What are you getting at child?" I smiled and held my hands out, fingers spread.

"I have a memory of a story. There was a man who led his horse to the edge of a pond to drink. Out in the middle of the water there was a beautiful woman sitting on a rock. She called to him and asked him to go swimming with her. The man was very eager to be with her, because she was so gorgeous that he shucked all of his clothes off and dove in. When he reached her, he saw that she was also naked and she used her long hair to cover them both. After a while, the man grew tired of swimming, but the woman wouldn't let him leave. He tried to swim away but he was tangled in her hair and her limbs were wrapped around him stronger than ten men. So the man was trapped in the water and lived with the woman until he died." Gwyn was shaking her head, but smiling.

"I told your father not to be telling you those scary stories." She chuckled. It made me smile.

"All well and good for story time, but what does that have to do with Ergot?" Olione interjected. I turned to him.

"Well I thought, if we could lure him to the water, maybe we could somehow trap him in it." Olione slowly nodded and scratched his chin.

"You forget that Ergot is a creature of the water himself. Even if we got him to the water he would have more control of it than we and the tables would turn." Leila said, but she was leaning forward, her brows knitting. I looked around and there were similar looks on everyone's faces. It was Oulwihn who broke the silence, with a clap of her hands. She was smiling and her face was luminous.

"I was traveling abroad in the dead of winter. When I spied at the heart of a frozen lake, a farmer who had fallen to his death." She said joyfully and my face crumpled in horror. Ew. She saw my look and clapped her hands again.

"I do not mean to exalt the death of the poor man. I mean only to make an example of his predicament. He was in the lake, frozen, *in* the lake." She was almost giddy with her idea and it spread to the rest of us.

"So you can freeze the water if we get him in it?" I asked, to which she immediately shook her head.

"My power is not in that particular realm. But I know someone who can." Her head turn to the left and I followed. Those citrine eyes of hers were on Leila, who was shaking her head vigorously.

"I will not subject myself to the company of that wart." She snapped, crossing her arms over her chest. I was about to beg and plead, but Malcolm's fist came down softly on the arm of his chair.

"You will do what is necessary. For all of us." He growled. Her face tightened and flushed deep red. I waited for the outburst but it didn't come and her color subsided.

"Then it is settled. Tomorrow we begin." Gwyn said, clapping her own hands. I nodded my head along with Kamac and Olione, and Oulwihn and Malcolm. Leila skulked in her chair, lower lip stuck out. I looked around at everyone and my heart began beating faster. Tomorrow.

Well rested and well fed, I stood in the middle of an over grown orchard. The day was bright and sparkling with a crisp, cool bite to the air that I could feel even through my jeans and thick, pine green sweater. Tiny white butterflies flitted about on their rice paper wings. The trees were laden with shiny fruit, ready to be picked. The sun shone bright through red gold leaves kissed by autumn's lusty lips and rippling gilded grasses stretched to our knees. It would have been a completely magical moment, except for the company.

I wasn't exactly sure how I'd gotten stuck with her for my partner, but I sure as hell wanted a recount on that particular vote. She sat on a large rock with her arms crossed, back to me. *Don't touch the trees. Don't touch the leaves. Hurry up. Slow down. Keep moving.* Bitch, bitch, bitch, piss and moan, the whole way through the forest. She was worse than Malcolm. Where he ignored me, she couldn't seem to stop scolding me. Until we'd come to the orchard. I'd tried to ask her about it but she had only scowled at me.

"Don't touch the trees. And don't pick any of the fruit. Keep your hands in your pockets, and your mouth closed." She had snapped and stomped off to her rock. I was left standing alone in the tall grass by myself. For all of the new found friends I had, without her, I was very lonely.

I slowly shuffled over to the others side of the boulder and leaned my butt on it so my back was to her. I felt terrible. About everything. I blamed myself for everything that had happened. Her whole life had been taken away just like mine, except I was allowed to have some semblance of one and she was left as an onlooker. It had never been just about *her*. It was all about watching *me* and protecting *me*, and sheltering *me*. Growing up, it had been nice to have such an attentive friend. But now I could see what a burden I had been to her. A sigh rattled out of my chest. And now I was sending her off in to the mouth of danger against her will.

"Lei?" I said softly, turning myself towards her. She was hunched in the thick, burgundy robe she was wearing. It was thick and had a wide cream colored collar and cuffs.

"What?" she snapped, not turning in the slightest. I fumbled on the apology that had been on my lips, and tried for something else.

"If it gets too dangerous, you know you're going to abort right away, right?" I stammered. She snorted at me and tossed her shoulders.

"I have lived my entire life on the cusp of danger Cross. I don't need you to give me pointers." I turned back to my side of the rock, thoroughly stung. I looked out into the trees and let the sun warm my face. It was a beautiful place. We would have played in a place like this as kids, or gone hiking as adults. It was hard to believe that we would probably never do any of those things again.

"Leila?" She didn't answer and I had to turn to make sure she was still there. The breeze moved softly through her hair, tied loosely at the nape of her neck.

"Leila, I'm sorry." I began, rubbing my hand over the back of my neck.

"I never meant to be such a burden to you and I'm sorry that everything was so shitty. I didn't know. It's not a very good excuse but I want you to know that I'm grateful for everything you've ever done. And you'll always be my friend. That's all I wanted to say. Now I promise I'll leave you alone." I said and turned away from her. My eyes started to burn. I was gaining so much, but losing the pieces of my life I loved the most. It was all so unfair.

"You damn Cross' and your damn good intentions." I heard her grumble. I turned back around to find she had turned too, but she was looking out into the trees. The sunlight soaked into her delicate skin. I didn't say a word. I was trying not to even breathe too loud.

"The worst part about it was that you were so oblivious. And yet you seemed to *know*, deep down inside yourself that there was this part of you that was born to help people. You never hesitated to help someone in need, even when you were hurting yourself. And so goddamn humble. I wanted to puke. I was so mad, so jealous that even unaware, you were so sure of your place in the world. So at peace with yourself." She said, and I started to shake my head, but stopped myself.

"I didn't really mind watching after you at first. It was an honor, and a privilege to protect you. But when I found out that you were never going to wake up, that you were never going to take your place with us, or remember the life that you left. I was so angry. I hated you so much for living a life aside from everything else we knew. It wasn't fair." Her voice cracked. I wanted to hug her but I didn't want to ruin the moment. My heart ached for her.

"And even now, I've never been able to understand how you couldn't remember us. How you couldn't remember *me*. I was supposed to be your second. I would have sat at your right and we would have been friends forever. But you couldn't break the geas. You didn't love us enough to remember." She said bitterly, wiping her face on her sleeve. I felt anger build up inside me at the injustice of it all.

"That's not true!" I shouted, and her head snapped in my direction. Her chocolate eyes were burning with dark fire. I jumped up away from the rock and stamped my foot on the ground.

"That's not even true and you're an idiot for even saying that! Of course I loved you! You are my sister, my forever friend! I lost a part of my soul the day you were all taken away from me. How could you even think those horrible things? You think I don't feel lost? You think I don't wonder what the heck is wrong with *me*? Why everyone I love keeps dying on me? And do you really think I didn't pace a hundred miles across my yard the day I had to give Max my damn car?" I yelled. Leila was staring at me in wide eyed disbelief. I took a step towards her and she jerked back on her rock.

"I have memories in my head of a time when you and I were like two toes on the same stinky foot. And there isn't anything in any recollection I have that would lead me to believe that I would have ever wanted to part my life from yours. Not then, not now, not ever." I said, hot tears running down my face. Her image blurred but I could swear that she was crying too.

"I can't change what was. I can't undo what my grandmother and everyone did to me all those years ago. But as of right now, I want your solemn oath that you will be my friend. And you'll get old with me like we always planned." I was weeping as I said it, and I had to rub my nose on the back of my hand. After a long minute, Leila reached out and used her sleeve to wipe the tears from my face.

"I don't know what kind of friend I could be to you. I've made my heart so hard against everyone. But I swear, from this day forward, I will be your right hand until the end of time. You *are* my sister. I swear it." She said softly, and a cool wind rushed up around us. Leaves rose in a whirlwind so that I had to shut my eyes against them. I saw Leila pull her robe tight around her, and duck her head into her collar as I did. I stood there with my hand over my face, the wind stinging around me. I could hear the trees crashing together, the foliage rustling at their feet. And as quickly as it started, the wind withdrew. I uncovered my face slowly, and found Leila doing the same. There were leaves stuck in her hair and it looked like a crazy bird's nest.

"The Mother is always listening." Leila whispered. It made me look around, eyes wide. I turned back to her and smiled. I sat down on the rock beside her, tilting my face up to the sun. A feeling of contentment was creeping into my bones. Only some bad guys to vanquish and a lord High and Mighty to knock off his horse, and life would be on its way back to normal. I felt Leila pulling at my hair and opened my eyes.

"You have leaves in your hair." She said, handing me a crinkled brown oak leaf. I looked at the mop of her hair, and burst out laughing. Yep, we were on our way back to normalcy.

The sun was high in the sky, a lemon yellow orb over our heads. A fragrant breeze pressed into our skin. A lark sat in a nearby tree and warbled his sweet song. I wanted to shoot him. The same bird had been a-warbling for the longest time *ever*.

Leila and I sat in comfortable silence, but the waiting was killing me. We were waiting for our guides, she had informed me. I hadn't been privy to the most intimate details of the plan. The basics seemed simple enough though. Leila was the bait and would also be the one to trap Ergot in the designated pond. Malcolm and Kamac would be nearby to rescue her in case things went horribly awry. Gwyn and Oulwihn were hashing up some kind of spell or binding to make sure that Ergot wouldn't get free until such time as deemed necessary. I.E. Never. Which was the best plan I had ever heard.

Meanwhile, Olione had gone off to find me a place to sit and wait. And do nothing. I was so excited I could shit. It was hoped that I could remain in this chosen place in relative safety from Gannon and the shadow men until I was retrieved.

The others had obviously taken Leila's words in the green dome to heart. I didn't have any powers I could use at will; I didn't have any great knowledge that I could protect myself with, and the only weapons I knew how to wield were sitting on my workbench at home. So the long and short of it was that I was about as useful as a bump on a log. The up side was no one wanted me to get whacked by the bad guys. So into the woods I went.

Leila stood up away from the rock, drawing me out of my revere. She was looking out into the orchard at something. I looked in the same direction, squinting my eyes, head tilted to one side and couldn't see a damn thing. I looked up at her and then back out into the trees. There were trees, and grass, and more trees. I was about to ask her what she was looking at, when one of those trees detached itself from the earth and started walking towards us.

I lurched away from the rock, ready to make a run for it, but Leila was calmly standing her ground, hands tucked into the pockets of her robe. I watched her out of the corner of my eye, unable to keep my attention from our visitor.

It had crossed nearly fifteen feet and the closer it got, the more it looked like a woman. Well, if you can call someone with splotchy, white, birch bark skin and long tendrils of green-brown hair trimmed in golden spade-shaped leaves a woman. She walked to us until she was less than six feet away and stopped. Her white hands were long and graceful, beckoning to us. Even from my petrified position, the green glass of her eyes was astounding. My eyes flickered to her feet, which wiggled through the long grass like the exposed roots of a tree.

Leila turned her face to me. It was a look I was becoming familiar with, her alter personality. It was cold and bitter as a winter wind.

"You will remain here until your escort arrives. Do not leave the orchard. And do not-"

"I know, I know, don't eat the fruit." I finished for her, rolling my eyes. She squinted hard at me, before giving a sharp nod. There was no hug, no reassurances. She just turned and left, following close on the heels of the tree woman. They were almost out of sight when Leila turned and pointed her finger at me. *Stay.* I could almost hear her say. I resisted the urge to flip her the bird, settling myself back against the rock.

When I looked back into the trees, they were gone. And I was alone in the gold washed day.

14

I've never been good at being idle. *An idle mind is the devil's playground.* My grandfather would say. And in my case he would have been right. Less than ten minutes had lapsed and I found myself looking out into the trees, my eyes tracing the outlines of their rosy fruit. My mouth watered just looking at them. I could clearly imagine their sweetness, their juice filling my mouth and dribbling down my chin. I frantically shook my head.

Leila said no fruit. She was very clear about no fruit. I bent down and started gathering armfuls of long grass. With steady fixation, I separated the grass into small bundles and began weaving them into thick springy wreaths, a trick I learned from my grandmother. When I had one finished, I got up and started picking handfuls of bright wildflowers and colorful bits of leaves.

As a child in my grandmother's house, I always remembered the tangy sweet smell of wild grass and flowers lingering through every room. There would be wild wreaths on every door and thick garlands of flowers in my hair all through the spring up until the first kiss of winter. There were always tiny bouquets left on my pillow and on my backpack before school.

I was sitting back on my rock, weaving flowers in shades of lavender, bright violet, aching vermillion, shocking cerulean, and powdery blue. My fingers deftly trimmed their stems and plucked the odd petal. I was so focused on the task at hand that it was a long moment before I realized I was being watched. The little alert system that I was becoming more aware of as time passed had gone off. All the little hairs on my arms stood on end. I froze, unable to help myself. I've never been a good liar, and I sure as hell couldn't make my body lie. I raised my eyes to the sun-drenched trees and there she was.

She was tall and well made. The line of her back could have made an iron rod weep. Long, supple legs helped her stalk through the grass with ease. Silver glinted like a spark off of her glossy hair. As she neared, I could see that it wasn't even hair, but a magnificent crest of silvery feathers. They cascaded down her neck and draped over her bosom like some expensive stole. The bare flesh of her arms, stomach and legs were a mottled shade of gray-brown. More silver feathers draped over delicate hips and covered what modesty demanded.

I would have been afraid, if I hadn't been so in awe of her. She was a creature of regal bearing, to be feared and respected in the same token. She drew near and stopped, pinning me with shrewd hazel eyes. The moment of recognition was so sudden I nearly choked on my own spit. I snorted a little, my hand over my mouth, and coughed. One silvery feathered eyebrow inched up her high forehead. I don't think I could have been more surprised if Santa Claus had jumped out of the bushes.

"M-Michelina, what-I mean . . . what the heck?" was all I could manage. I was absently crushing the wreath in my lap, unable to process this new bit of information. A very sly smile slid across her ample mouth.

"I can't go to PTA meetings all the time. A girl has to have hobbies." She said smoothly. I almost choked again. I was so used to treating her like she belonged on a pedestal. I wasn't exactly sure how to react to the new version of her. She was still regal and poised, just . . . feathered.

"Sure . . . I suppose." I said, setting my wreath aside. She cocked her head at me in a very bird-like way.

"You may finish your project before we leave. There is plenty of daytime left." There was a curl, an almost-accent to her voice that I couldn't pin down. As if she were speaking from the back of her throat at times. I shook my head, standing.

"Naw, it's alright, it was just something to pass the time until you got here. You *are* here to take me to wherever right?" I asked, watching her very carefully. My skin started tingling with anxiety, but she smiled and canted her head to one side.

"I am. I serve the lady Oulwihn." She said. It was a lot to digest, but the last few days had been full of crazy new things. I slowly nodded.

She turned without comment and I followed. It seemed to be the way of things lately, following strange people into the woods. I know my mother had probably warned me against it at some point, but it hadn't seemed to stick. Here little girl, want some candy? Maybe a trip through a magical forest where pretty much everything is trying to kill you? Yea, that sounded about right.

I thought about what to say Michelina, but nothing came. My voice was caught in my throat like a wad of gum. I watched her well-formed back and tried not to think too much. She turned her head in my direction and slowed her pace so that we were nearly side by side.

"It is good that you have come back to us. How is your adjustment progressing?" She asked. It was very formal sounding, like the way Leila now spoke. As if even their speech changed with their forms. I supposed it was like matching your shoes with your purse.

"Well, I haven't quite crossed all the way over. I have bits and pieces of memories and the odd power surge, but nothing big. People are trying to kill me, and the people who aren't, don't seem to like me very much. I'm really pretty confused most of the time. Everything seems new, but vaguely familiar. Other than that, it's not bad." I said shrugging. Michelina was nodding.

"I can see how it would be terribly disorienting. You do not have much to go on, having been bound as a child. We are lucky as children. We are more apt to react on instinct, to trust our hearts, and to believe without the taint of experience. It would be easy to say that even as a child you would not have been knowledgeable in the ways of the supernatural world. You would only trust what your inner voice told you. I believe it is this way for everyone. Now you must fight against all things that you have become. But even still, it is good that you have come to us once more." She said, her shining eyes focused on the path ahead. I wasn't sure whether to be shocked or confused some more. It was the longest I'd ever heard her talk outside of a city council board or town hall meeting. And she had never spoken more than two sentences to me. Her focused concern in the bakery suddenly came to mind. That, along with what Gwyn had said about the pixies. *They've been watching you since the day you were born.* I suddenly had the strangest sensation.

"You've been watching me." I exclaimed, and her silvery head turned briefly in my direction. I realized it was another of those strange bird-like sideways nods.

"It has been my honor." She said. I stepped over a fallen branch, a deep furrow forming between my eye brows. Stalking faeries, killer trees, and bird ladies. I didn't really want to know what else was following me around. I got an image of a dancing wash bin in my head and shook it off.

"Who told you to watch me?" There was a twitch in her shoulders and the feathers down the back of her neck ruffled ever so slightly. If I hadn't been looking hard at her, I would have blamed it at the wind.

"Junviere was my friend. Somehow she knew there would come a time when she would not be with you. She bade me watch over you." She said softly. I focused my attention on stepping around a group of saplings. It was strange how alone I had felt just a short time ago. How lost. But it was becoming very clear that I was never alone, no matter where I went, what I did, there was always someone looking out for me. It gave me a warm fuzzy in my guts.

"I swear on my life that I will do anything in my power to keep the dark ones from hurting you." Michelina said. I turned my head and found her watching me with burning intensity. I didn't need to think about the level of her sincerity. I didn't need to mull it over. I just nodded.

"I know you will." I watched her, watching me. There was a fringe of tiny feathers sparkling at the corners of her eyes. All at once her feathers poofed up and she shook herself. I heard a deep sigh ease out of her accompanied by a high keening whistle. Her plumage settled and she smiled at me. After a moment, she turned her face back to the trees and came to an abrupt halt. It was so sudden, I nearly ran into her. She placed a steadying hand on my shoulder, her eye brow quirked.

"We have arrived." She announced and I quickly looked around. The forest was settled in shades of gold and yellow and dull bronze. We were surrounded by sturdy oaks with their girthy trunks and cypress trees that twisted their bodies in every direction. The leaves were thick under our feet. I blinked, trying to see what she saw. The only thing out of the ordinary, was the smoothly cut trunk of a tree nearly six feet in diameter sticking out of a drift of leaves. I guess she saw that I wasn't seeing what ever there was to be seen, so she walked over to the trunk and started brushing away the leaves.

She cleared away a good foot of room around the trunk, revealing several things. The first, I saw right away. It was a bulging ruck sack like the ones in the cave where Malcolm and I had slept. It sat on the ground, tucked into the juncture of two thick root legs. I wondered briefly if it was one of the same bags, but decided not to ask. Michelina had proclaimed herself my ally, but there was no telling who was allowed to know about that special place.

The second thing I noticed was the ring of stones. Upon closer inspection, I saw that they were large chunks of smoky quartz. They sparkled as her shadow moved over them. Michelina stepped back, and pointed at the bag. I realized she had been very careful not to touch it. It was still partially buried in leaves.

"This is for you. It contains items of a repelling and protecting nature. Lord Olione had it delivered here for you." She said giving me a broad grin. I cocked my head to one side questioningly, to which she shook her head.

"The small one would have brought it himself, but he was made aware of his limitations. His ego overshadows his brain." She continued, stifling a chuckle. I guess I still looked confused because she gestured at the bag with one hand.

"Our kind cannot touch such things as that which lay within. Some are so strong, even covered in good cloth, we cannot even carry them. And only because your blood is so richly human will you be able to wield them to your advantage." I walked over to the bag, stepping into the circle of stones. I don't know what I expected. A flash of light or the blaring of trumpets, but nothing happened. I picked up the bag and put it on the table like surface of the trunk. Michelina had backed away as I moved. She was standing outside of the circle, watching me.

"I would ask you not to open that until I go. Just being this near, I can feel them attacking me." She said stiffly. I turned away from the bag looking at her. Her feathers were ruffled and her eyes looked enormous. I felt as if I were looking at the face of a hawk instead of a woman. Her eyes dilated strangely, swirling down like a bird's. Her words sank in and I found myself frowning.

"What do you mean go? I thought you were gonna stay and protect me?" she shook her head and shrugged and shook her feathers out trying to settle them.

"You will be safe here, so long as you don't leave the security of the circle. The life spirit of a very old tree went in to its construction and it has been given your name. Not even the most powerful of our kind could hurt you here. The trinkets are for creatures of a greater unseelie nature. They will make the more powerful ones pause, and the lesser would not even dare. You must not leave the circle until one of us comes to retrieve you. Do you understand?" I looked down at the circle of stones and nodded. I didn't like it. I didn't like it one bit. But what else could I do? I sat down on the trunk and frowned up at her. She smiled softly.

"It will be alright, someone will return for you before the sunset." I could only nod. I didn't want her to go. I didn't want to be left in the middle of the woods all alone. Michelina nodded once more before turning and walking off into the trees. She didn't say good-bye or turn to wave at the last. She simply walked into the trees, and disappeared in a rustle of golden brown foliage.

I sat there for a long time, looking in the direction she had gone. I was grateful that the sun was still shining over my head, warming my hair. The air hinted at moving currents but there was no evident wind. I rubbed my hands over the legs of my jeans and rubbed my whole face vigorously. Smoothing my sweater, I turned to the bag still sitting beside me.

The opening was a drawstring hole covered by a wide flap. I flipped it back and tugged on the loosely knotted strings. Wadded into a tight ball, on the very top, was Malcolm's leather jacket. I took it out and found a little white piece of paper pinned to the sleeve. In neat scrolling letters it read, 'turn all clothing backwards.' I placed the jacket next to me and went back to the bag. The next thing was a scarf of the palest pink, with red stitching all over it. At first I thought they were flowers, but when I looked closer, I found they were arcane little symbols sewn in bright crimson thread. I couldn't read them, but something inside me recognized them. That tingling of the familiar. I folded the scarf and placed it carefully on top of the jacket.

Next came a double strand of brightly tinkling bells. They were dull silver in color, but their music was painfully sweet. It was long enough to be a necklace and I suspected it was meant as a belt. I set it with the other things and continued, diving in with all the enthusiasm of a kid at Christmas time.

I pulled out a small wreath made of wood with more symbols carved into it. There was a piece of glass like a droplet of water that contained a large green four-leaf clover; a fragrant little pouch with a note on it that said, 'do not open'; a torque bracelet made of gold so fine it was like liquid sunlight in my hand and a small bundle of dried flowers tied with thick twine and what I suspected was dark hair of some kind. The last two items I pulled out were a sparkling piece of white crystal wrapped in a gnarl of wood the size of a softball hanging from a wide, leather thong and a pale circle of green jade on a long black cord. I laid all of the items out on the trunk.

It was a pretty motley of trinkets, even though I had no idea what any of them would do. Well, I knew what the jacket was for. I just hoped I didn't lose it. I had a proclivity for losing or destroying my clothing as of late. I shook my head at the insanity of it all, and stood up, careful to stay within the boundary of my stones. Taking a quick look around, I started systematically removing my clothing and turning it around. I hoped and prayed that no one came as my white ass was hanging out in the sunny autumn light.

When everything was turned, down to my socks and underwear, I started putting on the things laid out. I put on the belt of bells, making sure the opening was turned to my back. I twisted the scarf into a stylish knot, with the ends trailing back over my shoulders and put on the jacket with its wide shoulders and thick arms billowing around me. I could smell the faint odor of men's cologne and my guts tightened. I love the smell of a good clean man and nice cologne. I reached behind my back and pulled the coat closed. I can only imagine the sight I made as I stretched myself to zip it, arms at impossible angles, back curved, head tilted, tongue sticking out of the corner of my mouth.

I placed the wreath on my head when I had finished. The posy, I put in one pocket with the clover droplet and the leather pouch went in the other. The jade I placed around my neck and the torque around my wrist. The bracelet was warm against my skin and I couldn't be sure that it was the sunlight that had warmed it while it sat on the trunk. I picked up the strange piece of wood/crystal and sat down. With everything on, I felt warm and cozy.

I turned the thing over in my hands. The sun struck the crystal, reflecting rainbows on my body and into my eyes. The wood was smooth, delicately soft, like mole skin. The leather thong was connected in a loop that slid through a hole in one part of the gnarl. It fit nicely around my wrist so that the crystal gnarl dangled jauntily from it.

With all of my treasures on my person, I was suddenly sleepy. I felt my eyelids grow heavy and my body was steeped in warmth. I looked back at the ruck sack and thought about what a good pillow it would make. Wadding it up into a ball, I crawled onto the trunk and lay down. If I kept my legs bent slightly, I fit perfectly. I tucked my arms up inside of the jacket, the sun warming the black leather nicely. The sound of insects droned in the air. I closed my eyes, lulled by birdsong.

Vivian. My eyes snapped open, blinking in the rusty-gold sunlight. I sat up quickly, disoriented. I blinked around, unable to remember where I was. I'd been having a dream about two little children running through a field of Black Eyed Susan's. I looked blearily out into the trees and felt the wreath slide to one side of my head. I put up a hand to steady it and slowly remembered where I was.

I looked frantically up at the sky. How long had I been asleep? The sky was still well lit, but the shadows had grown long all around. I ran my hand through my hair, attempting to tame the bedhead I had developed. It had been such a nice nap. I was more than tempted to lie back down.

Vivian. The last traces of sleep were chased quickly away. I couldn't have been more awake if someone had thrown icy water on me. I looked all around, scooting in a circle on the trunk. The wind had picked up. The trees moved in its dancing fingers. Every movement was the enemy. I wanted to run away. To where, I wasn't sure, but anywhere other than here sounded like a fantastic idea. Anywhere outside of the vicinity of whispering voices in my mind would have been great.

Vivian. It was such a soft sound, barely a whisper, but it ricocheted through me like a red hot bullet. I lurched around on the stump, gasping for breath. The wind blew cold across my face, making me shiver. My flight instincts were in full gear. Adrenaline rushed through my veins.

Vivian. This time the sound was a little louder and vaguely persistent. I rolled it over in my head and found it familiar. The other whispering voice had stuck fear into my very core. It had been the scent of a predator upwind of its prey. This second voice was new. It's a trick! My inner voice screamed. Of course they wouldn't use the same voice, how smart would that be? There was no way in hell I was following some scary whispering voice this time.

I strained my eyes and ears to the surrounding forest. I was struck with a sense of dejá vu. Why? Why does this crap always happen to me? I thought. I sat on my stump with my knees under my chin, arms tucked into the sleeves of my jacket.

Vivian.

"Shut up!" I yelled, putting my hands over my ears. Just stay in the circle. You'll be safe so long as you stay in the circle. I thought, with my face buried against my knees.

Vivian . . . help . . . me . . . My head jerked up so fast, my wreath came off and fell out into the leaves. This time I could identify the voice. It was one that I had been hearing nearly my entire life. I got up off the stump, but stayed inside the circle of stones. What if it wasn't a trap? What if she was really in trouble? No, I thought, shaking my head, Malcolm and Kamac were there with her. She was as safe as could be.

I chewed on my bottom lip, staring out into the trees. The shadows there were deep and foreboding. I couldn't help thinking that I was wrong. That Leila needed me. I rubbed the back of my neck and pulled on my right ear lobe. What if I was wrong? The thought spiraled around in my head.

Taking a deep breath, I stepped out of the circle. The whole world seemed to lose about five watts. I was colder outside of the circle and a raging chill marched through my body. I carefully bent and picked up my wreath, placing it securely on my head with a few pieces of knotted hair. The gnarl bumped against my hand as if trying to reassure me.

This is bad. This is a bad thing to do. My little conscience whispered to me. I nodded to myself, wringing my hands. This was indeed a bad thing to do. I stepped into the trees and never looked back.

A steady clip was carrying me back towards the orchard. The bells around my waist tinkled as I went. The sun was starting to set and a multitude of reasons not to leave the circle were popping up in my head.

Michelina or whoever came to 'retrieve' me was going to give birth to a live farm animal when they found me gone. If I didn't die, Malcolm was going to kick my ass up into my shoulder blades. This was probably a trap. I told myself for the millionth time. I was sweating inside my jacket but I didn't dare take anything off. I had already left the circle, no sense in making myself an even easier target.

After leaving the circle, I had felt very clearly the sensation of being drawn. I was back to feeling like my body was the compass needle and the whispery voice, my true north. I didn't need it to keep whispering, I knew exactly where it was coming from. This was less reassuring than you would think. Normally you would want to run away from the danger. But Nooo. Of course not. Why would I do anything that smart? I pushed these thoughts away and trudged onward.

I reached the orchard in half the time it had taken to get away from it, when I felt a tug on the other end of my mental compass. It was an urgent, panicked feeling. It was strange and frightening. Then I realized that it wasn't my fear I was feeling. Someone down that long line was terrified and in great danger. I picked up my feet, and took off running.

I dodged through the trees as fast as I could. I could feel the sun waning at my back and it spurred me on. All I could think of was that Leila and the others were in the clutches of the shadow guys. I didn't know what I was going to do, but damnit, I couldn't just do nothing.

I flew through the forest, with the lives of my friends in my mind. I sped along that petrified shaft of fear that had suddenly turned icy cold and I knew in my heart that it was really Leila calling. I focused on her name, on the image of her face in my mind and I ran. It's amazing to me how I didn't run smack into any trees, but I didn't have much time to contemplate it as I suddenly spilled out into a clearing. I slid to a halt, nearly falling on my butt, and gapped at the scene before me.

There was a small pond with its banks covered in a carpet of short, emerald-toned clover. The trees created a canopy over the water and shielded it from the light of day. A thick stand of cattails created a veritable wall along the back half of the water's edge. It was all very picturesque. At least, it would have been if not for one little snafu.

At the center of the pond, there was a monster and in the grip of his telephone pole size arms was my very naked best friend. Half of the beast looked like a melted candle that someone had left out in the snow, while the other half of him was all sculpted male and torrid rippling muscle that showed pale and opalescent as the inside of an oyster shell. Leila was screaming and not from the throws of passion. The man monster was eight feet tall (give or take a couple inches) and was in the process of squeezing the life out of her. As if this wasn't enough, to the left, at the water's edge, Malcolm was battling with another creature that had the head of a horse, and the body of a naked man. They fought in the shallows, wrestling and thrashing in the water. Malcolm was tangled in the creature's long dark mane. Close by, Kamac was being dragged into the water by what looked like two beautiful naked women. Their skin was like mother-of-pearl, their hair dark as a moonless night, strung with bits of shell and long fronds of seaweed. Their bodies were lithe and nubile, any guy's wildest dream. At any other time, I think Kamac would have followed them both into the water with jovial abandon; but now, he clawed at the ground, leaving furrows in the dark earth. He struggled in earnest, but the two women were slowly and surely dragging him into the water. I turned my face from scene to scene, not knowing who to help first.

I watched as Leila got one of her arms free, and punched the giant right in the jaw. His arms opened and she fell into the water with a wide splash. She surfaced and went after the giant, grabbing ahold of one massive arm. She seemed to be in control for the moment, so I ran over to Kamac. Stuffing the crystal gnarl in my pocket, I grabbed both of his wrists with my hands. He looked up at me with his amazing yellow eyes, wide and full of fear.

"Guardian? No. What are you doing here?" He ground out and I could feel the shifting of his body as he tried to kick away from the women.

"Well it looks like I'm rescuing you." I yelled over the commotion nearby. I pulled on his arms, digging my heels into the bank. The women snarled and hissed at me, jagged white teeth showing between their lips.

"*Let go pretty pretty, we want to play.*" One said and it was like listening to a voice through a tin can. Fear ran me through with an icy blade and I almost let go. I was suddenly so cold inside, so very cold, the cold of the deepest darkest ocean, a frozen stream on a high mountain. I was shivering, and my breath misted in the air. Ice formed at the water's edge, clinging to Kamac's body. I was colder than I had ever been in my life. Colder than a snowman's bum, my grandmother would have said. I was so cold, burning cold. And then I realized I *was* burning. My frickin' arm was on fire!

My eyes opened without the memory of having closed them. White-gold flames were crawling up my arm. They spilled over onto Kamac and engulfed him. I tried to let go but to my horror I found I couldn't. It was as if my hands had welded themselves to his flesh. I waited for him to scream as the flames covered his body, sending his molten gold hair crackling around us. But he never made a sound.

Kamac looked up at me in profound awe. It was the maidens who screeched in terror. The cool water splashed my face as they tried to flee. The flames had eaten their way up to my face and through a veil of fire I watched the water foam and churn. One maiden was able to detach herself and dive into the murky depths, but the second wasn't so lucky. Her weedy hair was tangled around Kamac's legs. The fire was hungry, eager to fill up her cold flesh. I could feel the fire's fervor in my head. I knew the moment it touched her clammy skin. I heard her scream and felt the fire strike at her like the kiss of a lash. Only the smell of burning meat brought me back to myself.

With all the will power I could muster, I turned my eyes away from the gruesome scene. One by one, I peeled my fingers away from Kamac's wrist, the screams of the water maiden ringing in my ears. An almost audible sound like the release of a plug in a tub rushed through my ears and I tumbled back onto the bank. The fire on Kamac's body extinguished at once, leaving me nearly blind. The water maiden though was still aflame and her image was imprinted on my eye. I watched her give one last violent lurch and fall into the water with a hiss and a rush of steam.

I would have sat there for a long time looking at the spot where she disappeared, but Kamac was already scrambling to his feet and pulling on my arm.

"Rise Guardian, you must leave this place at once. You are in grave danger!" he shouted. I could only look up at him, dumbfounded. My wrist was still burning where the bracelet lay. Struggling to my feet with Kamac pulling on me, I took it off and threw it out into the trees. I probably should have thought about needing it later, but I wasn't too happy about burning people alive. Not even bad people. Kamac was yanking on my arm trying to get my attention. I'd been staring out into the rippling water.

"You must go! Go!" he shouted, pushing me towards the trees. It took me a moment to get started, my legs had turned to jelly. He kept pushing on me like a mother goose herding her gosling.

"What about Leila?" I asked, grabbing onto his arm. He shook his shining head and gave me another push.

"I will assist her, but you must go." He said. We were at the edge of the trees and a deafening roar split the air. The pond was now at our backs so we both turned. Two points of light like black fire were locked on us. The man-monster was wading through the water in our direction. Leila had her arms around his waist, but he dragged her along like a rag doll. A big, naked rag doll. I didn't think he was coming to invite us for tea and I started to tremble. Kamac gave me one last shove and stepped in direction of the pond.

"Go!" he shouted over his shoulder, before running and jumping into the water. I would have run. I should have run. But like a big dummy, I stood there, frozen to the spot. Like in every horror flick where the chick stands there and lets the monster come, I stood there. In the theater, I would have booed and hissed with the best of them.

Kamac was now latched onto the monster's arm, with Leila crawling up its back. Watching them, I could only assume that this giant lump of a man was Ergot. Sparks flew from Leila's hands as she struck him in the head several times. She rode his back like a mutant pony.

And speaking of ponies . . . the man-horse was making its way over the water. My eyes darted to where he had been wrestling with Malcolm and a gasp tore from my lips.

Malcolm was lying in a crumpled heap, with his right arm bent at a horrible angle. He was desperately trying to stand and I watched him lurch into the water. His head went under and I was spurred into action. I ran towards the pond intending to help. His head surfaced and I watched him splash through the water. It looked horribly deep, but only came up to his waist. I stopped in my tracks, five feet from the water's edge and someone screamed my name. Malcolm's face turned in my direction and I could see a gruesome bruise blossoming across the entire left half of his face. The look in his eyes was disbelieving.

I turned away, just in time to see the giant raising his hand at me. Leila and Kamac were hanging from his body like strange fleshy accessories.

The horse-man had one hand on Leila's leg, when the world did that terrible slowing down thing. The scope of my sight widened panoramically. I wasn't sure if I had suddenly stepped outside of my body or what, but I could suddenly see every detail of the scene before me.

Malcolm was hunched in the water, his hair falling just so over his stormy gray eyes. The water sluiced down his face and dripped like shining gems off of his chin. He had his good arm stretched out to me, large hand open, fingers spread wide. In the middle of his palm, there was a glowing red ember, red as the spout of a volcano. His mouth was moving, but I couldn't tell what he was saying. I recognized my name, but then my brain moved on.

Leila also had her hand out to me, palm up. The horse-man had his hand on her leg. I could see his fingers digging into her tender flesh, the flash of malice in his jet dark eyes. His black stallion's face gnashed its long square teeth, tossed its flowing mane, whipping water droplets into the air. A bright, blue-white light was growing in Leila's hand, a captive star shining in her palm. The light made harsh lines on her snarling face. Her teeth were bare as she gave a wordless scream, her free arm hooked around Ergot's neck.

Ergot, with Kamac dangling from it, raised a massive arm. The golden haired man had scaled his body and wrapped his legs around the appendage. His long, glorious hair trailed down into the water in a river of gilt. He pulled and jerked on the arm, but it wouldn't budge. Ergot had his enormous hand held out steadily, and in his palm there was a blinding ball of green fire.

Taking in everything, my mind gave a small sigh and said, 'Ah shit.' I stood there, unable to run, unable to protect myself and all I could think was that I wished I were home. Wished I were safe. Wished I could be anywhere but right there at that moment. I thought briefly of my father and lastly, my mother.

The shining orbs of light flew from their hands at the same time. I watched them grow; expand, until the entire world was illuminated by these three miniature suns. I watched them come for me. There's no place like home, I thought, feeling my body grow light. I closed my eyes against the brightness just before they struck. There's no place like home.

The earth was shaking. I was shaking. My teeth clacked painfully together and my head snapped back and forth on my scrawny neck. Vaguely I could taste blood where I'd bitten my tongue.

The quaking stilled and I was able to open my eyes. It was winter. There was snow all around us. The boy and I. His hands were on my shoulders. Even then his hands were strong. His eyes sparkled and his face was flushed from the cold. I wanted to give him my mittens, my scarf. I was so warm. It was a shame he should be so cold. He shook me again, pleading between gritted teeth.

"Wake up. Wake up." He said.

Such a strange boy. I knew him from school. He didn't have many friends. I looked at him in pity and began taking my gloves off for him. I had another pair at home anyways.

He slapped the gloves away. I watched the deep green material fall into the snow and he took me by the shoulders again.

"Wake up. Please you have to wake up. Don't leave me!" He said and there were tears in his eyes. I'm right here, I thought. I wasn't sure what he was talking about but I felt bad just the same. Poor boy. Don't cry. I would do anything just so that he wouldn't cry.

He started to speak again, but two tall men in black suits came and lifted him away. He fought them, kicking and scratching and trying to bite them. I had never seen a kid fight an adult before, much less two. I couldn't look away. My mouth was hanging open.

He almost got away at one point, trying to run back to me, but they scooped him up and held him tight.

"Wake up!" He yelled, "Please wake up!"

I picked up my gloves out of the snow and brushed them off as the two men took him away. I didn't think it was strange. They looked like two policemen my grandma knew. Perhaps they thought he was hurting me.

I put on my gloves and turned away. In the distance, the boy's voice rang out into the wintery day.

15

The sound of rustling leaves penetrated the tight seal of the closed window. It soaked in through the walls, dripped out of the ceiling. Not the crash and heave brought on by raging gales. Only a whisper, a secret hush. Each leaf rubbing against its neighbor, dancing rhythmically in a delicate breeze.

The pillow under my head was fragrant from its last wash. Sun kissed and air dried. Tiny spots of light drifted back and forth over my eyelids. They made lazy circles on the backs of my retinas. I was warm all over, my blanket tucked up to my chin. I couldn't remember that last time I'd been so comfortable, so peaceful.

The light continued its slow drift over my eyelids, leaving red imprints in its wake. It must be such a nice day out. All sunny and breezy through the trees. I love when the light shines in through my window. I should roll over and open it. Let the fresh morning air in.

A little furrow wedged itself between my eye brows. There's no window next to my bed, I thought. My heart started pumping faster. I struggled to control my breathing. Cautiously, I opened my eyes.

Over my head, a canopy of evergreen leaves swayed. Sunlight peeked through tiny chinks in the thick growth, but the spots were few and far between. Heavy branches sprawled in every direction, cast in cool twilight. The thought struck me. I was lying in a tree. I slowly sat up, pushing away a velvety blanket that looked suspiciously like moss. My soft bed turned out to be a thick drift of autumn leaves and my pillow a mound of dried flowers. As my eyes adjusted to the gloom, I found myself sitting in the biggest tree I had ever seen. The crook of the branch I lay in was nearly five feet wide and seven feet deep. It was one of many that I could make out. I squinted out into the distance but the far end of the leviathan was obscured by its numerous branches.

I didn't know where to begin. I was alone, in a tree, god only knows where. In the dark no less. With no food, no light, and no friends. This was usually the part where I went and locked myself in my room with The White album and a honkin' plate of scones. But alas, I was scone-less, and a strange smell was emanating from my person.

I ran my hands down my body, to make sure I was in one piece. The wreath was gone from my head, as was the belt of bells. I stuck my hands carefully into my pockets. One still held the pouch and clover droplet, while the other was full of ashes, with the crystal gnarl stuffed on top of it. I pulled the gnarl out of my pocket and brushed off pieces of burnt flower from it. What I wouldn't do for some light, I thought, rubbing at the crystal. Like someone had switched on some remote control dimmer, a light grew inside the gnarl until I had a twenty watt wireless bulb in my lap.

"Well I'll be dipped." I exclaimed aloud. I held out the little crystal lamp by its thong, tickled pink by my discovery. Not a lot was going my way these days, but at least now I had light. Yay me.

The circle of light spilled out in a pool about four feet around. At its edge, a branch shifted its weight, and watched me with small shining eyes. I froze, clutching the lamp tightly in my hand. There was no way in hell I was going to drop it and be left alone in the dark with this new foe. The branch shifted again and I could see the shape of a body with the knees tucked up to a bark covered chest. One spindly bark-skinned arm was tucked in close to its body, while the other was stretched up along the side of a neighboring branch. Its head was full of tiny branches covered in tiny leaves. If it hadn't moved, I would never have known it was there. It didn't seem to have a mouth, and when it closed its eyes, it blended perfectly with the other branches. A Homo Sapien-shaped chameleon.

Now it watched me openly, its almond shaped eyes shining bits of obsidian. I've never been the sort of person to commune well with nature, but it seemed to be gauging me as I was gauging it. I watched it slide its out-stretched arm down the branch and hold it out in front of its body. It took me a moment to realize that it was pointing a root-like finger past where I sat. I was apprehensive to turn my head away, but slowly I craned my head back over my shoulder.

Just beyond the edge of the enormous branch that formed this little nest, there were thick grooves in the bark, just thick enough for a foothold perhaps. I turned back just in time to see the tree person disappear into the upper reaches of the canopy. Taking this as a hint, I slipped the thong of the lantern over my wrist and crawled to the edge.

The steps were shallow, but thankfully well ridged. The foot of the tree was over sixty feet away, but from my vantage point, it might as well have been a thousand. The ground below was bathed in darkness, with tendrils of mist floating just so above its face. Tiny points of light drifted in the air. I felt as if the universe had turned upside down and I was trapped inside the sky. Looking out, I could see no other trees, and it added to the illusion.

I dreaded climbing down into that darkness. But I couldn't stay up in the branches with the tree guy, maybe more than one, lurking above me. Swinging my leg over the side, I felt around with the tip of my sneaker until I found a solid hold. A shaking breath rattled out of my chest as I slid my other leg over. I found at once that there wasn't enough room on a single step for both feet and I was forced to lower myself to the next. I gripped the bark of the tree with my fingertips. There was barely enough room for a mouse to dance on the meager ledges. Licking my lips and taking a moment to gnaw at the inside of my cheek, I carefully descended from the tree.

Progress was slow but steady. I stopped only once, to readjust the little lantern to keep it from bonking me in the forehead. My hands had started to sweat and a trickle had begun down my back. It was nerve rackingly slow going, but easier than I had expected. Three quarters of the way down, I changed my mind.

I was little less than twenty feet from the ground, craning my head over my shoulder to keep an eye on things below, when I stretched out my foot and found nothing. My muscles were screaming from the effort it took to cling to the side of the tree. My arms had developed a constant tremor. I skimmed my foot back and forth, thinking maybe they had placed them farther apart. When I still found nothing, I started to sweat even harder.

"You've got to be kidding me." I groaned, pressing the side of my face against the rough bark of the tree. I bumped my forehead repeatedly against it, silently cursing. I reached my foot out again, searching in vain for that next step. I just can't win, I thought, I just can't F-ing win.

I contemplated going back up, but the thought of being confronted by the tree person, made my stomach curl. It had been very specific about showing me the way down. A clear sign that I was no longer welcome up there. I groaned and bumped my head against the trunk a few more times. That's when something grabbed me.

My head snapped up and I came face to face with a tree person. I didn't know if it was the same one, but it had ahold of my wrists with its rough, rooty hands and was lifting them away from the steps.

"No! No!" I shouted, struggling in its grasp, but it was like trying to fight with a concrete python. It lifted my hands further and further away until I was clinging to the edge of the steps with my tip toes. At the last, my feet slipped away, and I was dangling in the open air. Those beady eyes shined brightly in the light of my lantern. I wanted to scream, to cry, anything but hang there like meat on a hook. I looked below, and that was a mistake. It was a long frickin' way down. Something was going to break when he dropped me. I looked back up at the tree person, frantically shaking my head. Of course they never teach you to speak to *Tree* in high school. I had a chilling realization that there was nothing I could do. So I closed my eyes, and gritted my teeth. What a way to go I thought, feeling the cool air gently move over my face. After a long moment, the hands opened, and I fell.

I dropped about two feet, before I connected with the ground and tumbled backwards into a soft patch of thick moss. I lay there, blinking up into the canopy, my chest heaving for breath. In the darkness above, I watched a long, snaky shadow gradually shrink itself back down to human size and disappear up the trunk of the tree.

I lay there for a good long minute. I wasn't sure I could have gotten up if I had wanted to. My arms felt like jell-o and my whole body was shaking. I had to coax my heart back down to its place in my chest from where it had launched itself in between my ears. When I was sure that I wasn't going to break down into a hysterical mess, I sat up. My lantern was still safely secured to my wrist. I rotated my limbs to make sure everything was still working. My left wrist felt stiff and sore.

Pushing back the sleeve of my jacket, I found a shiny pink band of flesh encircling my wrist with two rounded places where the ends of the torque had sat. It was tender to the touch and slightly blistered on the rounded ends. Just great, I thought. Scared to death, running for my life, and now I'm gonna be all scarred up. I turned my wrist back and forth in the light. At least it's an interesting looking scar, I mused.

I covered up the burn and heaved myself onto unsteady feet. Lifting my lantern, I turned my back on the tree and crept slowly into the misty dark.

I didn't go far before the feeling of someone near came over me. Instead of freezing as I had learned was a very dangerous habit, I spun around, lantern held high. The mist snaked through the air in curious ribbons. It was plentiful, but not so much so that I couldn't see a figure walking slowly towards me. Creeping, gliding on long, strange legs. I'm not ashamed to say I quaked in my shoes, watching that thing come. The shape of it made my heart leap in my throat. It reminded me of the shadow men. And if there was one, there were others, and I was screwed. Yet the creature that stepped in to the circle of light was not a shadow man.

I knew it was some kind of a man, but not quite. He towered over me and looked for all the world like a deer standing on its back legs. His satiny coat was ash gray and covered his entire well-muscled body. His face was that of a deer, but like no breed I had ever seen, large damp nose, enormous limpid eyes, and a rack that could have made an adult moose jealous. This glorious crown was covered in the same baby soft looking fur as his body. His long graceful arms were taut with muscle and very human looking. He stopped not three feet away and regarded me with solemn eyes the color of blueberries.

"You see me." He said. His voice was low, but clear, and very male. Since I've never had a conversation with a deer, I could only nod, tongue-tied.

"You are human." He said, and it sounded more like a statement than a question but I nodded. I was less sure about that particular avenue as time progressed, but it was more or less the truth.

"You will come." He said, and turned and walked away. I had half a second to think whether or not to follow him but decided to err on the side of caution and trotted after him through the mist. No sense in pissing off the natives. I didn't think he had gone far but it always seemed like his silhouette was ahead of me, just out of reach. He round the side of the giant tree and I had to pick my pace up to a jog. I suppose I should have been a little more cautious about running through a dark, mist filled clearing, but something told me that I needed to follow. I *needed* to keep up with him. I had the impression that bad things would happen if I didn't.

I was thoroughly out of breath when the canopy suddenly thinned and burst into a bright area at the back of the gigantic tree. I stopped dead in my tracks, gasping and sweating profusely.

Laid out before me, twenty or so feet from the base of the mammoth tree, was a pond. My recent experience with ponds made me a little nervous, but I had never seen anything so beautiful in my life. Some trick of nature had left a perfect opening in the canopy so that the sun light poured in in a magnificent stream. It reflected on the surface of the pond like diamonds flashing in my eyes. The air shimmered and cedar dander floated lazily by. Vivid purple violets bloomed near the banks in great fleshy clumps, while giant cattails nodded their heavy heads and frothy plumes of white lilac gently waved. A pair of pure white swans glided over the surface of the pool, their long necks regally poised. At the water's edge, on the thick carpet of deep green moss, there was white stone bench, and on it sat a woman.

I called her a woman, for the simple reason that she was wearing a flowing, white, gauzy dress and seemed to possess the bosoms necessary to fill it out. She too looked like a giant deer, but her fur was as blindingly white as fresh snow and her rack was as polished and gleaming as alabaster. She had draped herself beautifully on the stone bench, dress foaming around her, dainty hooved legs crossed and tucked under. She was looking out over the water, very picturesque.

The gray man-deer glided down to her and took a knee beside the bench, head bowed. I couldn't hear what he was saying, even though they were only a few yards away. She turned that magnificent head of hers, and looked right at me. Her large round eyes framed by impossibly long lashes were luminous orbs of amber. In the center of her forehead, there was a glittering red stone; a bright spot of blood in the pallor of her fur. She lifted her hand and beckoned to me with a graceful sweep of her fingers.

With less thought than I had given to chasing off after the deer-man, I walked down into the gently sloping valley. In the light I could make out another giant tree that had its branches intertwined with the other. I briefly wondered how many gigantic oak trees there were in this place. I stood a comfortable distance away and looked full into her wide, dreamy eyes. The deer-man stood off to the side, and a little behind her.

"Why have you come here human?" Her lips barely moved. Her voice was like the soft chiming of crystal. Both of my arms were loose at my sides and I gave a small shake of my head.

"I don't know. I don't know where *here* is. My friends were fighting this guy named Ergot and I got caught in the crossfire. I don't even know *how* I got here." The words tumbled out of me. She watched steadily, her eyes never blinking. I had the urge to fidget or shuffle around. Her avid attention made me nervous. It was a long moment before her long lacey lashes flickered.

"I sense that you speak the truth. The tree sylphs tell me you appeared quite suddenly and you slept a very long time. They believe you were in a magic sleep." She said with that barely moving mouth of hers. She raised her slender hand, and gestured to me.

"Sit and we will converse." I turned to the left and there was a large red toadstool where there hadn't been one before. It was about two feet high and a foot wide. I walked over and gingerly settled my bottom on it. It didn't move or threaten to crumble under me, so I let myself relax ever so slightly. The deer-woman was watching me, as I was sure she had the entire time. All at once, another rush of words came to me and spilled out of my mouth.

"Who are you? What is this place? How long have I been here?" My voice sounded loud and slightly out of place. The swans had stopped their gliding and turned their heads in our direction. The deer-woman's lashes fluttered and her head tilted ever so slightly.

"I am Hind and this is Hart." She said, motioning to the deer-man.

"I have no word in the human tongue to name this place. I will simply call it one of the many chambers in the heart of Gaia. Time does not exist here as it does in your world. So much as a week has passed since your arrival. But in your own time it has been only a few days."

I wanted to slap myself on the forehead. Instead I sat there gapping at her. A week. I'd slept for a whole week? Worse, was that I had been gone so long from my own time. God only knew what was happening while I was away. Anything could happen in a few days. I shook my head to clear away the avalanche of thoughts and closed my mouth.

"My name is Vivian Cross. I'm very grateful to you and the sylphs for letting me stay here, but I really need to get back. How do I get out of here?" There was that fluttering of lashes again but this time her head cocked itself to one side.

"You are a child of the Cross?" she said. I shrugged my shoulders and nodded.

"The one and only." I said, pulling up the sleeve of the jacket. I watched her lean forward and examine my wrist, the points of her antlers precariously close to my face. When she sat back, I almost thought she was smiling.

"This explains a great deal. I did not believe any ordinary human could have come here, even by accident. I am relieved to see that it is one of your ilk that has done so." She said. I felt exasperation bubbling up inside of me.

"You know who I am?" I asked. She tilted that heavy crown of hers and gave a long slow sweep of her lashes.

"All of our kind knows the Cross." She said enigmatically. I was flabbergasted. I was a frickin' celebrity. I shook the moment away trying to stay on track.

"Alright so how do I get back to my own world?" Her lashes fluttered.

"You may simply use your power and go. Nothing in this place can harm the child of a Cross." She said and I blanched. Use my power? A lump gathered in the pit of my stomach. I don't know what look was on my face, but I hope it didn't look as bad as I felt. I probably looked constipated.

"R-ight, um … about that … I don't really have any powers." I said. Her eyes widened about a centimeter and her shoulders lurched.

"What do you mean? You are a Cross, you are the Will and the Way." She said, biting off each word. It made me shrink back a little. So much for nothing in this place being able to hurt me.

"Well, my grandmother and my Aunt Gwyn and some other people put the hocus pocus on me to make me forget everything. And while they were at it, they bound my powers too. I've had stuff happen on accident, but I haven't figured out how to really use any of it." I watched her relax back on her bench, the sun glinting off her antlers. She was looking at me in that unblinking way of hers. The stone in the center of her forehead sparkled like a captive star. I waited for something to happen, maybe the brain puree that Gannon had put on me or the painful flashing that came when I got an especially important memory. But nothing happened. She kept staring at me and the sun was warm on the top of my head. I tried not to let my attention wander, my eyes starting to drift over the beautiful pond. The swans had continued their leisurely stroll. A family of mallard ducks was paddling along the edge of the opposite shore. A brisk shake of Hind's antlers brought my attention back immediately. Her eyes were sharp as the edge of a new blade.

"Absurd. A Cross bound rotten in geas from here to kingdom come. Whoever has done this to you has made quite the botch. Even I could not fix you without fear you would be irreparably harmed." Her voice was harsh with disgust.

"So does that mean I'm stuck like this forever?" I asked softly. Even though I wasn't sure I really wanted to know. She fluttered her lashes at me.

"It is a rare thing for me to admit, but I honestly don't know. You could be healed on the morrow. Or you could remain torn for the rest of your days." She said. That lump in the pit of my stomach suddenly grew into a pile of jagged rocks. Torn for the rest of my days. It didn't sound very appetizing. Then a second thought struck me.

"So does that mean I'm frickin' stuck here?" I shouted. Hart moved, but she waved him away. I had almost forgotten he was standing there. He watched me with hard, dark eyes.

"I have the power to return you to your realm, but it may not be exactly where you wish to go. The world beyond has changed much over the years. And not all for the better. We have no wish to be found out by other humans." She said. I stood up from my toadstool, the lantern bumping against my fingertips.

"Well I'm ready to go whenever you are. My friends could be in danger. I need to get back to them." She looked up at me for only a second before rising gracefully to her feet. It almost looked as if she were floating.

"I wish you luck in all of your endeavors Cross." She said, towering over me. She placed one cool hand on the top my head and bowed her own.

"In your current state I am not sure how you will react to the sending. Be prepared for anything." She said softly. I felt my eyes widen and my mouth go dry.

"What's happened to other humans that you've sent places?" I asked. Her eyes closed and her hand began to warm.

"You are the only human that has ever been here." I was about to argue with her. To say that maybe we should talk this over first. But it was too late.

There was a blinding flash of light and all of the air was crushed from my body. I was flying, falling, speeding through the air at a velocity the likes of which no human body has ever experienced. I had enough time to wonder if this trip came with airbags, when I felt myself come out the other side. I came out, and went crashing through a net of branches and leaves and growth. I slammed into the ground upside down with my back end on a tree trunk, legs in the air. All around the world was bright and sunny. The air was chill with the promise of the coming winter. Acid washed blue sky showed through the tree tops. The wind was fragrant with moist earth and the decay of autumn leaves.

With a groan, I rolled onto my knees and pressed my face to the damp carpet of fallen leaves. I love you ground. I love you gravity, I wept inside my head. I got to my feet, teetering like a drunk and wrapped my arms around the nearest tree. I love you tree, I thought, laying my cheek against its wonderful roughness. The sharp crack of a twig breaking nearby brought me to my senses.

I let go of my tree and turned. There was nothing but trees as far as the eye could see. I stood stalk still, barely daring to breath. A rustling of leaves and the crackling of undergrowth came to my ears. I would have been sweating, but the chill of the air had congealed it on my skin. My eyes scanned the vertical lines of trunks like soldiers popped to attention. A flickering of anger, the slightest spark, warmed my innards. I was so damn tired of running away. So damn tired of being chased. I was supposed to be this grand high poobah of heroes wasn't I?

I carefully squatted down in the growth, and picked up a fallen branch as wide as my arm. Which wasn't saying much, but it would work in a pinch. I stood, back pressed to the tree and waited. The snap-crackle came again, and I charged in that direction.

I crashed through the foliage, yelling at the top of my lungs. I swiped my stick back and forth through the brushes, attacking stands of vines, demolishing low shrubs. Weaving through the trees, I sought my sneaking foe. The ground turned rocky, but I didn't care. I stopped to listen for a noise and when it came, I ran in that direction, yelling like a complete maniac.

"Come out and fight me like a man!" I shouted, scrambling over a large boulder. I slipped on a patch of moist lichen and went head over heels backwards into a bush.

I lay on the ground gasping, grateful that I had landed on soft leaves and not on rocks. I climbed out of the bush, twigs and leaves making my hair stick up in all directions. I stood there panting, branch lose in my hand. The land was at an incline here, studded with boulders, stalwart trees growing wedged between them or sideways clinging to their faces.

With a sigh I walked over to the boulder I had fallen from and leaned my butt against it. Sweat oozed down my temple and there was dirt in my mouth. I spit into the leaves and the crackling came again, not four feet away from where I sat. I slowly turned my head to the left, eyes stretched wide. My heart raced, my fingers clenched around the branch. Out of the woods, from behind a heavy boulder and a clump of bushes, there stepped a trembling brown doe.

She was trembling all over, her enormous ears swiveling through the air. Her wet black nose sniffed the air and she regarded me with liquid brown eyes. I couldn't help myself, I busted up laughing. I whooped and cackled and guffawed, long and loud, until tears were streaming down my cheeks. The doe pricked her ears at me and bound away. Flee, I thought, flee from the blood crazed human. I laughed until my guts hurt.

Wiping my face, I pulled in a few deep breaths and eased my laughter down to a few sighing giggles. I started to toss my branch away, when something snapped off to my right. I turned quickly, just in time to see a flash of bronze skin and a very male arm through the trees.

Quickly and quietly, all traces of mirth wiped away, I set off after it. He was making enough noise for the both of us and it was easy for me to follow. Branch poised, I raced on, seeing glimpses of bare leg and wide tan shoulders through the foliage. Part of me knew I should have been running in the other direction. Another part of me was still mad as hell.

The growth grew thicker, until I was forced to push my way through. If this creature didn't know by now that I was following it, then maybe it deserved a couple whacks on the head. The forest was so dense, I started having trouble tracking. I could hear something moving up ahead, but I couldn't see it and I sure as hell didn't want to run in blind. What if it was one of Gannon's cronies? What if he had powers? Hell, what if he had a gun? That thought stopped me. Through all of the goings on of the past weeks, it was hard to remember that there was still a normal world out there. People hunted and people carried big guns.

I could still hear the crackle and shuffling of my quarry up ahead. Do I follow and get shot or do I stay here and wait for him to come chasing me? It boiled around in my brain until I stamped my foot down in the leaves. Dagblastit. If I was going to be damned, I'd rather be damned for doing.

With a mighty shove, I rushed through the growth at full speed. Add another one to the list of dumb things I've done.

Sadly, I didn't have time to yell or even turn back. The bushes opened up and I ran smack into the guy I was looking for. And I do mean smacked into him. And he was as naked as the day he was born.

I screamed. He screamed. I screamed and he screamed. We stood there, screaming at each other. He had ahold of my upper arms and was shaking me. I lifted the branch, and smacked it over the top of his head. To my surprise, the damn thing disintegrated in my hands. Musty, rotted pieces of wood flew everywhere. The look on his face was almost comical. We both stopped screaming and stared at each other.

His skin gleamed like molten copper. Over terribly blue eyes, there was a ridge of orangey amber scales that ran up his forehead and disappeared into his white-blond hair. The tips of two short spiraling horns peeked out of his wavy locks. There was a moment of shock before he wrapped his arms around me and held me in a tight embrace.

"Oh my god, Viv! I'm so glad to see you! I thought it was Gannon's bitch coming for me. I'm so glad it's you." Reed stammered in my hair. I was still in shock. It took me another long minute before I could return his hug in full. The first thing I noticed was that his back was whole and unscarred. This made me very happy. My friend, my Reed, was whole and alive. And . . . and frickin' naked! I frantically pushed him away.

"Geez oh frickin' Pete, Reed! You're frickin' naked! Ew, get away from me!" I shrieked, slapping at him as he tried to hug me again. There was a huge grin on his handsome face.

"Aw come on, you know you want me!" he chuckled, wiggling around. I slapped a hand over my eyes.

"For the love of god, please put some clothes on." I said, exasperated. Reed laughed. It was a wonderful sound, but irritating all the same.

"I would, but I don't have any. I haven't been able to go near town since Keely grabbed me. And none of the things that live out here really care about clothing." He said. I took my hand away from my eyes and gapped at him.

"What the hell do you mean Keely grabbed you?" I shouted. Reed shrugged his lean, well-muscled shoulders.

"Just what I said, she snagged me up that first night, and I figured they might be looking for me after I got loose. So I just took off. I've been running around in the buff ever since. But its California, so I figured no one would notice." He said chuckling. I slapped him in the arm

"This is no time for joking. Keely is in league with Gannon? And how the hell did you get free?" He gave me that irritating shrug of his.

"Yea she's his, ya know, 'main squeeze.'" Reed said, making the quotations with his fingers. I snorted. More like dirty, stinking slut, I thought.

"After I had a chance to cool down, I busted out of that damn stone coffin you left me in and high tailed it out. You guys left the door open so it was pretty easy." He continued, smiling. I was so glad to see him alive and it *almost* made me want to hug him again. Almost, but not quite.

"I heard down the grapevine that you hooked up with Mother Gwyn and the other council members though, so that's good. 'Spose your memory and stuff is all back huh?" he asked. I shook my head.

"I was with them, but we got separated trying to take down Ergot. I've got some memories back but no powers I can use at will. Most things have just been happening by accident . . . I'm sorry I buried you in stone." I said, feeling my face grow hot. I really was embarrassed even if he had been trying to eat me at the time.

"No sweat, I needed the time to meditate anyways. It's been a while since I've been able to just let it all hang out. It was hard to put it all back in." For a minute I was going to slap him in the arm again, thinking he was making a dirty joke, but his face was so solemn.

It struck me how hard it must have been for everyone. Not just my family or my friends, but for everyone that had ever come to me for help. They had come to me seeking solace and asylum and what they had gotten was another place they had to hide in. They had to hide their real lives because I wasn't allowed to be a part of it. If I hadn't already felt bad about everything that was going on, now I felt even worse. Reed must have read it on my face because he put a reassuring hand on my shoulder.

"Hey, why the long face. Everything's okay now." I tried to smile but I couldn't quite get it up all the way. I had ruined everyone's lives. It made me want to cry. Where the hell were my scones when I needed them!

"Well yea whatever. We gotta get going. God only knows what's been happening since I've been gone." I said, shrugging off his hand.

"Yea, seriously. I don't know what's up, but I do know everyone is holed up at your house and more than half the town has gone into hiding." He said. My eyebrows popped up on my forehead.

"My house? Why the heck is everyone at my house? What's everyone hiding from?" I yelled. Reed shrugged.

"Hell if I know. Been hiding in the woods remember?" I glowered at him. There are very big reasons why we are friends, but sometimes he infuriates me. My mind dwelt on the fact that there were people living in my house without me and unseen forces were on the move.

"Alright come on. Lead the way. We're going to my house." I said and Reed smiled.

"I'm really glad to see you." He said and lightening quick, squeezed me in another tight hug. I screamed and would have punched him right in the head, but as quickly as it started, the hug was over, and I was glaring at his bronze, naked ass running off into the forest.

16

The whole way back, Reed and I chattered to one another. Through all the strangeness and difficulties, he was still my friend. Even if he got a little weird and horny sometimes.

It was nice. Walking together, pretending for even a moment that all was right and even in the world. When we reached the house, it was a cold splash of reality.

The days that passed between the now and then seemed few, yet endless. The stiff mustache of my front porch roof and the shining picture windows were familiar, but it was as if a handful of years had passed since last I had been there. Everything looked the same, blooming roses, porch swing, tinkling wind chime. Yet they significantly changed.

There was a big gap in one of the box hedges and rectangles of tar paper littered the grass, which was yellowed slightly from lack of water. Like my house, I too had subtly changed. Yet completely unchanged, I felt my heart swell at the sight of it.

Reed stood next to me, wearing my shirt like a cloth diaper. I would have said it looked funny, but in a way it fit him. Otherwise, he looked pretty normal now. All the ruddy scales and pointy horns were gone and he was his adorable old self. He trailed behind me as we walked up to the house, sniffing the air like a dog. Very *not* adorable. He had been doing it nearly the whole way.

"You sure as hell didn't smell me coming." I had snarked at him. He had shrugged and looked at me very seriously.

"Your smell has changed. I would say you smell kind of like Leila and the others, but it's different. Not like anything I've smelled before." He had said. I hadn't asked him any more questions. It was just another nail in the coffin of how not normal I was becoming. Not that I minded being different, but in regular life, being different is excellence in sportsmanship, making the fluffiest scrambled eggs, having a sixth toe. Being different does not mean you suddenly have weird powers and you're the Guardian of all races of oogie-boogie things. And it's a crying shame, because I make excellent eggs.

We walked up the path and up the steps and I stood in front of the solid oak door. It was strange, knocking on my own front door. I couldn't hear anyone beyond. I knocked hard, hard enough to bruise my knuckles. There was the sound of feet, something shuffling, the locks disengaged and the door swung open.

Malcolm stood there, red eyed and disheveled. His clothes were rumpled and his hair a mess. He was barefoot. The entire left side of his face looked like it had taken a trip down a cheese grater. One eye was full of blood from a blown a vessel. His bottom lip was split and swollen on the left side. He just stood there staring at me. He opened his mouth and then shut it again and repeated, looking for all the world like a land locked fish. I reached out and touch his arm gently.

"Malcolm? Are you ok? What's wrong?" I asked. He didn't answer. He clamped his mouth shut and just stood there. And then he grabbed me. All the air was squeezed out of my lungs for the fourth time that day. I was about to tell him to let go when I realized he was hugging me. His face was buried in my messy hair, and he was hugging me. I couldn't have been more shocked if he had taken out a gun and shot me. Things had to be really shitty for Malcolm to go all touchy feely on me. That's when I had a horrible thought.

"Malcolm. Malcolm? Where are Leila and Gwyn? Is Kamac alright?" I asked, patting him on the back. He eased away from me, blinking rapidly. He set me away from him and took a step back. I could almost see the emotional shutters coming down. I grabbed his arm and shook it hard.

"Where is Leila? Where are Gwyn and Kamac?" I shouted. He just kept blinking at me and took another step back. Just then, a small pale figure pushed him out of the way.

"Vivian? Oh god, Vivian is that you?" Gwyn sobbed and latched on to me. A ghostly pale Leila appeared behind her in the dark foyer, her eyes and nose bright red, as if she had been crying. She stood next to Malcolm, her hands strangling each other. Gwyn was weeping all over me.

"Can somebody please tell me what the hell is going on!" I yelled, holding her away. Gwyn sniffled and fought to catch her breath. I looked from one face to the other, my own crumpled in confusion.

"Perhaps you should come inside." Malcolm suggested. His usually deep voice was soft and raspy around the edges. He took hold of Gwyn's shoulder and coaxed her back through the door. Her brown eyes were locked on me, great alligator tears still rolling down her cheeks. She sniffled, and took my hand.

"Yes, yes, come in. Come in." She said drawing my arm into hers. We all trooped through the foyer and into the spacious living. All of the lights were on, and the smell of burning herbs was thick in the air. I waved my hand in front of my face trying to brush it away. Behind me I could hear the deadbolts engage on the front door.

The living room is the most spacious room in the house. It has two fluffy white couches covered in giant embroidered heirloom roses, running parallel down the length of the space. A matching, oversized recliner that you can easily fit three people in sits near the entrance. Each overstuffed couch has two mahogany end tables, with their matching cousin the coffee table in the center. At the far end is a black, cast iron heating stove, it's stack going up into the wall to the outside. The walls are stark white, covered in pictures of me and my grandparents at various stages in our lives. It's quite possibly the most wonderful room I have ever been in.

There were candles burning on the coffee table and a tan wooden smudge bowl in the middle. A small bundle of white sage sat nearby with one end slightly charred. Malcolm and Leila put themselves on the couch under the picture window, while Reed flopped into the giant recliner. I was left with Gwyn on the other couch. She was attached to my arm like a limpet.

"Okay, so we're sitting, start explaining. What happened with Ergot? Is Kamac okay? What about Gannon?" I said, trying in vain to detach myself from Gwyn. Not that I didn't love her concern, but I was dirty and sweaty and in no mood to hold hands. Nobody said anything. They just sat there staring at me. Malcolm's throat kept doing this weird thing that looked like he was trying to swallow a frog and Leila had her hands gripping each other so hard they were mottled red and white.

"Guys?" I tried again. I looked at each of them trying to get some kind of response. Reed just shrugged at me.

"We . . . we have vanquished Ergot." Leila said. Her voice was strained, barely above a whisper.

"Well that's a good thing, right?" I said, finally extricating my arm from Gwyn's. She sat back a little, content to simply pat my hand. At least she wasn't crying anymore. There was another heavy silence. I could feel their intense focus on me.

"We thought . . . we thought you . . ." Leila began, and her eyes started filling with tears. Eegads, I thought. I'm not good around criers. Especially people I care about. Give me boogiemen in the forest any day against a mean weeper. I was nodding, trying to encourage her.

"We thought we killed you." Malcolm said at last. I blinked hard at him.

"What?" was all I could say. It was my turn to do a landed fish impression. My eyes darted around the room to each face. Reed's pale eyebrows were high on his forehead.

"Well obviously I'm not dead. I'm ok. Really." I said, patting Gwyn's hand. No wonder she had been so emotional. Malcolm was shaking his head, his eyes looking down at something on the coffee table.

"Everything happened so quickly. We weren't even sure who hit you first. It had been my intention to simply send you somewhere else. I thought if only I could be faster . . ." he trailed off, hands loose in his lap. They were bruised and cut in places, part of a nail missing. I assumed it had happen fighting the horseman. Even through all of our recent adventures, he had never looked so bad. I wanted to make a joke, say something colorful about his appearance, anything that would bring back some kind of normalcy. Yet nothing came and I could only stare helplessly at him.

"I too thought I could be faster. It was stupid, so stupid . . . And then you were gone . . . Just gone." Leila said in her whispering voice. Gwyn held my hand in both of hers, giving in a light squeeze.

"When they returned, I tried searching for you. I read the crystals, sent out messengers, made sacrifice. I tried everything, but you had vanished. Just vanished." She said, shaking her head.

"Every human leaves a mark on the world, a fingerprint if you will, of their presence. And the only way a human could disappear so completely is if their *soul* has been destroyed." She said softly. I smiled and shook her hands.

"But I'm not dead, so everything's alright. Its ok, I'm ok. And-" I said gesturing towards my white haired friend in his diaper.

"I found Reed. All's well that ends well." I said, earning myself a few strained smiles. Gwyn hugged me.

"And very glad we are to see you." She said with a sniffle. Blast.

"Yep, and I'll tell you guys all about it, over some food. I'm starving." I blustered a bit, patting my ever thinning belly. There was a snort and a half choked chuckle from Leila.

"God, you must be alright. Though even half dead, you'd still think with your stomach." She chuckled, shaking her head. I couldn't argue with her. Food makes the world go round.

Over a precariously stacked sandwich, a pile of barbeque chips and a tall icy glass of root beer, I told them all about Hind and Hart, and the place of the giant trees. We had moved to the dining room. There were more candles burning in ornate glass cups that I hadn't known I'd owned and strange items hanging over the windows. Some looked like stones, others were small bundles of herbs or pouches like the one still in my pocket. I picked an onion sprout off my plate and nibbled it while they mulled the story over.

"We deal in creatures of legend, but this place is a faerie tale. No one has ever seen the heart of Gaia." Gwyn said, shaking her head. There were deep frown lines in her forehead, lips pierced. Leila and Malcolm had similar looks, the latter slightly crooked.

"Well the Hind said that there had never been another human there before." I said smugly, stuffing a chip between my lips. The tangy-sweet shock made my taste buds ache. Reed sat next to me, elbow deep in his own mammoth sandwich. He grunted every so often as he chewed, head bobbing from side to side. There are very good reasons we're friends. And nothing beats a good eater.

"Even so, it is amazing that you got there at all. When I reached out to you the only thing I could think of was here in your grandmother's house." Leila said. She slowly twirled a glass of iced tea in her hand. The high collar of her white dress shirt covered a portion of her jaw.

She was wearing jeans so dark blue they looked black. It was only perhaps the third time in our lives I'd seen her in jeans.

"You could have ended up in a damn wall." She said in disgust.

"I was thinking of the earth place. Where we slept." Malcolm murmured. He also had a glass of iced tea, but it sat in front of him perspiring and untouched. He had said very little since the living room. If I knew him the way I thought I was beginning to, I knew that somewhere inside that handsome head of his, he was kicking himself. Repeatedly. With a steel toed, golf shoe. In his mind I knew he thought he had failed. Again.

"It makes sense if you think about it. You both thought of a place close to the earth. The home of my grandmother. My mother's *mother*. The place of everyone's mother. It was pretty neat. You guys should have seen it." I took a big bite of my sandwich, humming happily to myself. Malcolm snorted and rolled his eyes. Leila's lips twisted ever so slightly, fighting not to smile. I seem to have that effect on people.

When I had finished and was nibbling on the last of my chips I returned my attention to my table companions.

"So what happened to Kamac? And the water boy and his weirdo friends?" I asked. Leila smiled into her glass of tea, but it was Malcolm who answered.

"Kamac was badly wounded. The Lady Oulwihn took him to a healing place to rest. Ergot is gone, and the water horse has been exiled. He broke a solemn oath given by his king to do no harm to the Guardians and their line. He will return at his peril." He said gravely. Leila sat to his right. Her eyes flickered over him full of something I could not name, and then back to her glass. Any other time and I would have needled them persistently for an answer, but I wasn't ready to get them riled up just yet.

"So what now? Gannon's lost his biggest ally. I'm not dead, and the shadow guys are going to figure that out some time soon. What's the plan?" I asked. Leila's eyes flickered to Malcolm again, and I found that Gwyn was looking at him as well. I was really beginning to hate being outside of the loop. I decided to start pushing buttons.

"Alright guys, I know you're all used to keeping secrets and stuff, but I'd like to be let in on whatever's *not* going on." I said, pushing my plate away. They'd ruined the last of the chips for me, drat them. It was Gwyn who finally turned to me.

"Now that Gannon has lost his right hand, he is vulnerable, but the only one who can challenge him, is a child of his house. Leila is not strong enough. There are others, but none who are close enough in the hierarchy. None except . . ." She trailed off, her eyes like sun touched earth falling on Malcolm. He was staring at his hands, limp on the table top. I pounded my fist on the table enthusiastically.

"Well okay then, DeHaven is a tough guy. He fights Gannon and we find a way to give those shadow guys the boot. We win the day! Hah, nobody crosses a Cross! It's a great plan." I said, thumping my fist on the table top. Everyone grabbed their drinks to save them from my tenacity. Reed's root beer slopped over into his plate.

"Hey watch it." He grumbled through a mouthful. He had been busy pillaging the leftover chips on my plate.

"It is not so simple. I am . . . I mean I can't . . ." Malcolm was waving his hands in the air as if trying to grasp some thought or word. After a moment, he looked to Gwyn, who turned and patted my hand.

"The DeHaven line is very old and over the years they have had to make certain adjustments to living among humans. One of those adjustments has forced them to limit the extent of their power." She said. It sounded like a big load of horse crap to me, so I just shook my head.

"Well what good is that? Why would you do something that would make you weaker?" I asked. Malcolm looked up at me. His one bloody eye made him seem almost cyclopean, his normally tanned face was pale and flushed on his high cheeks.

"You see my face?" he said and I nodded. How could I not?

"If I were to allow myself to delve into that closed side, I could be healed within the hour. It is the same kind of power that allowed the Lady Oulwihn to heal my broken arm. With it, I could overthrow Gannon and any other being that dared come against me." The irises of his eyes flashed like shiny new dimes. A prickling sensation crawled up my spine and over the top of my head.

"Well that seems pretty awesome. What's the catch?" The only catch I was aware of was the one in my throat and I was glad my voice didn't betray me. Malcolm's eyes shifted with that inner light.

173

"Once the door is opened, it can never be closed. It is like the releasing of a dam, the water that has escaped cannot be retrieved." He said. Gwyn was nodding and Leila was mirroring her. Reed was licking the crumbs off of his fingers completely uninterested in our conversation. A pet, Leila had said. I wonder if he knew what she thought of him. One thing at a time, I told myself.

"So, I know you guys have a lot of ways and you know a lot of stuff, but I don't get it. Why do you make it seem like a bad thing? You forget. I barely know what's going on half the time under normal circumstances. Try it in laymen's terms." For a second the old Malcolm surfaced in his eyes. Completely annoyed and disgruntled. Leila cleared her throat. The moment was gone suddenly and he looked away from me.

"If I may, I believe I can be of assistance in this." Leila said. Malcolm gave her a long, hard look before a curt nod of his head. Leila turned to me with her large dark eyes. I had never seen her look as otherworldly as she had lately. Her skin seemed lit from the inside.

"Along with a great deal of strength, our line gave up many things in order to serve the House of Cross. Our senses are dulled, our natural abilities are stinted. But most of all, we have given up our longevity." She said. I let her words sink in like a slow blow to the head, barely wanting to comprehend. I stared at her, my lips clamped tightly shut.

"It was seen early on that to serve a human, our kind must change our very way of life. The way we see the world. The way our emotions run. We had to change everything in order to serve beside them. Worst of all though, was the dying. A human life is such a short and fragile thing. Generations upon generations fell away, with the companions of our house gliding into eternity. We stayed young, healthy, vibrant. And because the Cross' were so good and pure, there was no resentment in them. Even while their hair became streaked with gray and the lines of years etched on their faces and we constantly remained the same.

"I think, from my own experience, this was the worst, to see them so gracious to the very end. Our kind could not fathom it. The pain of their loss was great. Every time one of your kind died, it was a knife twisting in their souls. It was so great in fact, the First Son of our house returned to our king and asked him for a way to make it stop. It is similar to the geas that was placed upon you, but it is more within our control. To open the door, is to stop the hands of time in their tracks." I could barely breathe. They had given up immortality to be with my family.

"No wonder you always look so good." I joked, but it was half-hearted.

"So, if you were to let yourself go back to these powers, you would never age?" I asked slowly. Malcolm looked up at me with those strange shining eyes of his and nodded. I turned to Leila and I realized her eyes glowed with the same inner light. Was this how it was? Was this how they really looked? What else had I taken from them?

"And what about you? Do you have the same thing?" Her eyes flashed and she looked away. It was enough. I felt so bad for them both. They had given up their very existence to serve my family. And for what? It was like Gannon had said; they were making themselves less because of me. It was like taking away a dog's sense of smell or clipping the wings of a bird.

"No. How do I make it stop? How do I reverse the king's decree? This isn't fair, that you guys should have to change your lives for me or anyone else. And what makes it even worse now is I can't even help you guys. Not like my ancestors helped everyone else. Maybe Gannon was right. You guys should just end this and go on with your lives." I said. It suddenly hurt to breath. My eyes started to burn. I supposed it won't be so bad. I'd literally have them forever. But what if they don't want to stay here? What if they realize how good they could have it and went off to somewhere else?

"Firstly, you have obviously not listened to anything we have said. Our kind *chose* to serve. We were not forced. We *chose* to follow, we were not dragged. Gannon has been blinded by his own self-righteous greed. He chose to open the door out of self-service, not service to others. There is no honor in what he does, no matter what he would say. Secondly, the only way for the spell to be broken is for the death of last Cross. It is the only way. It is written." Malcolm said. The rasp had gone out of his voice so that his tone was clear and solid. I ran my hand through my hair, and came away with an oak leaf.

175

"So then what's stopping you? You would have enough power to protect the Cross' forever. Your house would be safe. My house would be safe. What's the hang up?" There was that flickering of eyes between the two glow twins, and Gwyn lowered her own to the table top.

"Okay guys no more secrets, out with it." I said, but Malcolm pressed his lips together tightly. Leila opened her mouth but at a glance from him, she closed it. Needless to say it pretty much pissed me off.

"Fine. Feckin' *be* that way. But if you don't mind, this poor little human would like to know what were gonna do about Gannon or maybe the shadow guys if that's not too much to ask. I'd hate to step all over your precious FECKING secrets!" Heat flushed up my neck and into my cheeks. I don't get really mad very often. The heat of it spread all the way down into my belly. It was instantaneous and consuming.

"It's just great to know that everyone you care about is really stabbing you in the back. Feckin' secret keeping, two-faced assholes." I shouted. Even the roots of my hair felt hot.

"Vivian, calm down. There will come a time when you will know everything. I promise." This from Leila. Bitch, I thought, clenching my teeth. Lying, betraying bitch. She was going to leave me anyways, what does she care? A red haze had slid through my vision until the whole world was bathed in blood.

"Oh yea? You feckin' promise? You promised to be my friend forever. You promised to always be by my side. You're a feckin' liar!" I snapped. I had never been so angry in my life. It was a geyser, bubbling up and spewing out. The root beer in my hand had started to boil. I was so angry, I couldn't catch my breath. I couldn't even remember why I was angry. No, make that enraged. The clear thin glass of my cup burst in my hand. The boiling root beer gushed through my fingers and shards sank in to my flesh. Swirling darkness oozed into my vision until I thought I was going to pass out. But it wasn't that infinite kind of darkness, no blanket of unconsciousness. This was a curtain of shadow drifting over my mind. Somewhere deep in my guts I could feel that little shadow humming contentedly, feeding off my anger. All it had needed was a spark.

I blinked and was looking down at a bloody mess on the table. Something cool and soft was pressed against my forehead. There were shards of glass and pools of candle wax everywhere. It looked like one of those paintings where the artist drops paint filled water balloons from the ceiling on to the canvas. Malcolm and Leila were smothering a section of smoldering table cloth. The cool thing across my forehead moved, making me give a long slow blink off to my left. Gwyn had her hand pressed against my scorched skin.

"Well that sucked." I croaked. I would have taken a drink of my root beer, but it was spread out in a wide blotch dripping off the edge of the table. Reed pushed through the kitchen door with a gallon bag full of ice.

"I was saving that for margaritas." I joked as he placed it on the back of my neck. It was pure heaven. Someone across the table snorted.

"I see you've inherited a little more from your father then we expected." Gwyn said. She was waving a clear crystal in from of my face and mumbling something unintelligible with every pass. The world was moving in slow motion. Everyone had carefully reseated themselves. Reed was rummaging around in the emergency bag still sitting at one end of the table. He pulled out a heavy first aid bag and began cleaning my wounded hand.

I watched him pull out the pieces of glass and felt nothing. Part of me was really stoked. Another part of me was little worried. Come to think of it, I couldn't really feel anything but the bag of ice on my neck and Gwyn's soft old hand. I was also having trouble trying to piece a coherent thought together.

"I feel a little lost inside my brain." I told them all a bit sluggishly. No one laughed or cracked any jokes. Leila and Malcolm looked poised on their side of the table, ready for attack. Leila's eyes were wider than ever, I could make out the smallest wrinkles and white lines on either side of nose as her nostrils flared, the most minute dilation of her pupils, the weave of her shirt. I could see everything as if it were under some sort of magnifying glass. Interesting. Slightly weird, but interesting.

"I'm trying to help you control yourself a bit. That's the problem with having so many holes in the bind. You never know what's going to pop out." Gwyn said, and I could only nod. I was very detached from my body at the moment. It was like that time in the eighth grade when Jody Melon got me to smoke some weed. But hopefully this time I wasn't going to throw up, or go flying out of the swings at full speed.

"I'm sorry Lei. I don't think you're a liar." I mumbled. She nodded but didn't say anything in return. With the flip of a switch, I was suddenly back in my body. And my hand hurt like a mother F-er. Not to mention I instantly started sweating like a pig.

"Oowww! Holy crap. What the hell?" I yelled trying to jerk my hand out of Reed's grasp. He held on tight, tweezers pointed at the tip of my nose.

"Hold still! Or else I'll just gnaw the damn thing off." He threatened. I had a glimpse of razor sharp teeth and spiraling horns in my mind. It was more than enough to make me clench my jaw and swallow the pain.

I sat under the pointed scrutiny of the glow twins and shuttered gaze of Gwyn while Reed prodded and dug at my hand. A cold sweat had started at my temples by the time he was finished. I turned, expecting Gwyn would heal my hurts, but Reed took out a long roll of gauze and mummified my hand.

My eyes drifted over the mess on the table, catching on shining bits of glass, wax that was still opaque and warm. There were little piles of ash where sweet smelling posies had once sat. My eyes wandered everywhere but to the people watching me like an insect under a glass.

My hand hurt. My head felt like I'd been electrocuted. Again. I was all fuzzy and warm in that heat stroke kind of way and down in my guts, I was cold. The kind of cold where the sun never warms, fire never melts. I could feel that little shadowy particle of myself curled up into a ball, crouched in the corner, a regular feral dog. Like any feral dog, I knew it was ready to bite again without warning.

I picked at the tape on my bandage. The silence was growing, so much more than that pink elephant in the living room. Were there pink sperm whales? No, it felt like a techni-colored sperm whale hiding under a fine lace doily. What was I supposed to tell them? Oh yea, just so you know there's this little piece of shadow thing hiding inside me. I didn't really think it was a big deal. Surprise.

I scowled at the table top, frantically picking at a loose edge of tape. Reed reached over and took hold of my hand. He didn't say anything, just gentle pressure and then he let go. I put my hands down in my lap.

"That must be how they found you." Malcolm said. His hands were flat on the table top, ready for action.

"Maybe that's how they got in the house. They didn't need permission from one of their own." Was from Leila. My head snapped up.

"I did. Not. Let them in." I protested, staring hard at her. Her skin had lost that otherworldly glow. Her pupils had shrunk to mere pinpoints. She too looked ready to jump, flee, fight, anything. It made me feel even worse than I already did, if that was even possible.

"You don't seem very surprised about this." Malcolm said, his jaw tightly clenched. My face flushed and I couldn't stop it.

"You're usually such an influx of questions. A veritable chatterbox." I could only shrug. My face was on fire. Gwyn reached over and turned my face to hers. It hurt to look into her eyes. Those liquid orbs searched my face. For what, I didn't know but whatever she saw, I could tell she wasn't pleased.

"Why did you say nothing of this?" she asked, taking her hand away from my chin. I tried not to shrug again. I hated it when people just shrugged at me. It was the kind of thing that drove me nuts.

"I don't know. Everything's been happening so fast. I just kind of forgot about it." I said. It was a lame frickin' excuse. I knew it, they knew it. Malcolm snorted. Once upon a time I had thought it a very amusing sound. There was nothing but distain when I looked in his eyes.

"You forgot that you were carrying a possible homing beacon to the very creatures that are trying to destroy us? That you were putting everyone around you in danger? That you perhaps put the very existence of the Ancients at risk? It surprising how much you *forget.*" He spat. His neck was flushed deep crimson and his hands were balled into fists in front of him. An apology sprang to my lips. It surprised me. I had never apologized to him for anything. He was my arch enemy and my valiant protector. The whirlwind of emotions was intense. My breath caught in my throat. Our eyes had locked. I was drowning in stormy gray skies. The tingle of a memory touched the back of my mind. The room started to fade away. I could hear birds and feel warm wind running tricky fingers in my hair. It felt like something horribly important so I clutched at it, and like a butterfly held too tight, it disintegrated. Leila's voice filled the void.

"Perhaps we can use this to our advantage." She said. Malcolm was blinking at me, his face gone ghostly pale so that his wounds stood out in vivid relief. His breath rattled out from between his lips. His fists were trembling. We both turned our faces in Leila's direction, neither willing to admit that something had just happened.

"If they can track her, why not set a trap? We use Vivian as bait. Draw them into a place of power and destroy them. If she has joined the legions of darkness then she too will be trapped and easily taken care of." Leila said coldly. She spoke as if about a chair or a lamp. My mouth gapped a little and the feeling of anxiety only increased when Gwyn nodded.

"It might work if we are able to coordinate properly. But what of Gannon?" she looked to Malcolm, who nodded and unclenched his hands.

"I will do what is necessary. Even if the Guardian is lost to us we must assure the security of Red Glen." I couldn't believe what I was hearing. They were talking like I wasn't even here.

"Wait just a second. Bait? Are you guy's crazy? I'm not lost." I shouted. The three of them ignored me.

"We will need as many Houses to join us as possible. It will be the only way to ensure their destruction. If we take out Gannon and the Darklings in a single stroke, you will not be at your full power. I wish no further appearances from these beings." Gwyn said. She had turned her whole body towards them and I was suddenly outside of the circle. I literally *felt* like an outsider.

"The more leaders the better. Though I do not know if it will be needed. I too have decided to take certain steps to ensure our survival." Leila said. Her eyes were back to being all magical. I started to interject again, but Gwyn cut me off.

"I cannot make the choice for either of you. But know that I will stand behind you whatever you decide. I will contact the others and we will consider a place to hold the Darklings. As for Gannon, I'm sure you have your own plans." They all nodded to each other, faces grave. I slapped my bandaged hand down on the table and winced.

"What about me?" I asked. It came out kind of whiny. I was that kid that had been left out of the grown up conversation. Three pairs of closed, emotionless eyes turned in my direction. It made me sit back in my chair a little.

"You will remain here, until we are ready for your assistance." Malcolm said coldly. I clenched my good hand.

"The hell I am. I'm not going to stay here while you're off fighting bad guys. I know I can't do much but I could help. I don't know how but I know it would be a lot better than sitting around." I shouted. I knew I was little more than useless to them. I just didn't want to be left behind. Malcolm pinned me with his gimlet eyes.

"You will be no help. You're forever in the way and a hindrance to everything we do. And now not only are you a burden, but you are a danger to us and everyone allied to us." He said. His voice dripped with venom. I struggled up out of my chair and everyone followed suit. Everything he had said was true. I knew it in my heart and it was agony. Still I couldn't help but fight him. I'd been doing it for so long, it only seemed natural.

"Well fine then. But I'm not staying here!" I yelled, trying to push my chair away so I could escape. No one else moved. I had Reed at my back so I couldn't see what he was doing. My fight or flight reflexes were in full gear. I didn't want to but I *would* fight them to get away.

"You don't really have any choice dear." Gwyn said softly. Her beautiful brown eyes were sad and she gave a small nod. It took me a moment to realize she wasn't nodding to me. I started to turn, but strong arms wrapped around me in a vice-like grip.

"This will be easier if you don't struggle." Reed said in my ear. Of course I struggled. Who did he think he was man handling? Fay Rey? I kicked my feet and wiggled as hard as I could. I couldn't get my arms or much of anything free for that matter. He had never been this strong. I could count numerous times I'd beaten him at arm wrestling or having to help him lift boxes in the store. Even holding me with one arm, I couldn't seem to get away from him.

"Don't struggle Viv, you won't like it." He said, putting his left hand over my eyes. I wanted to scream. I already didn't like it. I couldn't get out anything but pathetic grunting noises. His hand was warm and slightly sweaty over my eyes.

"Please let me go. Let me go Reed!" I yelled.

At the very last, I thought I heard him apologize. Right before a giant wave hit me. It swallowed the world in a rush, filling my ears, my eyes, my lungs. My muscles turned to warm liquid. I was floating. I tried to swim away, but strong arms held me. Far away I heard a voice.

"Don't struggle Viv. Just go with the flow." It said down a long, long tunnel. What was it talking about? I was going. I was floating away. I was a raft on a calm river. A boat on a still pond. A feather on a summer breeze.

17

I was a flaming dumbass. At least that's how I felt when I woke up to my empty house the next day. I had on pink flannel pjs that I knew I hadn't put on myself. They were the pale pink of cotton candy, with garish blue cartoon characters on them. I'd never worn them before. They'd been a present on some long ago Christmas which I had tactfully hidden but not thrown away. Hours into the day, I was still wearing them, sitting on my front porch. I was as far as I could go.

I had tried numerous times to leave. Keys in hand. Flip flops on my feet. Raring to go. But I couldn't. I physically could not walk off the bottom step of my porch. I'd tried the back door too and got the same result. And running full speed off of the porch was a bad idea. I had a lump on the back of my head to prove it. I even tried going out a window, but I could barely stand to stick my head out, it was like a million angry bees doing the mambo in your gray matter.

Thoroughly thwarted, I'd gone to the kitchen and made myself a king sized breakfast. A slab of fried pork, eggs (my wonderful fluffy eggs), hash browns, a stack of toast and a tall glass of orange juice. I had wanted coffee but I was too cranked up for it. Totally wired and pissed off. But at least I was fortified against the coming of the day.

Out of spite, I had prowled the entire house and destroyed anything that had been left by my quartet of wardens. I burned every pouch, every posy, and shattered every crystal out on the walkway.

I sat watching the pieces glitter in the sun. The air was slightly frosty, and ashy rain clouds scudded by. Still I stayed perched on the top step, brooding. I didn't really care at that moment that I had probably left myself wide open to danger. But that was the point wasn't it? I was their bait now. They *wanted* the bad guys to come get me.

I shook my head hard. I couldn't even stand to think about it. They were all so hot and cold. One minute I was the center of the world and the next, a pimple between their butt cheeks. I desperately felt the need to fix something and I couldn't even go to the garage. They hadn't even left me that. The urge to cry crept up, but I smashed it down. I was well and good simmering as I was.

I put both hands on either side of my head and struggled with myself not to yank on my own hair. If my grandmother was here she would know what to do, I thought. The idea was a flash bulb in my brain. You know those ones from back in the day that exploded every time you took a picture? It was fantastic! I jumped up and rushed into the house. Every curtain was open. Every light was on. I ran up the stairs, and nearly fell down them in my rush. I stumbled to my grandparent's room and threw open the door.

It looked exactly as it had every day I had lived in this house. Except for the rare dusting, when I felt the need to be even closer to them, I hadn't touched a thing since my grandmother's death. Her enormous cedar vanity with its big round mirror sat just to the right of the door. There were bottles of oil and perfume and nail polish covered in many months of dust. There were even cobwebs draped on some things. I knew there was one tube of lipstick and a small compact of blush that my grandmother had used on special occasions. The fluffy queen bed was flanked by two white square tables, each with its own flowery Tiffany lamp. On the left side, my grandmother's side, a dark, wooden jewelry box sat under the lamp. It was plain but glossy even under the accumulation of dust.

The wash of emotion that flooded through me as I entered the room was almost more than I could bear. I almost abandoned my quest at once. Instead, I swallowed my hurt, batted away the memories and hurried towards the jewelry box.

Without ceremony, I grabbed it up and carried it to the clear space in the middle of the room. I plopped down on the carpet in a warm square of sunlight and place the box in front of me. Dust was all over my hands and smeared down the sleeve of my pajamas. I allowed myself to feel a moment of shame for letting my grandparent's things get so dirty. But I didn't have time to sit and dwell. I pushed the thought aside and flipped open the lid. I knew at once that I had hit the jackpot.

There were several pieces of jewelry in the box that glowed and I knew instinctually that it wasn't from the sun or some trick of the light. The items themself were imbued with some kind of power. There was a big men's ring that looked like a piece of raw gold bent into a circle. It still had bits of stone attached to it. I picked it up and placed it on my thumb because it was the only finger it would fit on. The ring was warm as if it had been on someone else's finger all day.

A spectacular bracelet of diamonds seemed to call out to me. Its glow brightened and receded, a slowly flashing signal. Pick me, it seemed to say. I held it up to the light. Nine stones, each the size of my thumb, with shiny silver links between, flashed in the sunlight like a captive rainbows. It was so beautiful, for a moment I forgot about everything else. I forgot why I'd even come up stairs, until Malcolm's cold words came back to haunt me. *It is surprising how much you forget.* His voice hissed in my head. I gripped the bracelet hard in my hand until the memory faded. Screw him, I thought. I never asked for any of this. I just wanted to live a simple life, help people and be happy. That's it, not too much to ask.

I wrapped the bracelet around my left wrist, over the pink burn scar that still lay there. My hand had been healed when I woke, but the burn had only turned into a soft new scar.

I rummaged through the box, picking up several other items. Each sent prickly shock waves up my arm. I quickly put them back, reading the message very clearly. They were not for me. The only other thing that seemed available to me was a silver ring with a small rough ruby in a square setting. It was simple and it fit the ring finger of my right hand perfectly. Closing the box, I got up and placed it back on the side table where it belonged.

The next venture was harder than I expected. I turned around to face my grandparent's closet. I wasn't even sure if anything in there would help me. Could magic be tricked? A huge part of me wasn't even sure it was worth the emotional anguish. I shambled over to the closet doors and placed both hands on the shiny white knobs with their lacquered blue-bells. I felt a great pressure build up in my head. The air was suddenly too heavy. I almost let go of the doors. Something inside me yelled, *run, stop, don't.* The feeling tumbled around in my skull until I was panting. At the last second I gripped the handles and yanked hard.

I literally heard a *pop* inside of myself and a breeze rushed past me. The air was full of herbs, full of magic. My skin tingled with it.

An ice cube did the luge down my back. I blinked into the closet waiting for my eyes to adjust, before I realized I didn't have to.

An eerie sense of the otherworldly hit me so that I shivered. In the middle of the small walk-in closet sat a white iron wrought table, a smaller twin to the one in the garden. On top of it was a glowing cardboard box tied with a thick ribbon and a bundle of herbs. Leaning against the box was an envelope, with my name on it.

I cautiously walked in and pick up the box. It was heavy but not unbearable and when nothing undo occurred I carried it out along with the envelope. I plopped myself back down on the sunny carpet, setting the box down in front of me. I held the envelope in my hands, slowly turning it over.

The neat scrawling of my name was distinctly my grandmother's handwriting. I pressed the paper to my nose and inhaled deeply. It still smelled like the honeysuckle oil she rubbed on her hands. The flap was closed by blob of green wax with a strange looking symbol pressed into it. After a second, I realized it was just a stylized version of a shepherd's crook. With an indrawn breath, I quickly broke it. Like a band aide, I thought.

The paper unfolded into two pieces of thick vellum. I could see threads of fiber in them when I looked closely and they smelled faintly of beeswax. I don't know what I expected, but my throat tightened as my eyes traced the first achingly familiar words.

My Dearest One,

If you are reading this, then I fear the worst. The opening of this letter means that your grandfather and I have passed before the time came to give you these items ourselves. And for this, I grieve.

I suppose also that the knowledge of your parent's death has been brought to light. For only with this action would you find it in yourself to come to my room. Part of me rejoices at this. I was never one for keeping secrets from my loved ones. And I am glad that you finally know the truth about all of us.

My heart was broken when I placed your mother in the earth. And it was broken even further with the wiping of your mind. How, I often ask myself, could I do this to my own grandchild? Blood of my blood? I was counseled by many that it was the best thing for you. And against my better judgment, I allowed myself to be led astray. Had I not been so steeped in grief, I would never have allowed them to do what was done. Through pain and strife our people have served others. Nothing should have changed the course of this path.

Even now, I look upon your young face and I see the stranger I have helped make you. Even though you do not long for them or question me on their departure, I can see the hole in your life where your parents once dwelt. For that other life, I can see you searching. I see you searching for that missing part of you, like a tiger cleansed of its stripes. I see you hurting and not knowing why. I see all of these things and can do nothing.

In this moment of clarity, I have begun collecting as many memories as I could find, for you to have. I have placed items in this box that will be of some use to you, and others that will hopefully be a balm for your aching heart.

The two earth bound books are the volumes passed down from parent to child since the first, first born Guardian. Hopefully they will be enough to help you find your way in this strange world. I pray one day you will pass them on to your own child with a happy heart, as I once did to your mother and my father did for me.

The way of the Guardian is a hard road. But the best things in life are always hard won. Always remember that we were chosen in gratitude and honor to serve others. Never let anyone take that from you. It is a gift the like of which others only dream.

I must go now my heart. You are curious about my doings and I fear what would happen if you should figure things out too soon. Please know that you have always been well loved. Your mother and father. Your grandfather and I. Many people in our community. We all love you so very much. You are the light in the darkness that guides us all and you will never be alone.

Blessed be the way and the light.
Love Grandma

Tears rolled down my face and splattered onto the letter like rain. I gently tried to blot the moisture away with my shirt but only succeeded in smudging it a bit. Setting it carefully aside, I covered my face with both hands and had myself a good cry. Well, more like sobbed. Wept. Bawled. Yea, bawled my eyes out like a frickin' baby. I cried until I couldn't cry anymore. Until my head felt all full and floaty.

I sniffled and snorted and wiped my face on my sleeve, which was damp anyways from the onslaught. I blinked wet lashes down at the letter and then snatched it back up. On the back of the second page at the very bottom, there was more writing.

P.s. Take good care of Leila and Malcolm. They love you much more than they'll ever let on. xoxo

I was flabbergasted. Leila I already knew loved me. But Malcolm? No frickin' way. I think she may have been thinking of someone else. Maybe grandma had a little nip of the good stuff before writing this letter. I read the two lines twice before setting the letter aside again. Yep, completely off her rocker.

I put it, and thoughts of love for any of my *friends* gently aside. I was still pretty miffed at them. Besides, I had a box from my grandma to keep me company. With barely contained enthusiasm, I tore off the ribbon and tossed aside the flowers. There was a sigh and a puff of air as I drew aside the flaps. This should have made me pause, but I was too excited.

Right on top, were what I assumed to be the 'earth bound' books. Both looked like they were made out of leaves. One was green, first shoots of Spring green. The leaves forming the cover looked fresh and alive. Pressing it to my nose, they smelled tangy and moist. Up and down the spine thin, deep green vines twined.

The second book was formed of red, yellow and fragile brown autumnal leaves and bits of wrinkled bark. It had a little white mushroom sprouting from one corner. I tried to pluck the fungus away but it shrank in my hand, only to reappear in another corner, this time as a small, fuzzy, brown cluster of them.

I was enchanted with the books. I instantly felt proprietary towards them and hugged them to my chest. They were warm in my hands. I wanted to sit there and read them, but each volume was nearly two inches thick. I set them aside promising to make time later.

The next thing I pulled out was a stack of photographs. They were of many different sizes and in different degrees of wear but all contained scenes of familiarity. Me, my mom, and my dad at my first birthday. My dad pushing me on the swings at the park. My mom dancing with me and Leila and several other little girls around a pile of pillows. My dad holding me and a shining yellow fish. My dad holding an infant wrapped in a pink blanket with my mom gazing over his shoulder. The pictures flew through my hands. I couldn't flip through them fast enough. I wanted to absorb every moment, every memory, because that's what it was.

I wasn't just looking at pictures and seeing them for the first time. I was seeing pictures and *remembering*. With every picture there was a memory, instant recognition. Smells, tastes, sounds. No memorizing the moment like an outsider. These were my memories. Mine all mine! I could roll them around in my mind like a piece of candy. On the bottom of the pile there were pictures of my parents when they were young and unmarried. My parents at prom. My parents at the lake. My dad helping my grandpa in the garage. I came to the last picture, and stopped.

I felt full all the way to the top. My heart was pounding in my ears. I felt radiant inside, as if a tiny sun had been born in my soul. I'd never been so happy in my life. I looked down at the last picture, and everything froze.

It was a picture of two little children. Hand in hand. Their backs were to the camera, but they couldn't have been more than three or four years old. The little girl was wearing a pale green dress with lace along the hem, white patent leather shoes and those little white socks with lace on the cuff. The little boy had on overalls and a little white dress shirt and shiny black shoes. It was a very adorable photo. My eyes caught on the little girl's free hand. It held a single Black-eyed Susan.

Something stabbed me in the eye. Not literally, but I screamed and all of the pictures fluttered to the ground. There was no memory attached to the pain, it was just a splitting migraine. It was an atomic eyelash in the eye. I thought for a moment that my eyeball had burst. Shaking and cursing, I took my hands away expecting blood to pore out. But there was nothing, just a single hot tear. The pain faded until it was only a throbbing and I could see something other than bright stars. My hands were quaking.

I picked up the scattered pictures, shuffling them back into a pile. I was very careful not to look for the picture of the two children again. I was very careful to not even think about it. I set the pile aside and went back to my box.

The bottom was filled with papers and three long white candles. There was a coil of slick black rope and a little gold hand bell with a tiny sheep on it. I rang the bell next to my ear and smiled. It was a familiar sound, though I couldn't place it. Setting it aside, I drew out the papers and shuffled through them.

There were honor roll awards, and birth certificates. One mine and one my mother's. There were ancient looking parchments with faded brown ink on it. I couldn't read any of it except for some numbers at the top of one that said, '1104', which looked suspiciously like a date.

There were deeds. One for my grandmother's house and twenty acres of land and another for a parcel of land on the other side of town with eight acres. I read each embossed and notarized deed closely and found my name on both of them.

There were smaller pieces of notebook paper in half familiar handwriting. After a moment I realized it was my mother's hasty penmanship. I pressed each little paper to my lips. Some had oily stains on them or large water rings. They were recipes. I read each one and could remember every single time I had tasted them.

The memories grew in me like a flower opening its petals. It was so much better than the bursts of images I'd been getting so far. It was so warm and welcome. I could recall smells, and places and names. It made me eager to sop up anything else. I placed the pile of papers on the floor between the candlesticks and the black rope.

Tipping the box on its side, I saw that only two things remained; a glossy white shell and a ball of gold twine. The shell was a large scallop. It was pure white, save for three little ochre flecks on its ridged outer part. The ball weighed almost nothing and the way it gleamed made me think it might actually be real gold. Neither item gave me any recognition. But I was hardly deflated.

With everything laid out before me on the pale peach carpet, I sat back and expelled a deep sigh. This then was an accumulation of my past. My eyes drifted over every item, every paper, a picture of my parents hugging me between them. My heart was so full. No matter what else happened, I knew that I had this moment and the return of so many memories.

I flicker of apprehension shimmered in the back of my mind. I had to get out of here. But this was my grandmother's house. I couldn't let the place go to shit because some bad guys were after me. This was my home. My house. The idea erupted in my mind. I realized it was the first time since coming here that I had ever really thought of this place as *my* home. *My* house. It was almost overwhelming. I had the most terrible urge to run down stairs and make scones.

I laughed at myself. At least now I knew that eating myself out of house and home was a family quirk and not some sort of eating disorder. I thought about the recipes and how Leila might like to have them.

Leila. Holy cow. I had forgotten all about them. I scrambled around, shoving the papers, the books, and the photographs back into the box. The candles and the rest I kept out. I used the thick brown ribbon to secure the box and sealed it with a tight bow. Hurrying to my feet I picked it up and put it back in the closet.

Rummaging through the long racks of clothing, I pulled out a ruffled, purple house coat. As a last thought, I grabbed one of my grandmother's lace shawls to put over my head.

When I had finished, I walked out and closed the door. Yet it didn't seem very secure. I walked back into the closet a couple of times and was about to pick the box back up, when an idea struck me.

I exited the closet and picked up the piece of black rope. This could be used to close the door, I thought. I don't know how I knew, but I was sure that once it was on the door, only I would be able to take it off. As a precaution, I put the jewelry box inside as well. When the doors were closed and the rope wrapped tightly around the knobs, the strands seemed to blend together at once, until there was only one. I would have stood there gawking in amazement, but I reminded myself that there was no time. I picked up the rest of the stuff and ran to my room.

It was barely mid-morning, but I scrambled around, throwing the things on my bed and rummaging through my drawers for something to wear.

Twenty minutes later, I had showered and was dressed. I had on a thick, high necked, cable-knit sweater the color of granny smith apples. It was long sleeved and perfectly warm. I had on a good pair of faded work jeans and my favorite pair of tan, steel-toed hiking boots. I don't hike but they were sinfully comfortable. Not to mention they were perfect for any kind of dirty work.

Over my sweater I put on a dark green flannel sweater vest with a hood. Into its pockets, I shoved the ball of twine, one of the candles, a liter, and the little bell. I couldn't get the other candles to fit without falling out so I put them on my dresser with the shell. The diamonds glittered brightly on my wrist and the two rings shined merrily.

A level of apprehension had built while I'd taken my shower. As I descended the stairs, my grandmother's housecoat over my clothes and the shawl secured over my head, it started to peak. It was full blown by the time I hit the front porch. All of the warm fuzzies I'd had up in my grandmother's room had faded.

The truck keys jingled in my hand. I'd snatched them off the hook by the door as I'd walked out. I was suddenly too warm in my layers of clothing. Where the hell was I going to go? I asked myself. Even if I did manage to get away from the house, where was I going to go? I now had a greater accumulation of knowledge about some of the things I was getting into, but I still had nil in the power scale. And I sure as hell couldn't abandon everyone to the likes of Gannon and the shadow guys.

I walked across the porch and slowly down the three steps. On the last one, I stopped and took a deep breath. The weight of obligation was heavy on my shoulders and I knew I couldn't leave. Yet I had to at least prove I could do it. I had to prove I wasn't useless. I had to show the others I was strong enough to face them down. I was *not* useless.

I closed my eyes and jumped off the last step. It was very anticlimactic. There was a rush of icy cold wind in my face and then the sun was warming me again. No angry bees. No one running from the woods to tackle me. I opened my eyes to make sure of the second thing. There was no one but me and a couple of white butterflies fluttering over my rose bushes. I smiled. *My* rose bushes. I looked down the drive and thought, *my* garage, *my* cars. It felt so damn good. I laughed out loud and did a little jig.

When I was done making a fool of myself for the butterflies, I put the keys in my pocket and walked across the grass. At least, I thought, if I was going to stay, I'd make myself useful. I smiled happily to myself as I unraveled the long green hose and watered the lawn.

There was a commotion in the house. I could hear the front door slam and feet pounding throughout. Voices yelled and something glass broke. I listened, humming to myself, my wide brimmed straw hat perched on my head. There was a little man, about two feet tall, helping me pluck weeds. He had on cute little brown trousers with suspenders and a tan canvas shirt. He also had some of the ugliest feet I had ever seen, but he was sweet enough and had been helping me in the garden all afternoon.

I was on my knees beside a small round herb patch, when the back door burst open. My little companion disappeared instantly. Malcolm stood there filling up the entire door and boy did he look pissed. Yay me, I thought, exceedingly pleased with myself. He was in his usual spiffy monochromatic attire, black slacks, black dress shirt, wide gray tie and onyx cuff links. His black alligator shoes shone brightly in the sun as did his slicked locks. Someone knocked into him from behind and they both fell out the door.

Malcolm landed just past the last step on both feet, graceful as a cat, with Leila attached to the back of his shirt. Kamac of the gold hair stood with Reed in the door way. Both of them were red faced.

"I told you to watch out." Reed hissed at Kamac, who just shook his shiny head and frowned. Leila was the first to recover. She detached herself from Malcolm and stomped over to where I still knelt.

"What in the hell are you doing out here? You're supposed to be in the house!" She yelled. I held up my dirty gloved hands for her to see.

"I'm pulling weeds, duh. And what the hell to you too; you scared my helper away." I said pushing to my feet. I pulled off my gloves and slapped them together, a big goofy smile plastered on my face.

"How?" Was from Malcolm who was still rooted to the spot. Kamac and Reed stood to either side of him. I waited for them to break in to song like a scene from West Side Story. I waggled my fingers at him and twisted my wrist so all of my sparklies showed.

"I figured since this *was* my grandmother's house and you probably wouldn't have adjusted the spell to keep *her* in, for all the obvious reasons. I thought I could put some of her things on and it might think that *I* was *her*." They were all staring at me in different levels of awe and disbelief. I was tickled pink and purple and polka-dot. I continued, slapping both gloves into one hand.

"As you see, it worked very well. Besides, I figured that the worst that could happen was not being able to leave at all, or that whole angry bee feeling, which is quite effective by the way. Because I know how much you guys need me one way or the other. And I know you wouldn't do anything to jeopardize your own chances at success." I prowled around Leila, towards the stone path and she turned as I moved. I could see the anger draining from her face, melting into annoyance.

"You're a dumbass you know." She said, and I stopped walking. I used every inch of my height to tower over her, scowling. She was completely un-cowed in her marmalade colored jacket over a frilly shirt so pale orange it was almost white. Her brown chinos showed off finely turned ankles and small feet tucked into marmalade colored flats. All of the orange brought out the fiery red highlights in her hair.

"Didn't you even stop to think that those wards were made not just to keep you in, but to keep everything else out? You nearly gave us a damn heart attack." She said, stomping her foot. My feeling of superiority was quickly deflating. I'd been outside all day and I hadn't thought again about how I might have put *myself* in great danger. I twisted the gloves in my hands and nudged a stray clump of weeds with the toe of my shoe. I didn't want to apologize. It was their turn to feel shitty. I wasn't the one who put the knock-out on anyone or who was using people as bait. Damn and double damn.

"Well you guys just freaked me out. That sleeper hold was killer. I didn't know what you guys were going to do with me . . . I suppose this doesn't really gain me any points on the not-being-evil scale does it?" I said, giving the gloves another hard slap into my palm. Leila was shaking her head at me.

"The only thing that matters is that you're alright." She said, startling me. It was something the old Leila would say. I looked into her dark eyes and found real concern there. Her brow was furrowed with worry. It made me feel like an ass.

"I'm sorry. I was a dumbass. But I made scones. Let's all go in and have a scone." I walked past Leila, and started up the path. Malcolm stood aside to let me pass and just as I reached the door, someone grabbed me. I could smell Reed's spicy cologne. This time I really gave it my all in my flailing.

"Damn it Reed let me go. Aw shit, not again. Let me go!" I howled. The other three crowded close. So close, I could feel Kamac's hair brush my arm. Malcolm and I were nearly nose to nose.

"It will be better if you are sleeping for this part." He said. He did not look like his normal self. One thing I had missed before but saw now, was that his face was completely healed. There wasn't a single wrinkle on his tan face. His gray eyes were as deep as the ocean, gleaming like two polished lead orbs. He looked like he was glowing. Then I realized, he *was* glowing. He was luminescent in a way that no human could ever be. He fairly radiated. I stopped struggling, completely in awe of him. I could have filled my eyes with his image forever, until a warm hand covered them and I was engulfed in darkness.

18

I was not surprised, shocked, awed, astounded or any of those other words about waking up on the ground. I was looking up at a patch of azure through a hole in the canopy. On one side the evening was slowly creeping, a single bright star giving witness to its fall.

I sat up, and looked around. I was mad, tired, and completely exasperated. Reed sat on the ground directly across from me in blue jeans and a white polo shirt. There was a very cautious smile on his face.

"Don't you smile at me you piece of shit. That's twice!" I yelled, getting to my feet. The world wavered and I almost fell back down. I fought to keep the stars from my eyes. When it cleared, I found him standing.

"I was only doing what I was told." He had his hands up in front of him, palms out. I marched over to him, and slapped him on the back of the head.

"That's no frickin' excuse. If you ever put your hands on me again, I'll cut 'em off." I said shaking my fist in his face. Reed rubbed the back of his head wincing.

"Malcolm said without your powers, the way here would have incapacitated you. You would have been really sick and what would you have done then, huh? Barfed on the bad guys?" he said, rubbing the back of his neck. I let my temper cool ever so slightly and turned around. I wasn't about to apologized this time, no way Jose. Oulwihn sat nearby, in a long white dress with sleeves so long they covered her hands. Around her neck she wore a strange necklace that looked like a tangle of feathers and bone. She inclined her head ever so slightly and beckoned with one pale hand.

"If you are finished punishing the young man, come sit with me. I have missed your company." She said. Her hair was piled into a mountain of snow and diamonds on her head. I wanted to stay where I was. But as

196

far as I knew, the lady Oulwihn was still on my side. I walked over and plopped down on the unseasonably green grass near her.

"I gave that to your grandmother for her eighteenth birthing day." She said in her windy rustling voice. I looked down to where she pointed. The diamond bracelet was still safely attached to my wrist. I had two thoughts at once as I looked back up at her. They wrestled with one another until I had the right words.

"Malcolm said you had the power to heal him. Does that mean you're immortal too?" I asked. Her smile was gentle and she shook her head.

"None of us are truly immortal anymore. And if they say so, it is a lie. As for myself, I simply age much more slowly than you. In the span of your life, I may age only a single year, perhaps less."

I looked down at my hands, grasping at my second question with a heavy heart.

"When you chose to open yourself to the power, did you stop . . . I mean did you . . . did you leave all of your human friends behind?" I stumbled over my words, but couldn't help myself. My hands shook with the effort.

"Your friends care about you very much. I do not believe any power in this world could ever persuade them leave you behind." She said. I don't think she would say that if she knew all the things that had been going on. Her cool hand lifted my face to hers.

"You are not evil. I was present at your birth. I have been present all of days of your life and never have I seen a trace of malice or venom in your heart. Leave these thoughts behind and fret no more." I was shocked that she would know my thoughts. My sinuses started to burn and my throat grew tight as she let her hand fall away from my face. Her citrine eyes sparkled as brightly as the diamonds in her hair.

I couldn't think of anything worthwhile to say. How had she known what had been gnawing away at my heart? I sat quietly beside her, and listened to the night creatures of the forest waking all around us. Somewhere far off, and bird gave a long, lonely call.

An eternity seemed to pass as we sat silently together, watching the shadows lengthening, feeling the air cool settle. Reed came and sat Indian style on my right. I saw that his tan feet were bare and shook my head. Many things in this world would change for me, but it was the little things that counted.

"How did you do that?" I asked, gesturing towards the place where I'd woken up. He gave me a crooked smile.

"The sandman trick?" he said, and when I nodded, he shrugged.

"Every so often, a child in my family is 'blessed' with the power of the djinn. The story goes, that my great-great-something-grandmother got tangled up with a desert djinn. And by tangled, I mostly mean knocked up. And ever since then our family has gained certain . . . powers. I'm pretty lucky. The signs didn't show up till puberty. Some of us are born outright with a full set of sharp teeth and tail." He said. I winced. Childbirth was scary enough without pesky supernatural family traits popping up.

"The sandman thing is the only thing I do really well. Some can fly. My grandpa used to sleep on the ceiling." He said nonchalantly. I started to exclaim something extremely gullible, when he grinned. I punched him softly in the arm but it didn't stop him from laughing at my expense.

We sat there in companionable silence and it was full dark by the time a small glowing figure stepped out of the trees. She was still wearing her marmalade colored jacket. Her presence illuminated the clearing. Oulwihn's power reacted to her and she was suddenly a bright light beside me. Even Reed was a little glowy around the edges, his cornflower eyes vivid in his face. Leila glided towards us and as she neared, I noted other differences.

Like Malcolm's face, she showed no single line, no wrinkle. Her skin was perfect. Her eyes were enormous, almost doll-like with their dark fringe of lashes. She turned those coffee colored eyes on me and I felt it like a jolt. Her hair, pulled back in a loose bun, seemed touched by living fire. So this is it. I thought. This is what it is to be on the other side. She nodded to Oulwihn and Reed.

"The others are on their way. We have but to wait and see." Her voice was a pure note plucked from a harp. I'd never heard her voice so clear, so melodious. She put those magic brightened eyes on me and they were hard.

"The time has come for us to face the darkness. I cannot make you stay, no one here can, for to do so may mean your death. I can only *ask* that you stand with us." Her liquid voice filled my ears and ricocheted through the trees. I rose to my feet as if pulled by strings.

My heart felt full. I held my hand out to her, all of my anger and confusion evaporated.

"I've always been with you, and I always will be. Sister of my heart. Together to the end." I said. My voice was less magical, but it echoed. Reed bound to his feet and slapped his meaty paw into mine.

"To the end." He shouted, right in my ear. I was about to yell at him again, when a soft white hand was laid on top of his.

"To the end." Oulwihn said softly, but there was a firmness that warmed my bones. Leila watched me from behind the mask of her face. I couldn't tell what she was thinking but at the last, she placed her hand on the pile.

"To the end."

19

In a fight, every body on your side is a piece of armor, a weapon in your armory, a bullet in your gun. Sitting in the clearing, with all of my friends looking like two-legged glow-worms, there were way too many holes in our armor. Not enough rounds for the full magazine.

Olione had joined us with his blazing red beard and giant sword. His face was painted white and he was bare under his plaid. Two men flanked him, slightly shorter but no less impressive. One had long hair stiffened into a white crest, and the other had his head completely shaved so closely that the dome of his skull shined. Both had their faces painted white and their plaids draped from their waists.

Michelina arrived in full feathered regalia, her fingers curved with long silver talons. She arrived alone, but went to stand one step behind the lady Oulwihn, hazel eyes taking in every detail.

The lion-man from town, who introduced himself only as Leo, shook my hand with a beefy paw. He wore shiny gold armor that looked Roman and buckled leather sandals. There was a sword hanging from his waist that gleamed wickedly in the low light.

Evalia, lady of the water, had long weedy hair strung with pearls. Her skin was like the inside of an abalone shell and she wore thick plates of whale bone to cover her nakedness. The gleaming white was layered down her torso in albino scales the size of half dollars. In her hands she carried a staff with shining blades at both ends. She was attended by two well-muscled men with blue-grey skin and slick white armor similar to hers.

A man that towered over me by nearly a foot and a half, with skin white and speckled as the bark of birch tree took a knee when we met. His lemon yellow hair was thick with ragged spade-shaped leaves and his eyes were as green as the first tender shoots of spring.

His name was Alexander and carried nothing but a loin cloth and pair of muscled arms thick as telephone poles.

And that was it. No cavalry. No Gatling gun to cover the rear. Everyone was milling around the clearing with nervous flickering eyes. The darkness had grown thick around our little haven. I wasn't sure what we were waiting for, but we had been waiting for a good long time. I wanted to ask if everyone was here but the answer seemed rather dire.

I sat on the grass beside Oulwihn, with my legs tucked up. Reed was milling. Leila was standing on the other side of the clearing. She looked like she was listening to something no one else could hear. I looked around from person to person, admiring their glowing bodies, their fancy armor, when suddenly I couldn't breathe. As if a plastic bag had been vacuum sealed over my head so that even my ears were clogged. My hands clenched in the grass, struggling to keep me up-right. And all at once it was gone. I sat there, a little bit sideways, panting.

"What the hell was that?" I gasped, and my voice sounded too loud to my ears. There were nearly identical looks on everyone's faces. Pensive. Strained. They had all turned to look up, as if something might drop down from the sky.

"The ward has gone down." Oulwihn murmured. I turned my head and watched as she rose to her feet. The movement was smooth and graceful as a well-oiled machine. Gliding, she moved across the clearing towards Leila. The other's followed suit, forming a loose circle. I was last to reach them feeling nearly frantic in the absence of their light.

Standing with them, the darkness seemed to grow. It swallowed the trees, blacked out the sky and threw ink into the fragrant grass at our feet. I wedged myself in between Leo and Olione with Leila at our backs. A stifling hand, I could feel the night pressing down on me.

"No matter what happens, stay close." The small man said his lips barely moving. My pulse raced. I could feel it beating madly in my ears, taste it in the back of my tongue. Our small group shifted, moving closer together.

"Stay together." Leila hissed and I could feel the vibration of it up the back of my neck. The tension built and the night grew. A veritable tidal wave, I could sense it rising over us, looming over us. As waves batter the endless beaches of the world, this one crashed over us.

Faster than my eyes could follow, misshapen figures dropped from the roof of the sky. They tumbled from the walls of the forest, scuttling on cockroach legs. Bloated and screaming, they burst up from the ground in writhing geysers.

I saw them arrive only by the light that my companions shed and though I had no wish to be in true darkness with these malevolent creatures, the eldritch light forced me to see far more than I liked. At once it seemed as if we had been engulfed. A tiny speck of life crowded by the infinite blackness of space. And all was chaos.

To my left, Alexander roared and thrust himself into a mass of darkness. Evalia followed close behind, her staff a whirling vortex of destruction. Shreds of shadow flew through the air like pieces of confetti. I watched as Reed leapt at a thick, two headed shadow. He was fully horned, a long, whip-like tail sprouting from the seat of his jeans. I watched as he tore off the shadows arms and used them to bludgeon it. Olione had stepped forward and was fencing with a creature that looked like an over-grown primordial dwarf, but nowhere near as cute. Leo shoved me behind him and grappled with one of the snake necked shadows that I had encountered before.

I stumbled, planting my butt in the grass. I found myself sitting at Oulwihn's feet her gauzy dress floating around me like a cloud. The face I looked up into belonged to a different person completely. Her eyes were twin suns burning in her face. Her skin so completely illuminated, no crease, no line or feature in her face could be seen. It was a smooth canvas with two blinding lights punched through it. Her graceful hands were raised in claws and a bitter wind blew from them.

At Oulwihn's back, Leila hacked into a shrieking creature with a blade of ice. It flashed with captive lightning and the creature screamed, flesh sizzling in its wake. I felt a moment of awe before I remembered where I was.

Getting to my knees, my first thought was to get up and join the fight. All around me the battle raged, inky body parts flying through the air, piercing screams and echoing roars splitting the night.

Olione's bald companion hacked a shadow guy in two before turning and beheading another. Michelina was literally ripping one to bits with her formidable claws. Looking down at my empty hands it quickly occurred to me that I was weaponless. Why the thought hadn't struck *before* the excrement had struck the oscillating wind device, was beyond me. All I knew was that everyone seemed to be fighting but me.

Our circle of light had spread, so that the fighting seemed to span the length of the clearing. Our champions dotted the area like vigorous stars. Standing, I gasped as a large shadow dropped from the canopy, right behind Olione. Helplessly, I reached out towards him, a wordless scream spilling from my lips.

Olione had moved to follow his initial head-on foe, leaving me several feet behind. He turned just in time to catch a hand larger than a dinner plate across the back. Nearly un-phased, he did one of those really neat rolling falls they teach you in martial arts and was back on his feet in a blink.

I would have crowed in jubilation but something grabbed me. Enormous, black hands latched on to my upper arms and hoisted me off the ground. I screamed, thrust into the air, wind rushing past my body. I drew my arms up around my face as I careened into the lovely plush grass the next instant. All of the oxygen was compressed from my lungs. I looked up just in time to see Leo crush the head of the offending shadow man. Viscous masses rained down on me. Leo threw the body aside and without missing a beat, jerked me to my feet.

"Get behind me Guardian!" He shouted over the din. I stumbled, but did as he asked. I was still wiping pieces of shadow man off my face when Leo splattered me with another one, a part of a hand bouncing off my chest. It struck me that standing behind him wasn't the best place in the world to be. I back peddled, and bumped into someone. I turn and found myself staring into a yawning maw full of serrated shark teeth. The enormous mouth snapped closed and grinned at me.

"Lovely day for a battle, eh Guardian?" It was one of Evalia's companions. He now sported a formidable sharks head. I gapped and would have remained that way, but he grabbed me and thrust me to the side.

"Head's up." He shouted and I careened through the fighters. I was thankfully able to keep my feet and made a B-line down the clearing. There was a shadow attached to Reed's back. Weaponless I may have been, but my friend was in trouble and that was all that mattered.

I jumped on the shadow and all three of us tumbled into the grass. The thing flailed around in my hands. I could hear it gnashing and snapping its terrible teeth and held on for dear life. Reed's polished bronze hands closed over the creatures head. I closed my mouth and my eyes, preparing myself for another wash of monster innards. There was a sharp snap, and the shadow man went limp in my arms.

I opened my eyes and Reed was tugging me to my feet. The shadow man flopped limply on the ground.

"Are you ok?" Reed said with his glowing white eyes and glossy copper skin. There was a grizzly piece of shadow dangling from his hair.

"I'm good. What are they waiting for?" I shouted. We were at the center of the battle, safe for just a moment. Reed leaned in close to my ear. The smell of hot sand and tangy metal filled my nose.

"Duhán must be here. Without capturing him it will all be for naught." He hissed in my ear. A second later, he was jerked away, spinning head over heels to the ground, a large shadow man on top of him. I screamed and started to chase after him, when another scream echoed mine. My head snapped to the left.

A lithe figure was thrashing under a mound of bodies. Michelina was screaming. High, piteous shrieks piercing the air. I could make out three figures bent over her, tearing at her beautiful body with their clawed hands. Blood poured down her flesh as she fought to get away. I raced towards her, brandishing only my own two hands. I leapt on the back of the closest shadow guy, pummeling him with my fists.

Standing outside of the moment, we must have looked particularly comical. The shadow guy yelling and running in a tight circle, me attached to its back practicing my best Donkey Kong impression. The darkling squealed and disintegrated in a haze of white flames. The remaining two shadow guys turned from a very still Michelina and hurtled towards me.

I didn't even have time to wonder what had just happened. White flames still licked over my skin. The diamond bracelet felt very alive on my wrist. Teeth bared, I rushed the howling Svartálfar.

The first connected with my fist and burst like an over ripe fruit. White flames consumed the remains, catching parts of the ground on fire. Persistent as a rabid dog the second grabbed my arm, tossing me into the air. I screamed but had only a moment before I smashed into the ground.

Spitting out grass and dirt, I spun, fists ready. I had landed close to Michelina. I could see her from the corner of my eye. There was so much blood and I couldn't tell whether or not she was breathing. Adrenaline coursed in my veins, my heart raced. I blinked rapidly, not allowing myself to think about the possibility of her death right that moment.

I sat up and watched the shadow man come. It was backlit by my glowing friends, most of which were now covered in blood and guts and worse. It came, and at the same time, another figure leapt out from behind me. I didn't even have time to think, to breath. I raised my hands, lips pulled back from my clenched teeth. The shadow men never landed.

Two blazing figures barreled into them, crashing over me. Someone kicked me in the shoulder. Another foot nearly crushed my fingers. I rolled around on the ground desperately trying not to get stomped. Wiggling my way into a combat crawl, I scuttled over to Michelina. I looked back and saw Olione and Alexander kicking some serious shadow man butt. When the Svartálfar were little more than inky pieces on the ground, they came over to me.

Olione knelt and put two fingers to Michelina's throat. His white face was drawn in harsh lines.

"Not gone, but damn close. We're not gaining ground. Where the hell is that charcoal-assed bastard?" he growled. Alexander stood his ground, acting as a guard while we hovered over Michelina.

"What do we do? There's so many of them?" I was ashamed to hear a tremor in my voice. Olione's eyes were hard as diamonds.

"There's nothing we *can* do." He said. Just then, a scream echoed across the clearing. We both turned to look in one movement.

Several of our valiant fighters had moved to the far end of the clearing. There was a sea of Darklings between us and them. At the edge of the tree line, a mountain of a Svartálfar had Leila lifted into the air. The fighters were slashing at it but it was like fighting water. Where ever they struck, the flesh filled in unharmed. I scrambled to my feet nearly knocking Olione over in the process.

"Leila!" I screamed, rushing headlong into the shadows. I hit them with all my might, Olione and Alexander following close behind. The shadow men disintegrated in my wake. My eyes were locked on Leila's struggling form.

Blood dripped from her mouth and from a cut on her brow. She had lost her icy sword somewhere and her clothes were horribly torn. The towering shadow shook her in its grasp like a dog worrying a bone.

My heart fluttered madly. All I could see was her stricken face, her torn flesh. My friend. My sister. My blood boiled. I had fought my way to the backs of her would-be rescuers without remembering the way. With a rush of terror and rage, I saw that the mountain of a beast was the one and only Duhán Agas.

I stopped dead in my tracks, white fire crawling up my arms. Duhán's disease ridden eyes collided with mine. He shook Leila so that her head snapped back and forth on her neck. Awesome magical powers or not, she had taken a beating and looked near to a faint.

"I will crush you Guardian! I will rip out the heart of you and make a feast of your agony!" He roared and his vile laughter filled the clearing. I pushed forward trying to make my way past the fighters, but was repeatedly knocked back. Behind me I could hear Olione shouting.

"Close the circle! Close the circle!" I held my breath, waiting for the suffocating feeling to return, but nothing happened. I spun around. On the other side of the clearing, Oulwihn had her hands raised to the sky. Leo and Olione's bald companion were gathered around her, guarding her from the Svartálfar. I watched her strain her arms upwards. Her power beat the air, rippling over my skin and nothing happened.

She lowered her arms and looked out over the darkness helplessly. Her face had lost the extremity of its otherworldly glow. There was something dark smudged across her forehead. I watched her shake her head and a cold lump grew in the pit of my stomach. I spun back around, with Duhán's laughter vibrating through my body.

"Surprise, surprise little Halfing." He cackled. My eyes grew wide as realization dawned. The world slowed. Someone had betrayed us. Again.

What to do, I thought, what to do. All around us the shadow men were as vast as the sky. I blinked rapidly. The sky. The night. The night is chased away by the day. The idea clicked together in my mind like porcelain tiles. The day. The day is light. Light, we need light. Rummaging around in my pocket I pulled out the candle and the small blue lighter.

"I shall take great pleasure in tearing her limb from limb. Come to me if you dare." Duhán roared. I took a deep breath and flicked the lighter against the small white wick. As flame met wax, light exploded throughout the clearing. The Darklings screamed. I was nearly blind, yet at the last, I saw Duhán flee. He bolted into the forest, taking Leila and every last shadow with him.

20

I sat on the ground, legs out in front of me. I was shivering, from cold, from shock, I wasn't sure. The remaining fighters moved quietly around the clearing. Strange creatures had materialized from the trees and slunk amongst them, tending to hurts and the bodies of the fallen. Michelina, Oulwihn had informed me, was deeply unconscious. Though it was a wonder she was alive at all.

Both of Evalia's companions had sadly fallen, and Alexander had come up missing an arm in the final rush. Only one of Olione's warriors remained. He turned out to be one hell of a surgeon and was stitching together an ugly gash in Leo's leg. Reed was slightly tattered, but generally unscathed. He gently carried Michelina off into the trees attended by two, slight tree people bound for some unknown haven. Oulwihn returned to my side and knelt beside me.

"All is in order Guardian. We must leave this place." She said gently. I could only nod mutely, gazing at the little white nub of candle in my hand as I had been doing for the past twenty or so minutes. Days could have passed for all I knew. My plain of reality felt precarious at best.

"There is nothing we can do for her just now. We must regroup and plan anew." I looked up at her, feeling hallow all the way down. Only a single thought broke through the haze.

"Malcolm. We have to tell Malcolm. He'll know what to do." My voice was a whisper squeezed out from between my lips. Something dark and fragile danced behind her eyes. My senses roused themselves ever so slightly.

"What is it? What's wrong?" In the hush of the clearing my voice was horribly loud.

"I have repeatedly tried contacting the young DeHaven . . . to no avail." She said softly. Her airy voice grated on my ears. My face grew hot, anger coming to the surface at last. I beat my fists into the ground throwing the little piece of wax hard into the trees.

"What the hell do you mean? What's happening to us? I thought you guys had this all planned out. What the feck is going on?" I shouted, rising unsteadily to my feet. Oulwihn rose with me, her hands folded before her. Her face looked haggard, even to my angry eyes. She had aged so many years in just a few moments. I turned my emotions down a couple watts with the realization.

"There is a traitor amongst us. We have been betrayed, more so than anything I could have imagined. This is no mere game of thrones. I believe Gannon has found himself a very powerful friend. I am at a loss. Forgive me Guardian, but I know not what to do now. I have failed you." She said. The despondency in her eyes was almost more than I could bear. Her beautiful clothes were torn and filthy. Her hair was uncharacteristically messy. The weight of responsibility was mine alone and should not have been on her shoulders.

"I'm sorry. I shouldn't have yelled. It's not your fault. Where did Malcolm say he was going to take on Gannon? If the traitor knew about this plan, they probably know about that one as well." Her eyes flickered over me. I could see her slowly rebuilding herself.

"There is a place of power built into the earth between your grandmother's garden and the family cemetery. It was the only place we knew would be untainted and it would save us the time of having to build a place of power from scratch. If the traitor is able to access it before one of our people . . . all is lost." The wind of her voice was the most delicate of breezes. I rubbed my hands up and down my arms chafing my skin. So many thoughts raced through my mind but none of them were helpful.

I continued to go back to the thought of my grandmother and her power, and my mother and her knowledge. Mostly of how I had neither. I wanted to scream. I rubbed the back of my neck vigorously.

No matter what thought I had, what idea arose, they all came back to the same conclusion. Oulwihn watched me with wide, clear eyes.

"They only want me. There's no reason for anyone else to suffer. They only want me." I said. Oulwihn started to shake her but I held up a hand.

"So many people have died or been hurt because of me. Their lives have been ruined because my life was *more important*. But it's not true. The life's work of a Guardian is to protect and serve others. So I think it's time that I started acting like a Guardian, powers or no powers." She continued to shake her head even as I spoke.

"You cannot do this. It will be the death of you." She whispered. I felt my shoulders lift, the weight of my own words heavy inside my flesh.

"I'd rather die a thousand deaths than to be the cause of anyone else's." I replied.

We stood there looking at one another. I couldn't tell what she was thinking, but my heart grew light and peaceful. I had a sudden thought blossom in my mind. What a great adventure this all had been. Good and bad, through doom and gloom, it was worth it all. Never had I been so full of love and hope. Never had my life been so replete. I looked at her, hoping she could see in my eyes how deep my feelings ran. She smiled a very sad smile, and drew me into her arms.

"So proud, your parents would be of you. Never doubt that for a moment." She said softly, giving me a squeeze. I returned her hug whole heartedly, feeling my eyes grow hot. There was a tight lump in my throat and I could only nod against her shoulder.

We stood like that until a soft red light appeared over us. I drew away first to find Olione standing near. He held what looked like a tree branch in his hand with a red crystal glowing at one end.

"We're ready. Let us be away from this place. I shall take us all into the earth and we'll be safe among my people. Fear not Guardian, we will protect you." He said. I looked at him, feeling my heart swell. Here again, so loyal, so beautiful to me. It made my soul ache. I slowly shook my head.

"I won't be hiding anywhere Olione. I'm going to confront Agas and put an end to all of this." I told him. His reaction was one of anger. He slashed the air with his branch light.

"Ludacris! You cannot do this thing. We must find another way. I will not allow you to throw yourself into the jaws of death." He shouted. I could only shake my head at him, keeping firm in my resolution.

"It's not a topic for debate. And as your Guardian, Olione Alberichson, I *command* you not to do anything to stop me from turning myself over." I said and my voice seemed to fill the clearing. That tricky cold wind rushed over us and the crystal light flickered. I looked around, brows raised. Neat trick.

Even in the reddish light, Olione's face was nearly purple with rage. His hand tightened around the branch and the wood whined in protest.

"Your word is law. But at the very least you must let me guard your way. For my service, you must allow me that." He said. His voice was strained but clear. Half of me wanted to tell him no. I wasn't sure how far my powers of guardianship went, but I didn't want to test it. The other half of me would be glad for his company and I knew it my heart he would never dishonor himself by disobeying me. At last, I nodded.

"I would be honored to have you with me." The anger leaked out of his face, to be replaced with a look of brilliant loyalty. My heart gave another painful squeeze. Oulwihn placed a gentle hand on my shoulder.

"I too will remain with you. Though it is not my wish, I was with you in birth and shall be so in death." I looked at both of them, trying to memorize their faces. A tremble of apprehensive wiggled through my guts, making me look away. I would not chicken out. I could not. Leila was counting on me. Hell, everyone was counting on me.

"Well we better get started. The night's not getting any younger." I said. My companions were silent. I watched them drift past me towards the trees, Olione leading. Their shoulders sagged in defeat for all that they kept their heads high. I followed, feeling the same weight fall on me. Stepping through the line of trees I swallowed the bump in my throat, clenching my fists.

As we walked quietly through the night drenched forest, we stumbled on another of the nights hiccups. After only a short time, Olione announced that we were walking in circles. We stood bathed in red light, just outside of the clearing we had left, contemplating this new predicament.

"They have certainly thought of everything." Oulwihn murmured, touching her fingers to her lips. Olione grumbled and slapped the branch against his palm.

211

"Gaia be merciful." He swore. I stood there with my hands shoved in to my pants pockets at a loss. Oulwihn walked around us, one hand held away from her body, feeling at the air. After she had done three complete circles, she stopped.

"Powerful magic is at work. I cannot see through this glamour." She said, gesturing helplessly. We stood there, silent, each lost in our own brooding world. I took the gold ball of twine out of my pocket and passed it back and forth between my hands. I threw it up once, and Olione reached over and snatched it cleanly from the air.

"Vulcan's balls!" he shouted. Startled, I took a step back. Oulwihn began clapping her hands together, a smile on her face. I could only stare at them, thoroughly confused.

"Do you know what this is?" Olione asked, still shouting. I shook my head, wondering at his excitement. He grinned, shaking the gold ball in my face.

"We've beat those bastards at their own game. This will get us through the wall." He took my hand and plopped the ball back into it.

"Now take the end and throw the rest out that way." Olione said, pointing into the trees. I looked from him to Oulwihn. I really hoped they knew what they were doing. Turning, I took the end of the twine, leaned back and threw the rest out into the trees.

I expected the ball to rebound and come flying back towards us. It would have been my luck, with the way things were going. Yet it flew in a straight line, quickly disappearing into the forest. The line grew taught in my hand, thrumming like a plucked harp string.

"What now?" I asked, looking at them with brows raised. They came up on either side of me, standing almost too close.

"Now we go. If it's doing what it's supposed to, it will lead us right to the house." Olione said. I blinked from him to the twine in my hand. Even when I thought my threshold for amazement had been pushed to its limits, fate dealt me another hand.

Twine in hand, we began again. Picking our way through the forest, in halting whispers, we formed a plan. It was mediocre at best, but it was all we could do to keep our spirits from waning.

Lady Oulwihn tried again to contact Malcolm, to no avail. It was left unsaid, but there were only two reasons he wouldn't be able to answer. And neither reason thrilled me.

Taking the high road, we planned on rescuing him along with Leila. At all cost I said, they must be rescued. This idea was not met with enthusiasm. Mostly they were worried for me and not for themselves, but I wouldn't bend on that point. Olione marched ahead, muttering and grumbling to himself, while Lady Oulwihn remained silent, her lips firmly pierced.

We stopped beneath two leaning spruce trees and Lady Oulwihn turned.

"We will remain with you as long as possible. I have no way of knowing what lies beyond, but be prepared for anything. One never knows with creatures of the dark." She said. I watched her wring her hands, her eyes darting over my face. She was stalling, saving that last bittersweet moment. I felt detached. I was going towards my own certain death. There wasn't much else I could do.

After a long pregnant silence, I felt myself nod. I watched Oulwihn pass her hand over the air as you would wipe condensation from the bathroom mirror. Deep inside my bones, there was a tightening and that sense of breathlessness. I blinked and found myself standing in front of my house. The twine was gone from my hand.

Never had a darkness so deep penetrated my home. It was so profound, the light from Olione's crystal torch could barely part it. The red light shone dully on the wide windows and the chain of the swing. Yet the air around it was full of wavering shadows.

Anger boiled up in the pit of my stomach so fiercely I could taste bile at the back of my throat. How dare they defile my home. How dare they. I clenched my fists tightly, my nails biting into my palms. I couldn't stop to dwell on it. Olione and Oulwihn made their way around to the right side of the house. They didn't look too closely at the house or the lively darkness that breathed around us.

We reached the garden unmolested and even from the edge I could see lights flickering in the space between it and the cemetery. My heart dropped. We were too late. My companions walked closely together, making themselves a wall between me and whatever lay ahead. My breath lurched in my throat, fighting with the maddening play of my heart.

At the end of the garden, the tall field grass was cut close to the ground in every direction. Forty feet out, the earth was scorched in an enormous circle nearly thirty feet in diameter. There were six tall torches burning with low flames around a wide ornate table. It looked carved of some dark, glossy wood and it had wicked clawed feet. And on it, bathed in dark flames, was Leila.

I must have made a move towards her, because Lady Oulwihn placed a restraining hand on my arm. I turned to glowing eyes and a face full of caution. *Only fools rush in.* A tiny voice whispered in my head. I turned back to find Gannon DeHaven standing at the head of the table with a very satisfied smirk on his pale face. The cat who at the canary.

"Welcome Cross. I would say it is a pleasure, but I make it a point never to lie." He called with a chuckle. I don't know if the others were surprised in some way, but I sure as hell wasn't. I hadn't doubted for a second that he would side with the Svartálfar. With Olione on my left and Oulwihn on my right, we started across the shorn field. The shadows swirled and heaved as we went, like waves in a pond. I could almost hear them salivating at us. As we reached the circle, Duhán appeared across the table.

He simply appeared out of nothing. He was in the same man shape as when I first met him, in his coal dark attire, cloak churning out behind him. He glared at me with eyes so hot I felt the searing of them on my skin. My breath caught and my heart skipped a beat. His grotesque, fleshy lips parted in a wide grin. Cold sweat oozed down my spine.

"What is the phrase? Like fish in a barrel?" he said, leaning his head in Gannon's direction. His voice grated in my ears. Gannon gave another round of chuckles. Leila groaned and began writhing on the table. My anxiety level peaked so that I wanted to run screaming into the forest. Only the sight of Leila pale and squirming in pain stopped me.

"I've come for my friends. I want to trade myself for them." I said, and I gave myself ten brownie points when my voice remained steady. Duhán laughed. Gannon laughed. A bad sign all around.

When Gannon had brought himself under control and wiped at the corner of his eye, he grinned at us.

"Trade? Why would we trade with you my dear, when we already have you in our grasp?" he purred. My stomach tied itself in knots. I wanted to spit at him.

"I shall kill you *and* your devoted companions. So that all will be mine in one fell swoop." He said, gesturing with one graceful hand. I readied myself for the blow, but when none came, I looked around.

Bottle blond head bobbing from side to side, Keely strolled into the clearing. She had a wide, predatory smile on her face and was more than out of place in her white clam-diggers and pale pink polo shirt. In one small hand, she held a long, thick chain. On the end of the chain, was Malcolm.

He was bare chested, blood running from a gash in his brow. His hands were linked behind his back, leaving the front of him as a wide canvas of tan flesh. Wicked lacerations striped him like a zebra. Yet all in all, he seemed un-phased. His silver eyes flashed with simmering rage and his usual brand of disdain. My heart fluttered in my chest with fear, just on the edge of panic. I looked away from him, schooling my face to a careful blandness. Gannon watched me closely, face shining and bright. I gave him unconcerned eyes.

"It certainly seems like you have the ball in your court." I mused, trying to keep from clenching my hands. Gannon preened, brushing an invisible crumb from the breast of his burgundy coat. I couldn't help but feel a distinct amount of hatred for him.

"But there's one thing you don't have." I said, my voice filling the clear night air. His dark eyes flicked to my face, squinting. His perfect face twisted with haughty contempt.

"Pray enlighten me human." He snarled. His voice prickled up my skin, catching my breath in my throat. Duhán also watched me closely, one hand spread casually on the table top. He was far closer to Leila than I was comfortable with and I wanted to tell him to back off. One thing at a time, my inner voice whispered. I swallowed hard, looking Gannon full in the face.

"You don't have me." I said and gave myself a hundred brownie points when my voice came out steady. Gannon laughed. Threw his head back and had himself a good hardy-har. Duhán wasn't laughing. The look in his eyes sent a shiver down my spine. He was intent and full of hard suspicion.

"Silly, silly, girl." Gannon chuckled. He was so damn pleased with himself. I would have done anything to be able to smack the mirth right off his face.

"Perhaps I must speak a mite slower for your tiny human brain to understand." The corners of my mouth drooped down into a deep frown and my head cocked itself ever so slightly.

"No, it's you who doesn't understand, dumbass." I snapped. His head jerked straight and I watched anger fill the cup of his eyes. That swirling darkness grew hot, until I thought I might scald.

"You might have this body, but you don't have me. And you sure as hell don't have the power of the Guardians." Of all the things I can accredit to Gannon DeHaven, there was an acute intelligence behind all the bluff and theatrics. It sprang up behind that well of anger and pushed it back ever so slightly. It made me aware that deceiving him wouldn't be as easy as I thought. He fingered his creamy white cravat thoughtfully, and slid his free hand calmly into his trouser pocket. His eyes were piercing and shrewd.

The torches crackled in the silence. I was aware of being watched from all angles. The very night watched me. Malcolm was quiet beside Keely, his eyes bright with eldritch light. Duhán was still squinting at me from the other side of the table. Unknown thoughts flickered behind his diseased eyes. My gazed drifted back and forth between all of them and I was glad that Olione and the Lady Oulwihn were with me.

"Of your own free will, you would give me the power of your House?" Gannon said at last. I heard the slightest tremor in his voice, the thrill of anticipation. I started to reply, when Duhán slammed his fist down on the table.

"No, that was not part of the plan." He shouted. Leila writhed and groaned. Gannon turned towards him in a single movement. I don't know what he would have said, because at that moment, everyone started to move.

There was a high pitched yelp from Keely and then Malcolm was flying towards Gannon. He collided with the other man and they both tumbled to the ground.

A bright flash of light filled my right eye and flew past me in a javelin of crackling wind. It took Duhán in the midsection and sent him flying back from the table. Olione stepped forward, long gleaming sword in one hand and white crystal torch flaring in the other. I would have stood there in shock, quite unaware of this little plan, but Olione pushed past me, nudging my shoulder.

"Now." He shouted running for the table. I ran after him, glancing briefly at Oulwihn. Her entire body was a pillar of white light. Wind poured from her in screaming gales, holding the shadows at bay.

I hit the side of the table running. Leila had her eyes clamped shut, sweat beading on her brow.

"Leila! Leila, wake up!" I yelled, shaking her. She moaned, but her eyes remained closed. Olione let out a vibrant curse beside me, and I turned to see what new thing had arrived.

Blueboy, Deluk was running towards us, giant axe over his head. Olione met him head on and their weapons kissed in a shower of sparks. I turned back to Leila, grabbing her arm and pulling her across the table. I'd fireman carry her if I had to, I thought, then something jumped on my back.

A snarling, scratching something.

I yelled and whirled around with it attached to me. Sharp claws raked into my neck and one side of my face. I reached back and grabbed a hand full of soft hair just as a set of teeth clamped on to my shoulder.

I screamed and threw myself down on my back, smashing my attacker into the ground. It let go, and I frantically scrambled to my feet. A flash of red-gold light nearly blinded me again just in time for me to see Keely get up on all-fours and snarl at me.

Just behind her, Oulwihn was tangling with Duhán and a slew of Svartálfar. She was blasting them with shards of light and electrically charged gusts of wind. A swarming flock of white breasted sparrows flew from her and attacked anything within reach. Screeching owls dropped from the sky and tore into howling darklings. So far, she was valiantly keeping them away, but I knew it wouldn't hold for long.

My attention was brought back to a scuttling Keely. There was saliva dripping from her chin and strange jagged teeth filling her mouth. I thought briefly about the tetanus shot I was going to need if I survived all of this. Something wet oozed down my cheek. I raised my hand to it and found myself bleeding. I glared at Keely with a snarl of my own.

"You bitch!" I shouted and she was skittering towards me. The world slowed down just a smidgen as she leapt into the air towards me. How I had ever thought she was any kind of cute was beyond me. She now reminded me of some demonic cupiedoll. I never liked her anyways, I thought, leaning back, fist tight. I swung just in time to serve her up a tasty right hook.

She crumpled to the ground with a satisfying thump and lay very still. Part of me wanted to check her for a pulse, but the other part of me mentally high-fived myself. I turned, ready for a fight.

Olione was swapping blows with Deluk. Both men were grunting and sweating. Their weapons deeply notched from the staggering power of the assaults. Blood stained the white of Olione's arm from a wound in his shoulder and more poured from a gash in Deluk's massive chest. I looked away from them and on the other side of the table, Gannon and Malcolm were fighting. Both men stood in their own pulsating nimbus. Cascades of shining power flew from their hands, crashing into each other. Malcolm's was deep red-gold and Gannon's shone like black fire. I couldn't help any of them, so I ran back to the table.

Leila was right where I had left her, panting and sweating. Taking hold of one arm again, I bent at the waist and pulled her across my shoulders. She was lighter than I expected, which was a plus. I turned, intending to run to god-knows-where, when the temperature dropped about thirty degrees. It was suddenly hard to breath. I started forward, in the direction of the house, feeling as if my feet were sifting through molasses.

Stop, hissed through my brain, raking my skin and stealing all thought. I was frozen to the ground. All sound ceased. I wasn't sure if I had gone deaf, or if I had simply died. I felt my body turn itself around, Leila still draped over my shoulders like a fleshy cape. Everyone else in the field was also frozen in their places, poised in mid-motion. The torchlight flickered over them merrily and yet foreboding in the same.

Put her down and step away. The voice fizzled through me again. With no will of my own, I returned Leila to the table and took three steps back. Every muscle in my body hummed with a foreign energy. It was warm and tingling, yet invasive. I felt dirty, unclean, befouled. A million disquieting feelings at once. From the corner of my eye, a small figure stepped out of the trees and glided into the light.

Her pelt of slate gray hair was pulled back from her smooth, youthful face. It was a visage that I had seen in old photographs. I would recognize it from now till the end of days. Yet it was no face that should have been in the here and now. The shock of it went through me with the power of ten. For a moment I forgot where I was, forgot who I was. So powerful was the sight of that face.

She stopped at the end of the table and turned to me. A sneer lit her full lips and dark fire curled in her earth brown eyes.

"Surprise." She said, a chuckle spilling up from her throat. I was still too shocked to feel anything but. I strained against the power holding me, unable to make out more than a tremble.

Gwyn strolled around the table, long sable robes trailing over the ground. She reached out and absently brushed her hand across Leila's damp forehead. Anger boiled up inside of me. How dare she!

"I couldn't let you take my little sacrifice. That would ruin all the hard work I've put in to this night." Gwyn chided. I watched her, powerless as she came back around the table and walked towards me.

I wanted to run, to be anywhere but right there. Mostly, I didn't want her to touch me. I knew it would be bad.

That evil sneer was still pasted across her new young face. I could wonder only faintly how she had come to this. She stood before me, head tilted back ever so slightly and fluttered her lashes. It made my stomach sick.

"Since you are so fond of stories dear thing, I have one more that you should hear." She said. Her voice curled around me like a smothering cloth. My face twitched like a fly ridden horse. She tilted her head to one side and ran an index finger down the side of my cheek. I winced inwardly, feeling her trace the scratch there. She pulled her hand away and examined the blood on her finger tip.

"Once, a long time ago, two girl children were born to the house of Cross. Twins. Separated by only the merest of moments.

The girls were born under the fullness of the moon and all signs told that they would be very powerful." She began in a sing-song voice, walking away. She strode back to the table, her long rope of hair slithering down her back.

"Though only seconds apart from each other, only the first was born with the mark of the Guardian." Gwyn prowled around the table, her gazed locked on me.

"They grew up together, these powerful girls. One trained to the line of Guardians . . . and the other left to the creatures of the wild.

The father was very proud of his first daughter, but of the second, the second he cared little. All that mattered to him was the way of the Guardian." She said and her sweet, clear voice was a hot wash over me. Trailing her hand over the table top, she walked out into the field. I watched her stop close behind Malcolm and run her hand down his rippling back. I felt myself flush and couldn't stop it. The movement was so slight, yet terribly intimate. Gwyn smiled at me and continued her stalk around him.

"As they grew older, the second daughter found many ways to expand her power. She insinuated herself into every corner of the otherworld that she could. Learned every lesson she could. Even dabbled in the darkest of arts. She swore, that she would be more powerful than her sister and that in the end, all would bow to the flick of her hand." Gwyn's voice carried to me as she walked over to Gannon and slapped the back her hand against his chest with a smile. His lashes fluttered, but it was the only sign that he was still alive. I wondered the same about myself. I focused on each of my limbs, struggling to even make a finger flex. Gwyn was suddenly right in front of me, nearly breathing my breath, breaking my concentration. She placed that intruding finger under my chin.

"Some time ago, the second daughter felt she was close to reaching her goal. Her sister was as powerful as ever, yet she was distracted with training her own daughter. And then there was the birth of the *child*. One Guardian she could kill, but two . . . there is no knowing the strength of a mother protecting its child. Such a thing would have been terribly reckless. The second sister decided to bide her time. Until at last, an idea presented itself." She took hold of my arm and slowly pulled. My feet shuffled over the ground and like a zombie, I turned. I turned until I was facing Oulwihn and the immobile Svartálfar. Gwyn released me and walked over to them. She ducked her head past a murder of crow stilled on the wing. Lovingly, she twirled her fingers in Duhán's vest. Straining on tip-toes, she pressed her lips to his gnarled cheek. I thought I couldn't feel any sicker than I did and I was wrong. My guts were a ball of hot rage and nausea and I couldn't do anything about it. She pulled away from him with a small, tight smile.

"She enlisted the help of a powerful man and promised him rule over all the creatures of Red Glen, if only he would kill the Guardians for her. She told him where he could find the wayward darkling and his worthless family. She opened the way, so that he could reach them. He was successful in all things save one ... but as I said, there is no knowing the strength of a mother protecting its child." Gwyn ground out. Every word was a serrated knife grinding through my marrow. I gasped for breath, fighting internally with the power that held me. This, then was our betrayer. *Someone on our side would have to let them in.* Malcolm's voice trickled through my mind. *There is a traitor amongst us.* Oulwihn whispered. I blinked rapidly, the only thing I could manage in my frozen state. Gwyn glided back to me, and placed a hand on my arm once more. Inside, I screamed. The touch of her was a brand, the kiss of a lash. She turned me carefully back towards the table before stepping away. I was sweating from the contact and near to hyperventilating.

"Once the young Guardian was dealt with, it was an easy thing to convince Laurel to erase the child's mind. Everything was going so well, so very well, until the older sister had an attack of conscience." Gwyn spat, standing beside the table, her upper lip curled.

"*She's old enough to learn the truth. We must release her. For love of our line we must release her.*" Gwyn mimicked in that oh so familiar voice. Her head jerked back and forth angrily as she spoke.

"Such a worthless bleeding heart. It was easy in the end to deal with her and her beloved Andre." She snapped. I grew still all the way into my blood. I felt it slow and nearly stop in my veins. Murderer, I thought, willing myself to grow deadly calm. Down, way down deep, I felt the shadow of myself awaken. I felt it wake with a vengeance and begin sucking up every inch of rage I could muster inside myself. I felt it grow, and watched as Gwyn strolled around to the other side of the table. I prayed fervently she wouldn't notice anything.

"And now at last, I will finish what was begun. I will destroy every last Guardian and *I* will be the most powerful of all." Gwyn whipped a long shining dagger from the folds of her robes, holding it high over her head with both hands. Leila strained on the table top, torso bowing upward as if eager to greet the touch of death. I could see her teeth bared, fingers contorted in pain. My eyes grew painfully wide as realization dawned. She was going to kill Leila. My friend. My sister.

Every moment of turmoil. Every stitch of pent up anger. Every drop of sadness and melancholy I had ever felt because of the loss of my family, I put into the fury I felt. I fed it to bursting and at the same time, that shadow gorged itself.

It grew, until every part of me was filled with it. Until all the world was bathed in anger and seething with hatred. For this woman.

I watched the blade come down and at the same time, I lashed out with that frothing, boiling shadow. It spilled out of me, burst out of me. My arm raised and a wordless scream exploded from my mouth, terrible, primal. The wave of darkness sped through the air, and slammed into Gwyn.

She came off of her feet and flew back, skidding along the ground. I let the darkness pour out, consuming the power in the circle that was Gwyn. Devouring every part of her that it could find. I let it pour out until every last trace of her was clean from my home, save for the woman herself. When the last of it was gone, I dropped to the ground, near boneless.

It felt like a long time before I blinked and found Olione running towards me. I was sitting on the ground, slack faced. Deluk lay on the ground cleaved nearly in two. I looked at him from behind a curtain of haze. My head felt floaty and disconnected. Farther away, behind Olione I could see Malcolm starting in my direction and at the same time, Gannon following him. I didn't have the strength to raise my hand. I opened my mouth just as Gannon leapt onto Malcolm's back.

Olione had nearly reached me, when the Svartálfar began pouring from all around. He turned, sword ready and began fighting. A hand grabbed my arm and turned me. My eyes met an alabaster face with glowing citrine eyes. Oulwihn helped me to my feet, allowing me to lean heavily on her.

"The circle is broken Guardian, you must take Leila and flee. We will protect you." She yelled, one hand pointed in the opposite direction from us. A shower of snow flurries and a frigid blizzard wind slammed into a wall of lurching shadows. It fell back screaming into the trees.

"I don't know how long I can hold them, you must go." She yelled again. I tried to tell her that I couldn't, that I didn't have anything left, but then she was ushering me to the table.

We had barely reached it, when a silver blur flash between us, taking Oulwihn in the chest. I watched her fall away from me in slow motion, one hand clutching the blade, eyes wide and confused. Black blood poured down the whiteness of her. I stood there and dumbly watched her fall to the ground. Turning back, I found Gwyn standing a few yards away.

She had blood and black filth leaking from her eyes and nose. Her gray hair was bleached bone white, her skin ashen. She hobbled towards me, gasping and panting for air. Even in my haze I could see that the whole of her eyes had filled with blood, leaving only the pinpoints of her irises. She bared her teeth and gave a feral scream.

I searched down inside of myself for the shadow-me, but found it spent and unmoved. In a movement she shouldn't have been capable of, Gwyn came in a blur, flying through the air. She hit me and we both went to the ground. Her nails slashed at me, tearing through my clothes like tissue paper. Her head slammed into mine and white stars burst behind my eyes. Bleeding and dumb, I ogled up at her as she crouched over me.

"You've ruined everything!" she screamed, punching me hard in the face. I could barely lift my arms to protect myself and blood burst from the corner of my mouth.

"There will be so much pain for you, you'll pray for me to kill you." She said, hitting me again. I don't know if it was the rage in her that gave her strength or if it was whatever power was left inside her, but the second punch blacked out my vision and left my ears ringing. I blinked up just in time to see her raising her fist once more.

"You will beg me for death in end." She hissed. I raised my hands feebly, thinking to ward off the blow.

I don't know who was more surprised, me or her, when the biggest hawk I've ever seen landed on her face. It was magnificent, resplendent in its robe of silvery-brown feathers. It's four inch talons ripped into Gwyn's face and they both fell away screaming. I didn't wait for another stroke of luck. I rose unsteadily to my feet. The world spun and I flopped back down on the ground. Something small and metallic tumbled out of my pocket and went tinkling across the ground. At the same time, something unseen inside of me clicked. I stared at the little bell and began crawling after it. I picked it up, holding it upside down. Torch light glinted off the little inverted caricature of the lamb. This is important my brain told me. I held it up, willing my mind to give up its secrets.

"Duhán! Stop her!" Gwyn's voice screeched through the air. I turn to see both she and Duhán standing nearby by, frozen in place. He looked comically confused. She, horrified, her face and neck a mass of wounds.

I don't have them often, but I had one of those ah-ha moments. Great, big, cymbals crashing AH-HA. With a flick of my wrist, I flipped the bell over. The tiny clapper rang against the thin brass. The clearest note ever heard by any ear ever, filled the field. It vibrated up my arm, rattled my teeth, and skipped the beating of my heart.

The veils of time fell away. The spells, the wards, the geas. All fell away to a state of complete clarity. Like the breaking of a dam, I was filled. A whiteness filled me, a pure radiance. It spilled out of my skin, out of my eyes, the tips of my fingers, the roots of my hair. I was standing with no memory of having done so. The bell fell from my hand, end over end into the burned earth. It's job complete.

My earth. My home. I could feel the power raging through me. The knowledge of all things that would have been mine, restocking the empty shelves of my mind. I could feel the circle built deep into the earth. It was full of dazzling light all around, until the night was as bright as the day. I knew its purpose, the hum of its life strand burrowed deep into the heart of the Mother. Mine. This place was made for me, for mine, for all that would come after.

I felt a fleck of disease standing within my center and turned my eyes. The Lord Duhán and Gwyn stood unmoving, whether from terror or trapped by the power I didn't know. What I did know was that they would never be allowed to hurt anyone ever again. I raised a glowing hand to them and they screamed. They were echoed by their brethren who had also been unable to flee.

Without an ounce of pity, I let the circle consume them. I watched as one by one they disintegrated into the earth, screaming, howling, hissing, begging. Back to the place from whence they had come. I let the power run and run until every last darkling perished. And at the last, there was Gwyn. Unlike the Svartálfar, she didn't go quickly, or pleasantly.

She clawed at her own face until black blood gushed down her body. Her once smooth, flawless skin sank in around her bones until it was a skeletal horror that screamed its hatred at me. Gratefully, in her last moment, the earth simply opened up and received her like a welcomed guest.

The soil rumbled and heaved like a stomach digesting a full meal. When it was still, the field was whole and unblemished. The light in the circle slowly faded, but I cast my own light. I walked slowly over the ground, illuminating my path, until I reached Oulwihn where she lay.

Dark blood dripped from her beautiful face. Her gown, which had been in ruins before, was covered in gore. She smiled up at me and it was painfully sweet in my heart. She had one hand clenched around the dagger in her chest. Blackness spread from it in a wide patch.

"At least . . . I could see . . . you come into your own . . . at the end." She gasped. The wind was gone from her voice. To my magicked eyes she seemed so plain, so human. I knew without thinking, that the dagger was stealing her life, poisoning her from deep within. And there wasn't a thing I could do about it.

A deep and profound sadness filled me. I was losing another part of my family. Another part of my heart. Tears ran unchecked down my face as I knelt and gently leaned my forehead against hers. I held my hand over the dagger, dreading what I must do. Yet I couldn't let her suffer. Her free hand tightened around mine and our eyes locked.

"It has been . . . my honor." She whispered. I nodded my head against hers, unable to speak past the sorrow lodged in my throat. I could only hope in my heart that she would know that the *honor* had been *mine*.

Before my strength could fail me, I thrust the blade deep and hard into her heart with a single blow. I watched the light fade from her eyes, watched as the last breath eased past her lips.

As gently as I could, I laid her out on the ground and stood away. I whispered a rune of earth magic and the ground opened up once more to receive its loyalest of servants.

I stood there a long time, staring at the place where she had been. Out in the trees, the night birds keened a lament. I was so entranced; I didn't feel Gannon come up behind me.

His power lashed out and caught me in the head like a club. I did a summersault to the ground, kicking up bits of long grass as I went. I had enough sense to scramble away and ended up on my butt, facing him.

His thick black hair was a mess. The right sleeve of his elegant coat was missing and the entire left side of his clothing was torn down to the waist, leaving his pale chest bare. Blood candy coated his hands and the side of his face yet he remained unmarked.

"Why won't you just die!" he growled. Dark fire sparked in his eyes and crackled at his fingertips. He raised a hand back to strike and I jumped to my feet with a speed that startled us both. I had one of his hands locked in my own, blood cool on my skin. He snarled in my face, snapping his teeth like a dog at the end of its chain.

"I'll die, the day you spill your own blood to save me." I hiss at him. He gave a sharp bark of a laugh. It was a loud, angry sound. His power sizzled in the air in wild bolts of miniature chained lightning. It stung my skin and lifted my hair in its wake.

"The day I spill my blood for you, would be my last." He ground out, his hand clenching around mine painfully. I gave him a small smile and pressed the upper half of my body against his.

"You swear?" I whispered. Gannon bared his teeth at me and for a moment I thought he might actually bite me.

"I swear it." He snapped. I let go of him and we both fell back a step. At the same time, I lifted my blood coated hand and wiped it across his forehead.

"Blood of your blood." I whispered. His eyes widened in understanding. There was no time to scream. No in drawn breath. The light went out of Gannon DeHaven like a candle in the wind. His body fell to the ground with a hard thump.

I stood there, looking down at him and Olione limped over to me. I smiled as he came near, genuinely glad to see someone on my side on their feet. There was a terrible gash in his thigh, his shoulder and one side of his face, but he grinned out of his beard at me.

"We did it." He said, his voice raspy and harsh. I could only nod, my mind wandering to my other friends. To Leila still blissfully unconscious on the table. To Malcolm where ever he might be, torn and bleeding. To Kamac and how I was ever going to tell him about his sister. *But he already knows.* My power whispered inside of me.

Yes, I thought, he already knows. They always know when their people pass through the Dark Forest.

"How did you do it?" Olione's voice broke through my concentration. I blinked at him.

"Do what?" I said dumbly. He pointed down at the body of Gannon. I shrugged.

"I made him swear that he would never spill his own blood to save me." I said, raising my ensanguined hand. Olione's face crumpled in confusion so I decided to make it easy on him. It had been a long night.

"Malcolm is the son of his House. Blood of his blood. Whose blood was spilt trying to save me. This is Malcolm's blood, not Gannon's . . . but hey, technicalities right?" I said with a shrug. I ambled away from him and his look of complete chagrin. I walked past the table and the sleeping Leila. Deeper into the night. On the burned ground, Malcolm lay beaten and bloody.

His beautiful body was covered in blood. One silver eye was swollen completely shut. I knelt beside him and he blinked up at me with his good eye. He was still wonderful to me, no matter what he looked like. I pressed a hand to his chest. He was dying, I could feel it. He had never opened up that gateway to his true power. He was still as human as I was. For all that that meant.

"Why didn't you save yourself?" I asked. I knew the answer, but I wanted to hear him say it. He grimaced and shifted onto one elbow.

"I would rather spend a single moment listening to you bitch at me, than live an eternity without you." He said softly. I felt an instantaneous spurt of outrage, but held myself back from punching him in the arm. There was a crooked little smile on his face, mocking and loveable. A spasm racked his body, ruining the moment. He started to cough and hacked up a dark glob of something not so nice on to the ground.

Placing my hands on his body, one over his heart and the other on his back mirroring it, I held him to me. I drew up every shred of power I could muster. Above all other things, I must save him. It was the only thing in the world that mattered to me right then and there.

I became very aware of his heart sluggishly beating, his breath against my neck, the softness of his hair against my face. I could feel the rustling of the trees around us, the night animals scurrying through the undergrowth, birds calling, their wings beating the air over our heads. The pulsing of the stars sparkled behind my eyelids. The heart of the Mother beat in me as though I were the river through which her life blood flowed. And all at once, I shoved it inside of him.

In the back of my mind, I heard him scream. The power filled him up, mending his flesh, stitching the pieces of him back together. It flooded his veins and engulfed his arteries. I gave until there was no more to heal, sealing his life force to his flesh with a single brutal blow. And still I gave.

It traveled out of me, seeking others to heal. Olione was there and it consumed him. I had a moment to feel his surprise, before it moved on to Leila. In an instant, it filled her to the brim. I could see her in my mind's eye, gasping and flushed. Then the power moved on.

As sure as we are connected to the mother earth, I was connected to all the creatures of Red Glen. And I healed them all. Kamac, Michelina, Alexander. Old Bill at the fire station. Mrs. Bailey's colicky baby. Ann Burgess at the Lady's Boutique. On and on and on it went. Warming hearts, calming fears and drying tears. I gave and gave as has been the way of the Guardian forever and a day. I gave until the well of my being was dry. Gave until the light faded away. Gave until my soul cut lose and floated away into the sky.

21

A flash across my eyes. A face. A hand on my chest. Lips on my mouth. Voices yelling. Someone else's breath filling my lungs, their hands urging my still heart to beat.

My eyes fluttered again. Malcolm. Leila. An unfamiliar man. All scurrying around. Spinning. Spinning pell-mell around me.

"Clear!" Someone yelled. Fire. Red hot. White lightning. A contraction seized every muscle in my body. And yet my heart refused to beat.

Silly heart, I thought distantly. Another breath. Strange, familiar lips.

A single bulb gently swayed in the sapphire glass of its cone shaped fixture. The room beyond was pitch black and full of undulating shadows. Faces, familiar illuminated faces floated into my vision. Some were not so familiar, but I was mostly just happy to be alive.

"Viv, can you hear me?" Leila asked. Her voice seemed far away even as her silky, mahogany hair brushed my face. I tried to nod, but my head wouldn't move.

"I hear you." Whispered out of my throat, but my lips never moved. I found I couldn't blink either. An edge of panic crept up on me until Malcolm leaned in close and kissed me gently on the cheek.

"You're dying." He said in a voice that echoed. Yes, I knew this. I had died several times.

"It's the only way. The only way to save you." Leila's voice floated into my ears. I was still focused on the fact that I couldn't blink. When her words really sunk in.

"What is?" I asked, with my immobile mouth. Reed was suddenly there and he also laid a soft kiss on my other cheek.

"We love you too much. We love you enough to let you go." He said. That panic that had been building crested in my mind. What the hell were they talking about? I tried to struggle, but my body wouldn't follow. Olione stroked my cheek lovingly with a callused hand.

"It's the only way." He whispered. Other faces drifted about, touching my hair, stroking my face. They were all familiar and my fear built. Firm hands held my body down and someone began murmuring a spell. It too was familiar. Terrifyingly so. I tried to struggle, to cry out, anything. One by one other voices rose and with it, the walls.

"Don't! Please don't!" I cried in a very small voice. The walls were going up, slowly shutting me out. Sealing me away.

"It's the only way." A voice told me. The hell it was, I thought. I reached inside myself searching for the power that had been there. It was there, but it was all tuckered out. It was limp as a wet noodle, bone tired. I nudged it, pushed it, *willed* it to rise. Yet it lay quiet in my being and the walls grew.

I'm here, I thought. Don't do this. I remember. I have the power. It's all okay now. I wept. I cried. I begged them not to go on. I shouted at them inside my mind. Because it was the only thing left I could do. The chanting rose and fell around me, vibrating my marrow. My eyes locked on the single bare bulb and the drone of voices. The walls went up and up and up until they closed around completely.

22

Once upon a time, there were two children born on the same day of the same year. One was a boy and the other, a girl.

The boy was born to a house of privilege, wealth and power. He was taught by the very best teachers and attended the very best schools. He was given everything his heart desired. He was rich indeed, yet he was also very sad. And very lonely.

The girl was born to a small family of foresters. They who live off the land and give thanks for all the fruits it may bear. She was very loved by her parents and grandparents and had everything a child could ask for. But for all of her good fortune, the girl was very lonely.

One day, after giving his tutors the slip, the boy found himself traveling down a deep forest path. He had never been so far alone, but he was not afraid, having been so alone since birth. After walking a good long time, the boy came to a fork in the path. The day was growing long and people would be searching for him. He was just deciding to turn back, when the sound of weeping reached his ears.

The boy reacted with unease. The only time he ever heard someone crying, was when his parents were home. His mother cried often and it bothered him more than he would ever admit. He was more than ready to turn back, but some quality in the distress stopped him. His feet were wandering down the path once more before he could stop them.

Only a short way and the forest opened up to a small glade. There were bright orange flowers all around and a tall cypress leaning over as if to shield them from the harsh summer sun. At the foot of the tree, there sat the girl. She had her face buried against her knees and her shoulders were shaking with the force of her sobs.

The boy strode purposefully through the flowers. He didn't stop until he was merely a few feet away from her. With a gasp, her head lifted, her eyes were full of fear. They were the most beautiful eyes he had ever seen. The dappled sunlight played in her long, red hair. He knew, without knowing how, that this girl was special. That she was special to him.

"Why are you crying?" he asked. She wiped her face and sniffled at him. He wasn't sure why, but he felt he would do anything if it would make her happy again.

"The bad lady. The bad lady was chasing me." The girl sobbed, burying her face back in her knees. The boy felt a fierceness build in him that he had never known. He stepped up beside her and placed his hand tentatively on her shoulder.

"Don't cry. I'll protect you." He said. The girl looked up at him with her green eyes so wide and fearful. Then, something curious happened. She saw the boy in a strange light. She knew in her heart that he would indeed protect her. And she knew also that she must stay with him. Always.

The boy gently took her hand and helped her to stand beside him. Without thought or reason, he reached down into the patch of jolly orange flowers and plucked a single one. With his whole heart, he gave it to her. He watched her sniff it delicately, reveling in the smile that blossomed on her face. He knew in his heart that he would do anything for her. And that they would be together. Always.

23

Rain pattered down on the sturdy tin roof of the garage. The sound of it filled my ears and brought me awake. I blinked up at the garage ceiling with its multitude of spider webs and a tiny black bat roosting in a corner. The light through the small rectangular window to the right was the gloomy blue of a rainy midday.

I struggled to sit up, the taste of burnt flesh and pennies in my mouth. I groaned, rubbing my head and looking behind me. I'd come inches from braining myself on the rim of the Old Woody's wheel.

On unsteady legs, I stood and glared at the monstrosity that was the Bailey television.

"Bastard piece of shit." I grumbled, flicking the plug out of the wall. I continued to rub my head and turned around in a wide circle. How long had I been here? Long enough for the weather to go cock-eyed, I mused. I opened the garage door, only to be pelted by cold rain.

Ducking my head into the collar of my coveralls, I ran towards the house. The sky above was full of bright, boiling gray clouds. I reached the porch and looking out over the yard, shook the rain off my clothes. The wind chime behind me tinkled softly. I smiled in spite of myself. I loved sitting on the porch listening to my little wind chime, rain, sun or snow. Still smiling, I turned and stomped into the house.

It was cold, and every frickin' light was on. What the hell? I thought. The last thing I needed was a crazy electric bill. I strode around, turning off lights and closing windows. I briefly thought about what I was going to do about the TV situation.

My grandma left me a nice sized one up in her sitting room, I thought, pulling the lacy drapes closed in the dining room and running a smoothing hand over the clean white table cloth. It's not like I was using it, I thought, meandering into the kitchen.

Despite the bump on my head and the fact that I'd electrocuted myself, I was strangely in a good mood. I felt light and dare I sat it . . . kinda happy. I shrugged out of the top of my overalls and set about making myself a cup of tea. Might even make myself some scones, I thought. I started the water to boil, feeling very pleased with myself.

I finished dropping off the TV, waving out the truck window to one of the many little clones. It was a bright and sunny day, full of billowing white clouds scudding playfully across the sky. I had both windows down, letting the wind whip my hair around.

I was headed for town. I needed to stop at The Panner for a vacuum light bulb and a few other odds and ends. Not to mention it was a great day for cruising around the hills. The roads were clear and the air was cool and crisp.

I hit town and waved out my window to Mrs. Burke standing in front of her store. She raised a slow hand and waved back. Wonder what's wrong with her? I snorted, pulling in front of The Panner. I got out and eyeballed an ugly black skid mark on the sidewalk. Some bozo learning how to drive. I strode towards the door, calling out to a man on the sidewalk.

"Hey Carl. How's it going?" he stopped and turned, with a lift of his shoulders.

"Good as always." He said, continuing on his way. I nodded, more to myself than anything, and pushed through the shiny glass door of The Panner. The little bell rang out brightly. A young man at the front counter lifted his head and smiled. I paused, blinking at him.

He had gorgeous blond hair like spun gold. It was cut into that shaggy surfer do that's overly popular with younger guys. His smile was open and friendly. Woohoo. I pasted on my most flirtatious grin and ambled over to the counter.

"Hey. You're new in town yea? Where's that other fella . . . what's his name. Rick? Roy?" I asked, leaning one hand on the smooth counter top. Oh yea, I was smooth. The guy smiled even wider. He chuckled and shook his shining head. His eyes were sparkling bits of amber in the pallor of his face.

"The name's Kamac. And *Reed's* out to lunch. But I'm sure I can help you with anything you need." He said, setting down the measuring tape that was in his hands. I felt the smile on my face broaden of its own accord. Weird name, but what a cutie. You can help me any day of the week, my inner voice purred. I straightened away from the counter a bit and shrugged.

"Just here to pick up some packages." I said. Kamac wiggled his eye brows, still smiling away.

"I'll see what I can find." He said, and strode off towards the back. While, I may add, I took complete advantage of the opportunity to check out his back end. So-so, but nobody's perfect.

He returned with three small, manila wrapped packages. I studiously examined the measurements on the counter top until he was back in front of me. It wouldn't do to have him catch me looking.

"This was all there was." He said, pushing them across to me. I examined each one before valiantly trying to dig a twenty out of my pocket. Damn you, jeans that make my butt look fabulous. I almost had it, when Kamac waved me away.

"There was a note that said you already paid." I looked up at him in confusion, hand still stuck in my pocket. I started to shake my head. I didn't remember doing such a thing, but I could remember my shocking experience from the day before. Maybe it had slipped my mind. I shrugged again and yanked my hand ungracefully out of my pants.

"Well I guess that's all then, thanks." I scooped up my things and headed for the door. I turned back to wave and Kamac winked at me.

"Have a good one Vivian." He said. I had to jerk my chin at him, nearly dropping everything. Smooth Viv, real smooth, I scolded stepping out the door.

I tossed my stuff into the truck and had my hands braced on the door frame, when an intoxicating smell assaulted my nose. I stepped back, my eyes drifting to the bakery across the road. It was such a nice place to eat. And I hadn't had anything since that measly little breakfast early this morning. As if I really needed coercing. I laughed at myself and slammed the truck door.

I was half way across the street, thinking about the yummy Kamac, and it occurred to me. I never told him my name. The thought made me stop dead in the middle of the street. I started to turn back, suspicion creasing the deep furrow between my brows. I was about to go back and lock up my truck, but the blast of a car horn stopped me.

"Hey! Get the hell out of the road." Someone yelled. I whirled around, coming face to face with an ugly blue Mazda. All fearful thoughts vanquished, I trotted to the other side. I watched the car pull away, with its driver throwing up his hands and miming angrily to the steering wheel.

Blowing my breath out between my lips, I turned and made for the bakery. Swirling gold paint and giant flowers curled around the edge of the front window. I gave it a second glance but decided not to stop. There'd be time for pretty murals later. Especially when food was in demand. With a bounce in my step and dreams of savory meat pies dancing in my head, I pushed into the store.

The scent was heavenly. I stood for a moment on the threshold, breathing deep. I didn't care that the other customers might be watching. I just hope I didn't drool on myself before I had a chance to sit down. I sauntered to the long glass case and bent to examine the delectable morsels. Everything looked delicious. My eyes darted around in rabid mongoose circles. A clean white apron appeared on the other side of the glass and I straightened, ready to feast, feast, feast.

The woman watched me with big quiet eyes the color of fresh black coffee. Her wine-dark hair was pulled back from her pretty face by a long yellow ribbon. I tried to remember her name, worrying at the corner of my mouth. Lily? Lana?

"Can I help you?" she asked, one finely trimmed brow raised. Leila, that's what it was. Nice girl. Very fashionable.

"Sure, I'll have a small pork pie and a slab of your baklava." I said. Leila jerked her head at me and set about getting my order. She seemed like a nice person, it was a wonder we had never hung out.

Quick and efficient, she readied my order and I quickly paid her. Without a snag of trouble from my stupid jeans, I turned. I started to leave, when my eyes caught on two figures sitting together at a nearby table. I knew them both from high school. One was the owner of The Panner, the white haired Reed. The other was Malcolm. Malcolm De-something-or-other. Mister hoity-toity. He didn't say much, but it was doubtful he had anything worth hearing anyways. All beauty and no brains probably. Great hair though. Stunning, burnt orange V-neck sweater and black trouser combo.

My eyes were drifting down to scope out his footwear, but I stopped. There on the table top, squeezed into a small crystal vase, was a bunch of yellowy-orange Black Eyed Susan's. I walked over to the table, conscious of their eyes on me and plucked one happy little flower for myself.

"My favorite." I said softly, sticking my nose in it.

A prism of light flashed off of the vase and burst in the retina of my eye. An instant later, a wave of inertia crashed over me, bringing an instant cold sweat down my back. I pulled my face back, blinking hard.

Dazed and slightly dizzy, I made for the front door, little yellow food bag lose in my hand. I still held the flower close to my face examining every last velvety petal. My heart was on fire, my pulse racing a million miles a second. I reached the door and at the last, turned, looking the three of them in the face.

With a laugh, I threw the flower across the room and watched as Malcolm snatched it cleanly from the air.

"Silly rabbits, you can't cross a Cross." I laughed and saw the wonder dawn in their eyes. I chuckled and turned and walked out in to the sun.

AUTHOR BIOGRAPHY

Ashley was born in California, but raised all over the United States. She lived in thirty of the fifty states by the time she was sixteen. She joined the United States Navy when she turned eighteen and was able to use it as a means to travel the world. She has been to Ireland, Germany, Italy, France, and Crete to name a few. She seperated from service in 2007 and became a Peace Officer for the State of California in 2009. She worked for a maximum security mental hospital for two and a half years before leaving to pursue her own personal business and her love of writing. Ashley resides in California with her family and two beloved cats.